# An Unbeatable Foe?

Saying nothing, London reached out and grabbed McNeil's wrist, pulling her to himself. Dragging forth every ounce of stability around him, the detective heard the distant sound of the sidewalks outside collapsing into the ground. As the ceiling came crashing down around the trio, London managed to push the Life-A-Day Man back a handful of steps, as he shouted;

"She's not yours! Let the whole universe fall—you don't get *her!*"

West repositioned his glasses on his face. Taking a deep breath, he stepped forward once more, saying softly;

"Indeed. And how exactly do you propose stopping me?"

London's face went dark, his soul cooling to its lowest temperature. His lips pursed grimly, he stared at West, then lowered his head a fraction to look into McNeil's eyes. The priestess nodded her head, telling him;

"Dies On The Right Day was the only one of us aptly named, but we were all well chosen."

*The inscrutible Teddy London, the original paranormal investigator, returns to confront a menace of God-like stature — knowing that the Earth's fate may have already been decided!*

1-892669-80-3 Trade Paperback

1-892669-81-1 Ebook

1-892669-82-X Kindle edition

Retail cover price $15.99

Printed and bound in the United States by Lightning Source, Inc.

10 9 8 7 6 5 4 3 2 1

Cover art © 2012 Ben Fogletto. All Rights Reserved.

Design/Pre-Press: Rich Harvey

Published by Marietta Publishing
Bruce R. Gehweiler, Publisher
677 Valleyside Road
Dallas, GA, 30157
www.mariettapublishing.com

# AN ETERNITY
# OF SELF

## C.J. HENDERSON

MP
MARIETTA PUBLISHING

# ~ DEDICATION ~

Most of the authors I know, or have known,
I have met while their careers, like my own,
have been in their ascendence.

Jolly comrades,
standing against the evils of the industry.
Fighting the same enemies,
Making the same jokes,
Dreading the same rejection letters.

But there are some I have encountered
at the height of their fame.
Some have been egotistical jerks,
more than ready to prove
that idols can often come with feet of clay.

But there have also been some that still know
what it is to write for the fun of it—
for the thrill of it all.

They are the ones who never lose sight
of why we really do this—
the good reasons, and the bad ones—
who somehow manage to keep their sense of humor
through all the crap life loves to hurl at our breed.

## LIN CARTER
was one such writer.

He wrote the first Conan story I ever read, and ...
dear God, how I wish
he was still here to write more.

"If you wish to live forever you must be wicked enough to be irretrievably damned; in hell alone do people retain their sinful nature: that is to say, their individuality."

"What man is capable of the insane self-conceit of believing that an eternity of himself would be tolerable even to himself?"

George Bernard Shaw
(1856--1950)

# PROLOGUE

**W**ELL, ...

Although there were bodies everywhere, only one of them was still moving. Oh, one could find here and there the occasional twitchers, this or that corpse-in-waiting still mindlessly dragging itself across the face of oblivion—true enough.

*As usual, ...*

But, all in all, the tall, slender man with the pale blue eyes and the unconsciously sinister grin walking calmly through the still-smoldering devastation, was for all intents and purposes the only thing still moving with anything approaching thoughtful locomotion.

*That was easy.*

The master of all he surveyed nearly sighed. Running a fine-boned hand through his yellow hair instead, he merely shook his head sadly. It had been easy. Really, honestly, once again it had all been far too insanely easy; maddeningly without effort. Rubbing at his clean-shaven chin, the lone figure continued onward. Absently adjusting his spectacles, he walked out across the etched, burned crumble which had once been a highway, its brittle surface crunching into powder beneath his precisely clipped march.

Before him a world's proudest city lie in staggering ruin. Massive structures of every type in all directions had been utterly destroyed. Melted, knocked over, torn apart—their still-bubbling rubble was a steaming obliteration beyond the comprehension of most minds.

Baraz'naaka—it was that dimension's greatest metropolis by far. Storehouse of its most cherished art, home to its loftiest thinkers—the center of its planetary government—a hub of culture and learning for nearly fourteen thousand cycles. And yet, it had fallen to the grinning owner of the sinister blue eyes and precisely clipped gait with an incredible ease. And, the worst part of it was, he could not have accomplish any of what he had without the eager help of those he had sought to murder.

*But then, isn't that simply always the way?*

Of course, he could have winked them out of existence with but a casual thought if he had so desired—but where was the sport in that? No, he had set out the rules for his most recent visit ages earlier when his wanderings had first begun, and he had scrupulously followed them to the letter ever since. If there was going to be destruction and death and all manner of satisfying misery during any of his carefully timed sojourns, well, it was going to have to be caused by those who would endure it.

That was, after all, what made it all so satisfying.

And, as always, the number of pathetic fools eager to help him he found almost distressing. How desperate they continued to be, the back of his mind sneered with a private delight, to toss away the armor of civilized thought as if were nothing more than the slightest of veneers. He had made a handful of important figures the merest of offers, and they had shed their culture's twenty-seven millennia of customs, taboos and creeds in a disgustingly brief matter of hours.

And, as it had happened so countless many times before, all they had really done was put purchase forward for the destruction of their world.

*Really ...*

As the only man on the face of the planet continued to walk across the burning, ruined landscape, the thin curl of his smile widened, then cracked his thin lips. All about him, in every direction, over each hill and plane and mountain, across all bodies of water, his limitless touch had reached with a permanence which would allow no recovery. There was not a structure anywhere on the smoldering world, not hut nor skyscraper, not schoolhouse or reinforced bunker, hospital or home, where his horrible gift had not been felt. Not an orchard or field remained, not a hatchery or ranch had been spared.

Nowhere had been safe.

No where.

Nowhere was ever safe from him.

*Just much too easy.*

A new thought sparked within the back of the man's brain just as he caught sight of his objective. He had known he would find them in the Plaza. Once a waterway of a fascinatingly intricate, near-hypnotic design, now it was naught but broken stone smeared with tar and anguish, its shattered arches housing the last native life of the dying world.

"Well, well, Chancellor Byremmm, happy with our little arrangement, are we?"

The crab-armed, stalk-eyed creature shuddered with terror. At the sound of the soft voice behind it, its skin changed color, its already sickened green going more yellow with the clicking noise of each step of the alien which had seduced it—stolen its soul.

"Killed them," the former leader of eleven billion sputtered weakly. More creatures like the Chancellor hunkered together weakly further across the square. Their terror of the humanoid walking toward them was evident in the sunken manner in which they backed away from his approach, in the way their already fractured skin tone yellowed away to nothing. But Byremmm was too angry, still too shocked to cower completely. Waving its arms forlornly, bubbles of regret seeping from its gasbag, it cried;

"Destroyed them. Us, everything. All this devastation ... all this ...

"Why?"

"Oh, come now, Byremmm, old whateveryouare, you do see,

don't you, that this is what you asked for. Well, what you agreed to, at any rate. Right?"

"But, to these ends? I never believed, what was the need, how could you, why? Why would—"

Suddenly exasperated, the slender man's face went sullen as he kicked the thing before him roundly. It was a stiff shot, straight and hard, heavy leather digging deeply into the brain sack of the blubbering creature. It fell on its side, burned and broken and unable to die.

"You miserable, frightened, greedy slug. You sold the lives of your world for what I had to offer without hesitation. You rolled the dice on your planet for your own gain, soothing your fish-eyed conscience with the thought that no one would ever take you up on the deal you had made."

Byremmm floundered where it had fallen, not seeing the point in rising. What did it matter where it remained? Its world was in ashes, and no matter where it went, everything would look the same, sound the same, hold the same accusing images.

"But, you know ... I like you Byremmm," said the man with a false tone any other human would have recognized. His hand reaching beneath his jacket, fingering a leather pouch which he carried under his left arm, he undid the thong holding it closed as he said, "Unlike the rest of your council, you've at least got a bit of backbone."

The clean shaven man smiled at what he considered quite an amusing joke. Then, waving his hand before him to indicate the still steaming mountains of corpses everywhere about them, he offered;

"Not much left around here, I'll grant you that. So, tell you what Byremmm, how would you like a chance to actually die, as well?"

As the creature looked up, all its stalks waving attentively—desperately—the slender man held a vial filled with a glowing red elixir in the air. As Byremmm began to shake uncontrollably, the alien quoted a poem he had learned in his youth;

*"There once was a man from Gnu,*
*Who found a large rat in his stew.*
*The waiter said, Oh please ...,*
*Don't shout and wave it about,*
*Or the rest will be wanting one, too."*

And then, moving far faster than expected, the grinning man tossed the vial haphazardly through the air, instructing the Chancellor, "If you really have the nerve to join your people, just use this. You know how."

The vial hit the ground, bounced once, then again, finally rolling to a stop several feet away from Byremmm. As the thin glass container shuddered into immobility, the man began to walk away once more with his customary rapidity, calling over his shoulder as he did so.

"Better get to it fast, Byremmm," he cautioned, purposely shouting loud enough for all those others unable to die to hear, "before one of the others get to it first."

Continuing onward without a backward glance, the man began to retrace his steps away from the once magnificent square. He would leave shortly—

*But,* he wondered, *for where? Where this time?*

And then, a fascinating suggestion rolled across his mind. He considered it for a moment, practically stunned at the beauty in its simplicity. Stopping for a moment, he allowed a vulgar snickering to escape his skull, then said to himself with smug contentment;

"Ah, of course. Isn't it just as they say—there's no place like home."

The sounds of a world's last survivors fighting over the means of joining the dead had just begun to break out in earnest as the tall, slender man with the knowing blue eyes and the sinister grin winked out of existence.

# CHAPTER ONE

THE DOOR WAS ANCIENT. Thick and heavy, made of lead and stone and massive timbers, great impossible things hewn from ten thousand year old trees that at one time had reached beyond the sky. Its hinges were as thick as towers, their pins the breadth of whales. It was an awesomely mighty thing, but one set in the side of a mountain so thick and wide and tall that as mind-wrenchingly large as the door was, it was a lost and tiny speck in comparison.

The mountain was a dark and foreboding place, a sheer, rugged nightmare of cyclopean peaks and callosal summits all as inhospitable to every living thing as they were to the very concept of life itself. It was a vulgar, pulsating terror, pocketed with reeking thermal pits and frozen glacial shadows. It was larger than the mind's dimension and wider than possibility. It was beyond scope, existing not within its own dimension, but *as* its own dimension.

It was what the Tibetans called Mt. Meru. It was the center—the final threshold—the one and only crossroads *to* all places *from* all places.

And, as for the door in question—that ancient gateway locked so tightly to the cliff side was by no means an anomaly—the mountain was covered with as many doors as there were stars in the universe. As least, that was the perception of the climber working his way slowly toward that one gargantuan speck.

The man paused, pushing aside a weariness as despairing as age. Brushing his sandy hair back, he blinked hard, then stretched his arms out, working at the pain digging its way into his muscles. He had been moving upward, hand over hand, toe and knee, elbow and wrist—straining, hanging, surviving—for what seemed like a lifetime. An entire actual lifetime. An eternity of bunched seconds lined up and played out one yard one foot one inch after another. After another.

After another.

"This is it."

Private investigator Theodore London stopped. Every function and aspect of the man that dared rest shut down in gasping relief. He had come up over a sharp outcropping of splintered obsidian and found that for which he was looking. He had passed many other doors on his way up the face of the terrible peak, but he had not paused at any of them. They had not been the one he wanted. This one was.

He did not know how he had arrived at this certainty, of course. London did not even know exactly why he was searching for the door. He had never heard of it until a day before his departure for it. He did not know its name when he arrived, either. It did not matter.

London had left his friends, his co-workers, and his entire plane of existence several weeks earlier knowing that he would simply have to search, and keep searching—across the leagues of other wheres and whens for who knew how many eternities—until he found the shrieking darkness he could sense coming toward his world. He had no choice.

It had only been a dream—a vision reaching the detective in the supposed safety of sleep—of a great darkness descending on his universe. Once awake, the glance into the future held onto his imagination securely. London could not name this horror making its way to his world, or even give it form within his mind. He only knew that it's arrival was imminent—and that he was all that stood between it and all he held dear.

A challenge had been flung. Somewhere across time and space, some horrific consciousness had set its bloated golden eye on the dimension which housed London's world. Like hairs on the back of a person's neck—when they just *know* someone is watching them—people had registered uncomprehending receipt of the foul attention. Nightmares and despair had swept throughout the detective's world. Suicides had broken out in record numbers. Men called it the end of the world. They always do.

The problem was—this time they stood a good chance of being correct.

Whatever horror was headed toward his birth reality did not matter. London knew he was the only person in the world that had any chance of stopping it. He also knew that if he simply gave into his instincts that they would lead him to the correct spot of its arrival—at whatever place he could meet the whatever that was coming. Besides this, the detective also knew it would be a place both his senses and those of the approaching shambler could interpret in like manner—a commonality where they could meet and contest with one another. He had expected all of these things.

What he had not expected was to find someone else waiting on the same side of the door as him. That startled him enough to make him blink, an unexpected expenditure of energy that leaked bits of his soul off into the wind. Being caught off-guard was a new sensation for London. He was not a man used to being taken by surprise.

Some time earlier, the detective had become involved in a case which had pulled him beyond the veil of the ordinary into a new understanding of the world—one so alien to all which had gone before it that it had utterly destroyed all his previous perceptions. Since then he had contested with vampires and demons, with changelings and with godlike forms whose mere visage could shatter the fragile senses of most who beheld them. He had lost friends and comrades in many of the battles, had spilled a necessary ocean of innocent blood, but he had prevailed time and again, and his world was still safe.

"Who the Hell ...," London wondered, his mind as worn as

his body. "Who is *this* guy?"

Physically exhausted but determined—practically beyond reason—the detective threw his leg over the ledge before him. He released the braced position of his fingers, extracting them from the crevice he had used as his last handhold. After that he made his way over the crumbling edge, rolling several yards inward before he stopped to catch his breath. Clouds of dust were raised by his arrival. As he lay in the thin layer of detritus remaining, he studied the man sitting quietly further up the bluff.

London received no feeling that the man was a threat to him. Everything about the figure, in fact—the hooding of the eyes, angle of position before the door, bend of the knees, the casual iron in the spread of the fingers, et cetera—bespoke its intention to meet head on the same thing that London had come to stop.

The detective's perceptions also told him that his senses were not deceiving him—that what he saw was a man like himself. He was an older man, with a face unlined but whose eyes whispered of uncounted years. He was tall, slender and saturnine, with a fine-boned visage as sallow as antique ivory. His hair was thinning but still black as night, save for a dramatic silver streak that began at his right temple and zigzagged backward to the base of his skull.

At that moment, however, the detective did not care. Giving in to his weariness, he gave off wondering about the older man and closed his eyes. Instantly his depleted form snagged energy from all about him. Years earlier London had learned the secret of miracle, had realized the truth behind the monumental simplicity that the fabric of a universe *can* be manipulated simply by believing one could do so. It was a difficult trick, one achieved by equal parts pig-headedness and self-righteousness—a stunt where arrogance and pride were worth their weight in fantasy.

London had found his way to the mountain by entering the dreamplane, a side dimension linked to the subconscious and unconscious minds. Most people could reach only the palest outskirts of this realm—and then only in their dreams. London could travel them at will.

But, such parlor magic comes with a price tag. The detective had discovered long ago that playing God was weighted by a staggering set of consequences. Every dipping into the cosmic drinking fountain cost an equal ransom in force and power—for every action there is an equal and opposite reaction. And so on.

London did not travel the dreamplane lightly any more. Not, knowing as he did that to do so—to use his abilities to transmute time and matter and space—had to be purchased in like portions of fixed reality.

"Now," he thought, "here I am using up who knows how much energy to reach this spot, and here's some other guy who's doing the same thing."

Seeing no need to belabor the obvious any longer, London reined in his power. He could see that a great portion of the surrounding bluff had already disappeared, consumed by his need for compensatory energy. Walking forward, he called out to the older man.

"Enjoying the view?"

"Well," responded the figure without moving, evidencing no surprise at London's arrival, "that was more original than 'hello,' I suppose."

"Forgive me," answered the detective shortly. "I've never been certain what the correct bon mot is for this kind of situation."

"And what situation is that?"

London stopped walking. Tiny wisps powdered around his boots as his weight bit into the loamy soil there on the plateau. Ignoring the effect, the detective said, "The one that, and hopefully I'm not assuming incorrectly here, brought both of us to this spot."

"You're a guarded man, Mr. London. A handy attribute in some circumstances, but I'm not certain we have the time for such antics now."

"Okay, you know who I am," answered the detective. "Fair

enough. I'm listed in the phone book. You mind telling me who you are, though?"

The slender figure thought for a moment. Then, memory slid the proper answer to his tongue.

"Sorry—I haven't used my given name for ... for a while. But when I still needed to be, I was known as Dr. Anton Zarnak. Of late, the last resident of Number 13, China Alley. New York, New York."

"What," asked London, recognizing the address as being not terribly far from his own home—within the same city. The same borough, even.

"Yes, small multiverse, isn't it? It had been for some time before my arrival the home of Professor Roland Guicet. He was stationed there for some sixty-two years until his disappearance. Then I was sent to take his place."

"His place doing what?" asked the detective.

"Safeguarding humanity."

And then, before London could respond, something stirred the massive door before them. It was the slightest of shoves, but the noise reverberated across the landscape like the sonic blasts of an attacking squadron of jet fighters. Bits of rust the size of continents cracked and splintered with the movement, flecking away to drift lazily toward the ground below. Their crashing kicked up banks of dust and detritus that blotted the sky, plunging everything into darkness.

"Hummmm," said Zarnak absently, noting the destruction, "less time than I thought."

"Less time than you thought for what?" asked London.

"For putting off the end of the world," answered the older man curtly. "Why else did you think we were here?"

# INTERLUDE

THE TALL, SLENDER MAN with the pale blue eyes paused for a moment in between realities. At first his idea to return home had seemed a splendid idea, filled with possibilities he could scarcely imagine. And, while he had in no way changed his mind about the delicious possibilities of roaming its avenues once more, he did realize a certain wastefulness about simply dropping in, rolling into town as he had in so many other realities.

His stays on so many worlds were such brief things. How, he wondered, could so many different species, life forms so diverse and varied, all be motivated by the same base instincts? How, he asked himself, could their goals be so trite? Their vision so limited? So Childish?

He knew his home world would be no better. Yes, a certain amount of time had passed since he had left all he knew behind, but not enough to make a difference.

"Humanity is a vulgar, low-bred herd," he whispered, his usual, falsely pleasant disposition suddenly souring. "You know we can expect nothing better from them."

Staring off through the various transmuting realities abounding around him, the slender man shuddered. Closing his eyes, his mind fell back in time, back to when he was merely mortal, before he had discovered the secrets to all creation. His brain filled with memories, hundreds of thousands of flashes of abuse and cruelty, all of it aimed at himself, hurled at him by the slow-witted beasts which thought themselves his better. From his earliest days, throughout his school years and after, every different scene his mind showed him did nothing more than anger and torment him.

No wonder he had never before thought of returning.

"Why would anyone do such a thing?"

And then, his eyes opening suddenly, staring forward, he smiled to himself.

"Why wouldn't they?"

The slender man had not been chased away from the Earth. He had not retreated. When the full extent of his abilities had been revealed to him, he had simply wanted to explore, to escape the simple three dimensions he had lived within his entire life. There were before him in that first instance of revelation, a billion, trillion worlds to choose from, to explore ... to play with as he saw fit.

He had done so with reckless abandon. At first he had hoped to find a somewhere that would not fall before him—a dimension where he might find beings with the intelligence or harmony to refuse what he had to offer. After all, he never attempted to deceive anyone. He was always quite honest about what he could bestow, but where such a gift might lead.

But the end result never varied. A few times he had warned those to whom he was making his offer quite strenuously, hinting that they were most likely calling their own doom down upon themselves. It had never mattered. None had ever listened.

"And mankind will fare no better."

Knowing he was correct, the man adjusted his glasses upon his nose, smiling wryly at the affectation. As if he needed such things. But then, a notion struck him. Here he was, condemning his brethren for their weaknesses, all the while perhaps being as ridiculous as any of them. It was an unfair comparison, he told himself. He was not as moronic as those he had left behind. He simply liked the way he looked in glasses.

"Still," he thought, "perhaps I could give them a chance to ... think a bit. Expand their minds."

For some time the slender man merely existed, continuing

to hang between the swirl of temporalities where he had paused. Then, after some meaningless amount of linear time, he said;

"I know, I'll send them a present. Something to get them thinking. Something to shake a bit of the dust out of their pedestrian, cobwebbed brains."

The man with the pale blue eyes concentrated for a moment, shattering the walls of several realities, plucking something mad and grasping and dangerous from one world and then hurling it toward his long left-behind home.

"There," he thought, watching the thing crash against the western edge of the continent he had once called home, "that ought to teach them something."

Pleased with himself, the slender man waited a moment, inspecting his handiwork. As he expected, the rifts he had created healed themselves smoothly. As he wished. After all, destroying individual worlds was one thing, but it would not do to simply start collapsing entire dimensions.

Then, once he was certain all was well, he headed for a world he had visited often, but with which he had never toyed. When first he had walked its streets, he had come across a restaurant wherein he had found they served a broth and bread meal he found remarkably sustaining. Not that he needed to eat anymore, but he had always felt, what was life without an occasional foray into the quaint?

"Yes," he told himself, with his gift, sent seconds earlier, and yet already festering along the edge of the Pacific Ocean for countless millennia, "a short meal, a chance to relax, then we can go home. And if they remain the race of low brutes we left behind, then we shall wipe the universe free of them as we have all the others we have ever encountered."

# CHAPTER
# TWO

"**W**ELL," thought London, half-sitting, half-falling down onto a solid looking out-cropping of igneous rock, "you wanted an answer, and there you go."

The detective did not want to reveal how tired he was—how truly weary he felt down to the core of his bones—but he had no choice. Reaching the illusionary mountainside had taken nearly all his strength. The detective had walked the dreamplane many times. He had confronted all manner of monsters and gods and things in between when there. More than once he had come close to shuffling off his frail mortal shell. But, he thought, never before had he been so exhausted in the mere journeying to the site of his next confrontation. It had taken every bit of strength the detective possessed just to reach the dimension of the door.

And, it was obvious to him that Dr. Zarnak knew it.

"You don't belong here," the older man said casually as he checked his pockets absently, searching for something.

"Yeah," responded London, somewhat annoyed at Zarnak's assessment. "And what makes you think that?"

"You're exhausted. The color in your face says you're having trouble breathing. The set of your shoulders, the way they're folded in toward your head ... ummm, no, not good. Your heart rate is violently out of control. And your breathing is far too shallow and rapid."

The massive door rattled again. The thin, tattered gray clouds hanging in the air before it began to move off, frightened by the possibility the barrier might actually open. London's eyes went wide at the sight. Zarnak smiled.

"Nor do I think," added the doctor, "that you are as ready for a confrontation of this magnitude as you might think."

London did not bother to stand. He needed to collect his energy, organize his will, forge his ability to resist whatever overwhelming irresistibility was pushing at the other side of the door.

"You've had an interesting career, Mr. London, and you've conquered a number of enemies far beyond what one could reasonably expect from one as unlettered as yourself," admitted Zarnak. "I'll grant you that. But, what approaches now is more than you can handle."

"Oh, and you can?"

Zarnak continued the absent searching of his pockets. Finally discovering what he was looking for, he pulled his hands free.

"No, I actually don't believe so."

London looked up. Sweat dripped off his forehead into his eyes, blinding him as he stared at Zarnak. The doctor was busy filling a pipe from a small, folded-flap leather pouch. As the older man put flame to the bowl, again the massive door shook with the terrible reverberations of having taken a great hit. This time, however, the door moved forward on its hinges several yards.

A hideous squeal knifed through the air as the ancient hinges slid outward for the first time in over half a millennia. The metal surfaces tore against one other, the resulting din hammering at everything within a thousand miles.

London's eyes narrowed as he watched more of the door's decaying surface crash against the uneven plane all around him. Zarnak seemed too engrossed with his pipe to notice. Wiping at his brow, the detective said;

"Okay, let me get this straight. I've stopped things like Q'talu and Nyarlethotep, but I won't be able to handle whatever it is on the other side of that door. You, on the other hand, you're humanity's protector. But you can't handle what's coming, either."

"Yes," answered Zarnak between puffs, "that's essentially correct."

London stopped for a moment. He was not exactly bewildered, but he did not know what to say. He did not know what the doctor was proposing, either. Sensing this, Zarnak told him straight out.

"Go home, Mr. London. This one is mine."

"But you said you couldn't handle it."

"Correct." The doctor let a great cloud of smoke escape his lips. Rapturous enjoyment spreading across his face, he said;

"I don't believe that either one of us can stop what approaches. Nor hat we could halt it together. Ultimately, we are both but men, and men can but bar the door."

"But listen, maybe if ..."

Suddenly, the older man was no longer across the plane, but standing inches from London. His nostrils flaring, upper lip curling, the doctor shouted over the deafening shrillness of the opening passageway behind them.

"Listen to me, little man. It's my turn to quit. I've stood my post, I've paid my passage. It's over. This is my job. I get the sinecure now."

The door moved once more. Again the sky was blotted by the noise of it. Again boulders the size of moons fell from the mountain, smashing down around the two figures. Ignoring it all, Zarnak reached out and grabbed the edges of London's coat. His pipe suddenly gone, his once calm face rippled in passion, he snarled at the detective.

"Who do you think you are? Just who in all the possible Hells are *you*!? Stop a few minor elders with more luck than anything else and suddenly you're Jules de Grandin? I think not."

The plane they were standing on split apart as more rubble battered the landscape. As the ground fell away beneath London's feet, Zarnak held him aloft.

"Lose as much as I have," he shouted. "Bury as many near and dear as *I* have—*then* think yourself *ready!*"

With but the slightest effort, the doctor threw London up onto what remained of the knoll before the door. Another deafening blow splattered against the inside of the barrier, echoing across the various dimensions all tumbled together there at the nexus. This time, however, there was a difference. This time, the door cleared its massive jam. Suddenly, it was open.

"Your time will come, boy," said the doctor. "But it's not today."

Pipe in hand again, Zarnak stared at the few feet of darkness revealed by the cracking of the door as if expecting something to emerge from that tiny sliver of space. Inhaling one last time, savoring the final lungful of flavorful smoke with only minimal regrets, he smiled benignly at London and said;

"I always did enjoy a good bowl."

Then, the doctor's hands were free once more. Reaching under his coat, he pulled forth a grotesque mask of carved and painted wood. The scarlet, black and gold image depicted a hideous devil face with three glaring eyes and open-fanged jaws from which escaped painted gold whorls of stylized flames. As he slipped it on, he told London in a humorous tone;

"An old friend I brought along to lend a hand."

Spreading his arms, Zarnak raised his voice over the thundering squeal of the still grinding hinges.

"*Sub pat'kiaa, yef yef gerdic trum'el kuna.*" The words bellowed forth from the doctor's slender frame, "*Yama hidie'ay, Yama gibgib'conna gibgib'conna.*"

London listened to the spell as the words were repeated. Before him the door was being slammed open further—inch by torturous inch. Next to him, the doctor maintained his ritual. And then before them both, as all around debris continued to fall from the mountain, a new phenomenon began to stir. A curling mass of ambrosial flesh and fire swirled with a violet mist some dozen yards away.

"*Trum'el kuna,*" called the doctor once more. "*Yama hidie'ay, Yama gibgib'conna gibgib'conna bing shem!*"

*who calls me?*

"Anton Zarnak!" shouted the doctor.

*I remember you*

The voice crawled out of the growing sphere of violet fire. As the ground splintered and the mountain trembled, Zarnak demanded, "And do you remember your duty to they who speak the words?"

*is there sacrifice?*

"Behind that door," answered the doctor. "You want an opponent, Yama—he's there and waiting."

*we destroy it together?*

"If it can be destroyed."

*interesting*

The cloud continued its metamorphoses. As it flowed across the plane, the door opened wide enough for a massive appendage to begin to force its way outside. Long it was, covered in hairy scales that glowed with a dull orangish hue. Neither arm nor tentacle nor any other kind of flesh which London could understand, it bent in numerous spots, jointed in no fashion of which the detective could make sense.

As Yama flowed through the doorway, a great burning hissing filled the air. New tremors tossed the mountain savagely, throwing London to his feet. Green bolts of translucent lightning rained across the knoll, forcing the detective to seek shelter. By the time he dared raise his head, Yama was completely inside the doorway, Zarnak quick on his heels.

And then, the doctor motioned toward London. Somehow the detective found himself at Zarnak's side. Before he could ask what had happened, he was silenced by the sudden appearance of another man from inside the door.

Older he was, gaunt and gray and joyless. His hunched frame was feeble and covered with blistered and burned skin that reeked of the odor of running pus and rot. Pulling the man out of the doorway, Zarnak said;

"Professor Guicet, I presume?"

The man nodded feebly, falling against the doctor. Zarnak handled him delicately, moving his desiccated form gently to where London could catch him. The detective accepted the slight burden with a delicacy akin to reverence. Then, Zarnak was through the door, gesturing at it to close behind him.

Multitudinous blasts of fiery rock erupted from behind the door. The sounds of unbelievable confrontation shattered the very air, the noise alone filling the atmosphere with burning ozone. London watched the door slide quietly shut. Then, seconds before it closed completely, Zarnak's voice reached him one last time.

"Take good care of Guicet, Theodore. As you care for him, so shall he who comes next care for you."

London nodded. Suddenly, he remembered what the doctor had said to him earlier.

"Your time will come, boy," Zarnak had said. "But it's not today."

The detective turned his attention to the trembling old man hanging on his arm. How many years—decades—had he held the line against the thing behind the door? How many would Zarnak and his inhuman helper be able to stand?

"And," London wondered, "how many will I when it *is* my time?"

Knowing there would be no answer for him until he no longer needed one, the detective turned his attention to the tortured, dying man within his arms.

Behind him, the mountain rang with the sound of battle. Beyond that, the universe spun onward—cold and uncaring. A champion had fallen. Another had taken his place. Theodore London sighed, wondering exactly what was going to happen to him next. Then, deciding such things were better left unknown, he began the arduous task of returning home with Professor Guicet in tow, hoping he could keep the old man alive long enough to see 13 China Alley once more.

# INTERLUDE

"T HAT!" the woman said, her eyes darting, voice shaking with fear. "Did you hear it? Did you hear it *that* time? Did you?!"

The man stood motionless. Listening. Yes—he thought he might have heard something—maybe ...

"Oh God, what's wrong with you?" The woman was not so much chastising as pleading, desperate to discover what it was that had changed in her world, for something certainly had. Maybe her husband had lost his hearing. Worse—maybe he was playing some elaborate, hideous prank. Then again, maybe she was simply insane, and was not willing to admit it yet.

Yet.

"You can't do this to me and get away with it, Richie. Not *me,* goddamnit! You're going to stop this right now—you're going to make it go away."

She was to the world a supremely strong woman, a Hollywood powerhouse, a Broadway star. Critical acclaim followed her around the globe. When she left her Manhattan home for the country's sunny coast, she did not do so to merely star in movies. No—*she* went west to appeared in motion pictures—films she wrote and directed herself.

She was, and she knew she was, someone who mattered. She was a star. She was important. *Too* important to have to put up with any more of the nightmare she was suddenly living.

"Why don't you speak?"

"Kennedy," her husband answered, "you're upset and you know I don't know what to do with you when you're upset. No one does. After all," his tone fell an octave, began to shake ever so slightly, "none of us can *afford* to get you upset at us."

Kennedy Walker bristled. Why was every man in her life so weak? Why was she so cursed?

"You limp biscuit ... I'm telling you there's something wrong in this house." Her voice began to pick up speed with each sentence. It notched slightly shriller with each one as well. "With this house. About this house. You want to hear me use the word so you can use it against me? Fine—I will. There's something goddamned *evil* in this place. Do you hear me, somewhere in its deepest bowels—*evil!*"

The woman gasped for a breath, shock and fear draining her of some of her emotion as she stammered, "I-I'm telling you this and all you're worried about is your allowance."

"Bite me, bitch," Richie snapped. "You tell me the animals are acting funny. I go and look, and they're not doing anything. You tell me the birds are watching you. I do the dutiful and go out and look at them, too. Surprise, surprise, they don't seem to be going Hitchcock at all. I report my findings, and does that put an end to your current little personal insanity? Oh—no, no. That, of course, would be too easy."

The woman made to defend herself, to say something, but her husband cut her off, snarled at her, a deep noise he dragged from somewhere within his shattered limits. His eyes throbbing harshly in his head, he closed the space between himself and his wife with a single step, then began to walk around her in quick, tight circles as he added;

"After that it's sounds. Sounds! What kind of sounds, my dear, I ask. You say 'listen.' So I listen; But I don't hear anything. I tell you I think you're hearing things, and do you even consider the possibility? No—why would you? Being reasonable, that's for people who don't have Emmys and Tonys and Academy Awards. No, you—you start cranking up the snide show."

The air between the man and the woman heated drastically, currents of it moistening as they encountered the cooler draft everywhere else within the room. The man's torso moved into a position that appeared to be setting him up to strike his wife—most likely across the face. The fierce look in his eyes backed-up his aggressive, if yet unconscious, body language.

"You want me to act like a man? You want me to make it all go away," he snarled, reaching for her. Grabbing her by the wrist, Richie dragged his wife back toward him, shouting, "okay, baby—you got it!"

Slapping Kennedy once, he then caught her other hand as it reflectively came toward him. Holding both her wrists in one of his hands, he shouted;

"This is it then; this is me, taking charge—calming the out-of-control hysteric. Listen to my words, Kennedy; let them filter through what's left of your brain—you've lost your mind."

The superstar turned away, attempting to refuse to listen. Tired of so much, her husband twisted his hand, forcing her to spin back around toward him. Her face an inch from his, tears shaking free from her cheeks, pelting his, he shouted;

"Do you understand ... you're babbling. Do you know what they do to the people who babble the things you're babbling—they lock them up."

Kennedy Walker's tears ceased flowing.

"And do you know what they do to rich, powerful people who scream about their house being evil? They laugh at them, and they write about them in newspapers that get sold at checkout stands. And they take away their lovely careers."

Kennedy Walker stopped struggling.

"That's right," her husband growled. "What's wrong with me? With *me?!* Pots and kettles, little girl. You're looking to do a sanitarium stretch while the late night comedians and the conservative media whittle your career into hasbeen-kindling."

Richie let go of his wife's wrists then, moving his hands to her sides. He did not touch her; he merely held his palms near her body, invading her space—claiming it. His words sinking into her mind, past the terror a strong part of it still screamed she deserved to feel—needed to feel—she stayed where she was for the moment. Confused. Tired.

Almost ready.

"Now," he told her softly, "what you need to do is go to your room, take a long steam, relax in the hot tub, and then go to bed." One hand darting to a pocket, Richie produced several capsules from a small golden pill case.

"Take these, one now, one before you go to bed. You're Kennedy Walker. If you don't like your house, you don't start screaming about demons and ghosts and crap, you just dump it and move into some five star box until you find someplace new."

"But Richie ..."

"Kennedy, you think you hear something. I don't. Even if there is something, it can't be much of anything. Nothing has happened to anybody ... am I right? Has anything happen, like in the movies? Have you been attacked, or hurt in any way? Have you seen a ghost, or anything like one? Or anything?"

"It's not ..."

"*Have you?*"

"No." The word came out of her on a tiny breath—small and barely audible. "No, nothing. Not really. It's just this feeling, I, I just ..."

"Kennedy," Richie cooed, notching his voice to sound as if he cared for the woman before him beyond her capacity to pay his never-ending bills, "you've just come off a major shoot. You wrote ten songs, directed yourself and some of the biggest box office fag bags in the business through six months of hell. You've been fighting with every media outlet in the country. Because you had the nerve to attack the goddamned Republicans and stick it to them where it hurts, they're panning your picture before it's even in the can."

Richie calculated his pause, waiting the proper space of seconds before making his sympathy noise, then moving his fingers ever so slightly so they gently touched the woman's elbows. Grateful for the subtle signal, Kennedy folded herself against her husband, began gently crying once more, her tears and sobs growing larger with each moment.

"There, there, baby—you let it out. It's all right. Richie's here to make it all better."

With practiced dexterity, the man held his wife with one hand while grabbing up a glass of Scotch he had poured minutes earlier when he had realized another episode was about to start. Moving it into Kennedy's waiting hand, he made certain she took the first of the pills he had given her, then gently guided her to the stairway leading to her master bedroom.

"Now you just get a good rest, steam and soak and sleep and all this will be gone by the morning. And, if it isn't, then we'll just get you out of here and you'll never have to see this place again."

The woman took an extra drink from her glass, then another. After that she handed it back to her husband and slowly started up the stairs. Reaching the fifth one, she turned slightly, half-asking Richie, half-asking the ether;

"I really am good, aren't I? I deserve all their praise, don't I?" The man smiled slowly, shaking his head as if addressing a child.

"Like you have to ask."

Her drugs already taking affect, The woman smiled and began making her way upstairs once more. She was feeling better. Safer. More confident. She would show them. She would show them all just exactly who Kennedy Walker was.

They'd learn, by God, she assured herself that you just did not cross someone as powerful and intelligent and beautiful as her, someone who had her finger on the key to everything—everything, and get away with it. She'd show them. Bastards.

She'd show them.

The shields of her arrogance medicated back into place, Kennedy Walker disappeared into her bathroom to pamper herself as she deserved. Watching the door close behind her,

Richie sighed gratefully and returned to the bar to reward himself for having averted another crisis.

Pouring more Scotch, filling the tumbler in his hand for himself, he hefted it, then held it for a moment, staring at its marvelous color through the perfect crystal of his glass. He toasted himself and his ability to keep his wife sane enough to tolerate, having no idea that he had just sent her to her doom, and that he would never see her again.

# CHAPTER THREE

"THAT IS ONE WILD story, boss."

The balding man addressing London was Paul Morcey, one of his two partners in the London Agency. The other, Lisa Hutchinson, was seated next to Morcey in one of the two red leather chairs situation on the other side of the detective's desk in his office where London had taken his usual seat.

"I agree," said Lisa. "This Zarnak person, he really had so much more power than you?"

Months earlier, when the trio had first come together, Lisa had been trying to escape a nightmare of supernatural origin brought down upon her by her own family. She had actually met Morcey first, a janitor at that time who had been affecting repairs to the detective's office. The balding man and London, however, had quickly been pulled together in the young woman's defense against the horrors which came after her in ever-mounting numbers until the detective and Morcey finally triumphed.

"I'm not certain he was so much incredibly more powerful than me, as it was he knew what to do with it. Like a pro b-ball player who knows his way around the court as opposed to a guy who can sink a shot from anywhere, but doesn't know how to move the ball yet."

"Makes sense," offered the balding man. "I mean, we ain't been at this ghost-bustin' stuff very long. You really stumbled in to things, and good thing you did, considered we'd all be history twice over if you hadn't ... but, this Zarnak guy, he kinda made like he was passin' his protectin' the world gig off to you—

right?" London nodded absently, adding;

"Pretty much."

"Yeah, we got kinda a problem buildin', maybe ... with that sorta thing."

"How so?"

"Word's gettin' around that this is the place for people to come if they've got hoodoo problems." When the detective raised his eyebrows to indicate he would like a further explanation, Lisa interrupted the conversation, announcing;

"Paul's right. I've been doing some casting around on-line, in my capacity as the one in charge of running the day-to-day of this office. Just looking for what people are saying about us, what the buzz is—"

"Your point, sweetheart?"

"Rumors are floating. People don't connect us to the Conflagration, but there's plenty of chatter about the vampires, the Grand Canyon ... even the mass healing at the hospital ... Paul was registered as an ICU patient. There's a lot of people out there with nothing better to do that search piles of facts to see what they can find in them."

London shook his head slightly, trying to make sense of what he was being told. It was not that either of his partners were failing to explain themselves clearly. The detective was simply finding the ordinary routine of life growing constantly harder to take seriously. He had just finished explaining how, after days of brutal physical effort, an exertion he was compelled to undertake by a dream he did not even clearly understand, moving through the ether between dimensions in the same manner others leave their homes for a jog, he had been off-handedly dismissed.

Theodore London was wrestling with the idea of being the world's protector. Only months earlier he had simply been a man, a normal, average, everyday kind of fellow with normal, average, everyday kind of problems. Now, somehow he was finding himself being moved into the position of being responsible for anything that might go amiss on the planet that had some sort of supernatural element attached to it.

"Indeed," a voice from the back of his mind hissed at him, "this meeting with Zarnak ... you raced off to your big ass mountain without even considering what you were doing. That's the way it's going to be from now on? You have a dream of portent, and suddenly you drop everything and just rush off to throw yourself at the newest big damn son of a bitch on its way to consume the Earth? Might not be the best way to run a business."

And that, London realized, had to be his main concern at that moment. Yes, the things he had done so far had needed to be done. And, as far as he had known at the moment, he was the only person on the planet who stood a chance of getting them done. He had saved the world—twice. With just a handful of people, he had saved the lives of billions.

Twice.

But, the problem with such accomplishments, as the detective knew his partner was delicately attempting to point out, was that they did not put food on the table or money in the bank. Lisa's mention of the Grand Canyon flashed through his mind, emphasizing the very notion he was trying to make to himself. Yes again, he and his people had saved the world from a hellish fate, but only because they had been able to raise close to a million dollars by breaking several casinos backs with less than scrupulous tactics.

London was not trying to justify his actions at that time to himself there in his office. He had done so then, and had not changed his mind about what they had done. No, what he was attempting to do then was simply decide his next step. As much as every young boy wanted to grow up to be a superhero, to slay dragons, defeat bad guys, save the girl, et cetera, the world did not allow for a steady stream of such activities. Not without sufficient cash reserves on hand to allow one to indulge such fantasies.

"So, what you're saying is, at a time when we're still trying to get this agency back on its feet, trying to grab up some long-term contracts to provide security, or surveillance, to do corporate new-hire background checks—whatever—I've been letting my Clark Kent complex get the better of me—yes?"

"Actually," said Lisa, smiling warmly at London, "that's what I'm trying *not* say."

"Don't worry about it. You're both absolutely right," admitted the detective. "I've allowed us to get distracted one too many times. Playing hero is a great ego boost, but it doesn't do much for the checking account."

"So," asked Lisa, still smiling at London, "what exactly are you saying?"

"I'm saying we need to get serious, or, at least, more serious. I didn't make you two my partners simply to then just flush the company away out from under you—"

"And I for one," quipped Morcey, "appreciate your newly enlightened outlook on the subject."

The detective smiled himself. Leaning forward, propping his elbows on his desk so he might use his hands in a more animated fashion while talking, he said;

"Swell, that takes a lot of the pressure off." London waited a beat to allow the balding man a chance to throw him a disparaging look, then added;

"Seriously, all I'm trying to say is that from now on—and I know who's mainly at fault here—we're going to have to start concentrating on making some cash. For the time being, no matter who comes to us, or for what, if there's no check involved, we tell them to find someone else."

"Okay," said Morcey, digging through a folder of papers he had brought with him to the meeting, "that being the case, oh, do I have an e-mail for you to read."

# CHAPTER FOUR

IT WAS NOT THE kind of neighborhood in which such things were supposed to happen. For one, it did not seem to be of a proper age. The kinds of hoodoo events on which they based every summer's glut of horror movies were supposed to occur in older places—tumbled down, boarded up ruins. Used-up, elder, dead patches long forgotten. But certainly not in places like Seaside.

Indeed, until only a decade previous, the community of Seaside did not even exist. Situated along the ordinarily, incredibly desirable California coastline, the land had always thwarted any attempts at industrialization. Too hilly, too rocky, too unstable—too far from any major roads, the necessary utilities and all the other modern amenities city folk wanted to be near—even when escaping to the country so they could "get away from it all." There had always been simply too many monumentally expensive difficulties to overcome to make anyone think sending the bulldozers into such an area would be profitable.

Which is why it took someone not concerned with monetary profit to do so.

Wallace Beardsly, designer of the P7 Organizer, the multi-multi-millionaire who was lucky enough to stumble across the latest piece of downloadable technology everyone wanted, had found himself with the proverbial correct number of dollars all concerned agreed came to more than those possessed by the Almighty—all of which made him the man to finally do what the conventional wisdom considered impossible. Wanting a home where no one else had one, he had purchased the abnormally difficult pile of rocks and chasms and poured the necessary tens of millions into the area that would allow building to begin.

The project was the subject of the entertainment news medias for the entire two and a half years it took to transform the nightmare of mountainside forests, mud hills and swamp bogs into the most desired piece of real estate in the Western Hemisphere. His home was the talk of the world for several months, until the banal and the small-minded finally found some other shiny thing to captivate their limited fields of attention.

At this point, Beardsly decided he would not mind a few neighbors to help share the crippling tax burden he had created by building where he had, in the manner he had. Even billionaires, he quipped to some media outlet at the time, like to have the folks next door over for a few rounds of bridge once in a while.

Looking for just the right kind of card players, he broke his eleven hundred acres into five, more or less equal lots, and then recouped much of what he had spent, soaking others of the nouveau riche as they clamored to have one of the most exclusive mail box numbers in the world. Kennedy Walker had been the last to build, the property she purchased the most remote segment of Beardsly's little media-blessed paradise.

The end result was the rather banally named Seaside, an extremely modern, well-lit, well-appointed socially correct environment to which Beardsly retired, becoming almost as famous for his newly adapted reclusive ways as he had been for his computer discoveries. Of course, if one was to retire from the world, Seaside was certainly a comfortable locale in which to do so. The walled-in world was an extremely pleasant place, its walls not too tall, its machine-gun carrying defenders kept discretely out of sight. True, it was somewhat banal, but it was also well-groomed, smart looking and quite easy on eyes tired of cities, traffic and humanity's masses. Its communal trees were neatly manicured, its gardens nicely tended. Flowers stood straight in their freshly turned beds.

As the rental car came up to the security gate barring the

world's ordinary folks from entering the magnificence of Seaside, Morcey ran his eyes beyond the windshield and over the double bunker and those guards he could actually see. He could easily tell they had obviously been picked to be both ethnically diverse enough to keep the residents of the tiny community happy, while still being capable enough to perform their duties.

"I get the sense we're in the land of the liberals, boss," the balding man quipped to London, one of two passengers in the back seat. Looking up from the paperback he was reading, the detective took in the view, then answered;

"Well, we are in California. Really—what'd you think we were going to find?"

"Are you complaining, Paul," asked the other man in the back seat. He was the oldest of all those in the car, a tall, thin fellow with intense, blazing blue eyes—small boned, but square-shouldered. Pointing toward the opulent grounds beyond the bunkers, he added;

"After all, people that live in places like these are the only ones that can afford fees like our dear friend here coaxed out of your new client." The man to whom the speaker was referring added;

"*Our* new client, Zack. When you work for the Theodore London Agency, you're part of the team."

"Oh yes, that makes a difference. I imagine that will look quite smart enough on my tombstone," the older man answered with a wry grimace. "'He Was Part Of The Team.' Indeed, has a nice ring to it."

His voice contained a catch within it which implied he was about to say more, but the older man went silent instead as their vehicle rolled up to the front gate of the imposing bunker complex. Dropping the driver-side window, the balding man behind the wheel threw his most disarming tone to the waiting guard, telling him;

"Hey, we're expected. London Agency, outta New York. We got a ten o'clock with a Richard Dennton."

"ID, please, sir," was all the guard gave him in return.

The man behind the wheel handed over his driver's license. The guard accepted it, checking its particulars against facts on a sheet of paper attached to his clipboard. He was clean shaven and properly appointed. His uniform was crisp and non-threatening, his belt hung with official, but non-lethal articles, unlike those of his teammates. The other guards, mostly out of sight, wore helmets and armor and each stood to the ready with a weapon in their hands. All those in the vehicle noted the fact and wondered if Seaside's security force was always on such alert, or if it were only a result of their current situation.

After a reasonable amount of time, the guard returned the driver's identification, telling him;

"You'll proceed to the Walker estate now. It's some distance from here actually, and the way is a bit tricky. One of our security vehicles will lead you there. Please do not lag behind or stop your vehicle. If you have some sort of mechanical difficulty which forces you to stop, do not leave the vehicle for any reason. Assistance will come to you immediately." No one felt reassured by his statement. Continuing in the same near-monotone, the guard finished, saying;

"You should reach the estate in approximately twenty minutes. You'll be met there by representatives from the county sheriff's department and several others."

"No directors, no producers?" quipped the balding man. "And here I thought this was gonna be my big chance to make it to the silver screen."

"There's a long line for that kind of thing out here," the guard answered tightly, motioning with his clipboard-free hand for the waiting security vehicle to start for the Walker mansion. "If Mr. Dennton was the type to read random screenplays, I would have given him one of mine months ago."

Throwing their rental car into drive, the balding man said;

"Gee, boss, I thought everyone here in California was supposed to be ... I don't know, supportive and crap."

"Maybe he was attempting to be merely supportive, Mr. Morcey," suggested the woman sitting in the front passenger seat—one who was not their partner, Lisa. An Asian, she was tall and thin and wrapped in long robes, hooded and cuffed, accoutrements which disguised the details of her body quite effectively. While her face remained a quiet mask, while both the two passengers in the back seat both chuckled, the older one added;

"I think she means, don't quit your day job, Paul." Keeping his eyes on the car in front of him, the driver nonetheless raised one eyebrow as he answered;

"Man, with friends like youse all, a guy could find his ego hangin' down around his knees."

"If playtime is over," said London, "let's use our private time here to size this place up." Closing his eyes, he put his paperback aside and his head back against the cushioned rear padding of the car. Shifting his body to find the most comfortable spot he could, he asked, "Any observations?"

"They like their security," answered Morcey. "I'll give 'em that much."

"I got a sense our budding screenwriter with the clipboard was, despite his quite expert performance, somewhat nervous." The older man looked over to London as he spoke, wondering to himself how the detective could simply ride along with his eyes closed, not filled with excitement, or at least curiosity. Knowing no answer would be forthcoming at that moment, he added, "Now, our question is, was he nervous about *our* arrival, or over why we were summoned in the first place?"

"My thinking exactly, Zack," answered London. His eyes still closed, as if he were trying to take in more than simply the conversation there in the car, he asked the woman in the front seat;

"Lai Wan, any ideas?"

"The man who greeted us, all those within the bunker whom we were not permitted to meet, those in the car ahead of us as well, all of them are frightened."

"Any idea what it is they're scared of?"

"Yes," she replied. "Some are worried over possibly losing their jobs. Some are thinking that such a loss might be accompanied by legal repercussions—someone accusing them of not doing their jobs. Some believe that the incident we have come to investigate might not be isolated, that it might only be the beginning of something larger—something terrible."

"I'll bet," interrupted the balding man, "that more of 'em think we're a bunch of phonies than think somethin' supernatural happened here. Who's with me on that one?"

"You are quite correct," answered the woman. "But that is not to say that some of them are not quite uncomfortable with the idea that there is something wrong with this area. Indeed, apparently there was talk amongst the security teams and other workers, grounds-keepers, wait-staff, et cetera, long before the disappearance that brought us here." Her voice dropping a note, she added;

"Apparently a large number of those who do not own this property believe that the deeper one goes into this area, the stranger things become."

All within the rental vehicle went silent at that point. The woman seemed quite content to simply sit and wait for their car to reach their destination. But, it was quite obvious that the older man and Morcey were both waiting to hear what London was thinking. Before they could find out, however, the security team ahead of them turned off the main road onto a side leg leading off through a thick pine grove. In but a few minutes they came to a second security post. This one, however, was standing ready for them with its gates at the open. As the two vehicles passed through the opening, the balding man said;

"Man, you feel dem eyes watchin' us? Shivers—this bunch really is plenty spooked."

"You can feel it," answered the detective. Staring out the window, simply allowing herself to *feel* their surroundings, the woman added;

"Give yourself a few moments to take in the atmosphere around here, most likely all of you will begin to agree with them."

At that point the two vehicles came into a spacious clearing. In the distance stood a massive house, a sharply modernistic mansion seemingly made more of glass than stone and steel. The grounds leading up to the multi-leveled home were extremely elegant, and yet understated at the same time.

"Beautiful place," said the older man, his voice almost wistful. "Really—the gardening quite reminds me of that outside the palace at Versailles."

"Yeah, maybe," admitted Morcey, his voice dropping into a quieter range, "but I bet most days your palace don't have so many police cars parked outside it."

"Well, come on now, Paul," answered London, his eyes opening as he sat forward slightly. Straightening his suit, he said, "you didn't think anyone was going to make any of this easy on us, did you?"

"No," the balding man answered, rolling their rental car slowly into place amongst the menagerie of other vehicles. "But my rabbi tells me I should stay open to new experiences."

"Well, this could be your lucky day," answered the detective, studying the house before them, distrusting it more with each passing second, "because, little buddy, something tells me that we're about to have the newest experience of our lives."

# CHAPTER FIVE

"SO, YOU'RE THEODORE LONDON," snapped a grizzled individual at the detective as the quartet entered the mansion, "the fancy ghostbuster from New York City. I guess all us simple types can get back to our ordinary crimes now that you're here to show us how it's done."

"Hey, sounds good to me," offered the balding man. "Don't let the door hit you on the way out, Grumpy."

The speaker did not seem to be terribly amused. Within the mansion of Kennedy Walker, quite a number of law enforcement officials had gathered to await the arrival of the London Agency, along with a trio of others London immediately assumed to be lawyers. Introductions were quickly made which confirmed most of his guesses.

The head of the local crime scene investigation unit sat on one couch with the local district attorney and two state troopers. The first to speaker, a man of medium height and only a slightly overbearing paunch was the local sheriff. Frankly, he seemed quite out of place in the assembly to London, but due to an antique set of laws never updated, he actually held authority in the area over the local city, county and even state officials present. Standing boldly in the center of the room, he was flanked by two of his deputies—one male, one female. The woman handed him a slim folder when he motioned for it.

While the members of the London Agency found seats within the well-appointed living room, the speaker introduced himself bluntly as Sheriff Michael Tyrell. His tone was a growl which indicated he expected those present to already know who he was. While the newcomers waited, he flipped the manilla file open, narrowing his eyes as he focused on the balding man.

"Paul Morcey," he responded. "Caucasian male, forty-four years of age; 5' 7", 156 pounds; brown eyes; brown hair, mostly contained in a foot-long pony tail; no tattoos, birthmark on right thigh; employed as a janitor until seven months ago, at which point subject switched jobs and became a private detective." Looking over the edge of the folder, the sheriff asked;

"Not your usual transitional job choice, is it? What caused you to make such a switch, especially when you sacrificed a pension plan you'd put ... twelve years into to do so?"

"Just got tired of stickin' my head in toilets, I guess," answered Morcey. "I know that must be hard for you to understand. After all, cleanin' commodes must seem like a real glamor job to a guy like you." The sheriff ignored the comment's antagonism, choosing to ask instead;

"Ummm-huummm ... wouldn't have anything to do with the destruction of the town of Elizabeth, New Jersey, as well as the devastation that occurred across the lower twenty blocks of Manhattan Island, would it?"

"Heavens, sheriff," answered the balding man, his smile a thing both self-satisfied and goading, "me, go to Jersey? Of my own free will? Obviously you have no idea what it means to be from Queens."

London smiled to himself, impressed with his partner's ability to deflect such an unexpected question. As far as any of them had been able to determine, no one had as of yet connected the agency to the terrible tragedy which had unleashed so much destruction earlier in the year. From what the detective could tell from the rest of those gathered, none of them had made the connection Tyrell had. Suddenly London's respect for the sheriff increased dramatically, marking him as someone who would bear watching.

Turning away from Morcey for the moment, the lawman in

question focused his attention on Lai Wan. Pulling his prepared paper on her, he read aloud;

"Lai Wan; Asian female, no age listed—anywhere. Isn't that a bit strange?"

"I died on an operating table a number of years ago, Sheriff. I've seen no reason to worry about such things since then."

"That's not my point," snapped Tyrell. "Such information is kept by the government for a reason. So—"

"Do not presume to lecture me on why governments do as they will with people and their lives," growled the woman. Her voice a searing knife edge to the ear, she threw her words at the sheriff, telling him;

"My height, my weight, age, eye color, hair, what job I perform ... my profession ... yes, that much I'll tell you. I am a psychometrist. I peel open the lies of men and spit on them. Tell me one of your lies, Mr. Tyrell, so I might spit on it!"

"That's enough!" The sheriff's bellow silenced not only Lai Wan, but all the others looking to interrupt as well. Deciding to move on, the lawman shifted his attention to the oldest of the visitors. Shifting to another paper in his folder, he read;

"Zachery Goward; Caucasian male, sixty-three; 6' 2", 185 pounds; green eyes; grey hair; scar on his right temple; employed by Columbia University as a professor of philosophy and theology. You a detective, too, professor?"

"Anyone who investigates, my dear, sheriff," Goward responded, "who explores any avenue of human endeavor which is heretofore unknown is by the very definition of the words a detective of sorts, wouldn't you say?" Rising from his seat, the older man made a theatrical flourish with his arm, asking;

"I mean, seriously, sir, whenever you choose to look at something of which you have no, or little, understanding, there is always that desire, in any sentient being, perhaps even a primal, basic need, to learn exactly what it is with which one is dealing—especially when the unknown is involved. Mankind fears that which it does not understand, you know. For instance, you yourself have been wresting with an unknown, I'm certain, not knowing why someone would call for outside help when you are right here ..."

"Thank you, professor ..."

"One finds several immediate surface fears in such a situation, of course—the worry over dismissal, perceived inadequacy, then there are the obvious concerns over rejection, and job security—"

Goward paused for a moment, as if trying to think where he should go next. Then, pretending to have finally noticed the thin ridge of impatience building across the sheriff's face, he notched his tone to a cutting edge, offering;

"Why, my good lord of Nottingham, is something the matter? Oh, wait—of course. How foolish of me, how insensitive, you went to all the trouble to plan this little moment of intimidation ... oh, how frightfully sorry I am. I didn't act intimidated at all, did I? Oh dear me, the rejection you must be feeling ..."

"Watch out, Doc," interrupted Morcey. "This guy's a loose cannon. There's no tellin' what he might do. Why now, me—I'm practically shakin' in me boots. Really I am."

"These the kind of jokes you made while you asslicks destroyed billions of dollars worth of property? While you killed millions?"

"Fairly weighty accusations, sheriff," said London quietly, suddenly—drawing all attention. Seated in a comfortable pseudo-leather chair of modern design, legs uncrossed, arms seemingly relaxed on the armrests, he moved only enough to tilt his head in Tyrell's direction as he added;

"I don't know where you get your fairy tale notions, but if you've actually got something to say, why don't you spill it? Our client isn't paying us to waste time doing the long arm cha-cha. Or maybe it never dawned on you that every second is vital in a missing persons case."

"Don't try and tell me my job, London, and I won't—"

"You won't do anything, sheriff," came another voice. Rising from his seat on the couch, the district attorney came forward angrily, snapping;

"I told you your 'Heat-of-the-Night' tactics weren't going to work, and I agreed to come here today for two reasons. One, to see you knocked back a few feet, and two, to make certain you didn't turn what is at present merely a touchy mess into a full-blown disaster."

"Hey, boss," shouted Morcey, clapping his hands together with feigned enthusiasm, "they're gonna play good cop/bad cop. Just like in da movies. We shoulda brought popcorn. Maybe we could send a deputy out to get Slushies. I love Slushies, blue, of course. And then—"

"I wouldn't be quite so flippant, Mr. Morcey, is it," interjected one of the lawyers representing Walker's studio. "Your presence here, in violation with our client's contract with Ms. Walker, could mean—"

"Forget that nonsense," shouted the woman next to him, the studio's insurance representative. "If this dildo does a shout that brings down bad press on this project, we're in a dive for a hundred mill, plus." Turning toward London, she practically screamed;

"He's going to sue you? I'll have your balls on a silver platter, served in wine sauce. If you think—"

"*All right,*" a new voice snapped from the doorway. "That should be just about enough out of everyone. Welcome to the wonderful world of Californian one-up-manship, Mr. London. Is it all you expected?"

The newcomer proved to be one Walter Liston, a tall, powerfully built black man with graying temples and cold eyes most in the room already knew to be the State Attorney General. When his office had caught wind of what was going to happen that day at the Walker estate, he had cancelled everything on his docket, including a meeting with the governor and the state's energy brokers, a conclave which, as he put it;

"I would have thought not even the much-awaited Second

Coming could tear me away from what I had scheduled for today, but we serve where needed. And," he had paused, casting a glaring eye toward the sheriff, "as it has already been proven to me, today it seems this is where I'm needed most."

"All right," answered London, "swell. So we get to go from 'good cop' to 'better cop.' Fine by me. Now that you've shut this raving pack of gutter dogs up for a moment, let me throw my cards on the table and see if we can't get somewhere."

Liston took the offer as it was meant, visibly calming. His eyes gave away to anyone willing to give them careful scrutiny that he was tired and frightened, but still ready to be reasonable. Banking on that holding, the detective said;

"My name, as I'm certain you know or you wouldn't be here, is Theodore London. I'm one of three partners in the London Agency. I am sorry, and even a bit stunned, to come here on one matter only to find that the local government wants to make me responsible for the event known as the Conflagration, but well, how does anyone even begin to answer something like that?"

Sheriff Tyrell glared. Varying levels of interest, from very to extremely, filled the faces of all the others. The moment shuddered with mounting intensity, for private detective Theodore London was indeed responsible for the destruction listed earlier. Fantastical as it might sound, he had been given the choice of pulling a trigger which would kill over two million people, his best friend included, or not doing so, and letting every sentient being in the entire universe perish.

"From what I can tell, and this is offered simply to put this nonsense to rest so we can get on with things," offered the detective, "the Conflagration was a supernatural event. From what I know about the world, there are agencies and departments within almost all of our country's law enforcement agencies that handle such things. Apparently they were all caught flat-footed by the event. Being private, my agency was not one of the ones involved. Now, the sheriff might want to spend time no one else has on trying to deliver the blame for that tragedy to my doorstep, but important as he is here in the land of granola, I think Mr. Tyrell's a little out of even his extensive jurisdiction, so I'm going to let that debate rest for now as it really isn't going to get us anywhere."

Tyrell started to noticeably bristle at London's crack, but Liston deftly interceded, saying;

"Let's for a moment entertain the notion that the sheriff here is a dedicated lawman who is willing to believe even the most fantastic ideas in the line of duty. If you would concede that it's possible he was merely acting in the best interests of those he's sworn to protect, maybe we could get past the kindergarten atmosphere I found when I arrived and on to where some good could be done."

Everyone around the room granted Liston's premise and worked at getting their tempers and private agendas under control. London registered the fact, deciding to look for the man's good side. The detective realized he was in a sea filled with self-interested barracuda. Having a shark arrive from nowhere to run interference for him was not the kind of gift he often ignored.

He also had to concede that he knew why Liston and all the others were on edge; when the Conflagration had occurred, like most everyone in the world, London himself had not believed in demons, witches, vampires or any other kind of nightbumper. Not only had he been forced to believe such information— quickly—but ever since then, as more and more like situations had come his way, he had found himself the center of much unwanted attention.

"Bad enough," he thought as everyone settled in for whatever was coming next, "someone like Dennton is able to connect us to this kind of crap. But to get here and find half the Californian Civil Service waiting for us ..."

The detective sighed, trying his best not to predict the future. Goward had explained to him that by attempting to predict the future, one began creating it. Looking forward at that moment, he decided, was not a good idea. Taking another tact, he asked instead;

"So, Mr. Liston, tell us—not that I don't love communing with government officials as much as the next taxpayer, but could you tell us why you, and the rest of this 'assembly,' are here to greet us, and not our client, Mr. Dennton?"

"Probably a good place to start."

"Before you do ..." all heads turned toward the Asian woman. So quietly had she remained pulled in on herself while the others squared off with one another that she had almost been forgotten. Embarrassment rushing through the room as all anticipated her next words, the woman rose from her seat, saying;

"For those who were waiting for the sheriff's score card," she announced, "my name is Lai Wan. On the long flight here which I did not want to make, we were only served snacks. Racing to be here on time, such considerations as restrooms were forsaken. If the group of you think you could thump your chests at each other just as well without me, I would like to, as they used to say in a politer time, 'freshen up' a bit."

Immediately both the state troopers snapped upward out of their seats and hastened to show the woman the way to both the bathroom and the kitchen. Thanking them, she asked the room if they would all like some tea. When everyone answered in the positive, mostly to avoid her judgmental gaze than anything else, she said she would see what she could do and then quietly exited the main room. Then, as the others went back to their dickering, she set out to do what she had come to accomplish.

# CHAPTER
# SIX

"I'LL GET RIGHT TO it, Mr. London," said the Attorney General, leaning forward in his chair. "You're in California, and more of this state revolves around Hollywood than we'd care to admit. The various entertainment industries—movies, television, music—the dollars that flow through their hands and into the state coffers have kept a lot of unrealistic nonsense propped up for quite some time."

From the way Liston paused, London wondered if he expected some in the room to challenge this or that part of his statement. When no one did, however, the man continued, saying;

"Everyone knowing this, though, has always left California open to charges of general wackiness. The title 'LaLa Land' is something that will probably never be removed from the popular culture, no matter how much some of the rich and powerful wish for it to disappear." The Attorney General removed his glasses for a moment so he could apply a bit of pressure to the bridge of his nose, then added;

"To be perfectly blunt, there are major forces at work in the background out here maneuvering to project a saner image. But, there have been one too many scandals here lately for them to control, and so for lack of a better way to put it, we're looking to put a little spin on this one before the media sniffs it out and goes wild with it."

"Well," offered the detective, keeping his tone level so as to project an attitude of cooperation, "I'll give you this much, Mr. Liston, when you put your cards on the table, you put them there face up."

"I'd like to apologize if I might," offered Tyrell. In contrast to London, he allowed the inflection in his voice to express that what he was saying only meant he was being politically polite, not contrite, and that he did not care much either way how people took it.

"Maybe I snapped at folks before I was bit, but what I'm asking you to understand is that I'm under a few more guns over this one than any of you are aware of. This Seaside place, this is my own goddamned little time bomb. I've been waiting for something in this nuthouse to go off, and now it finally has."

"First purchased and developed by Wallace Beardsly," responded London, "this millennia's Bill Gates. We met his happy doormen on the way in. After carving out his own homestead, he then sold off the four remaining lots—one to the youngest of the Daltons of Wyoming, cattle and timber money. He wanted to escape the cold weather and start cashing in on the joys of being a movie producer. The second went to the clean branch of the Beretella family, the ivy league section of that particular mafia clan that handles all their face-to-the-public business."

"There's a recommendation," snipped one of the sheriff's deputies, "the lawyer is the clean one in the family." As some of those gathered chuckled, London merely nodded, then continued, saying;

"The third parcel sold went to political refugee Polimar Grenzenki, paid for with monies he looted from his corner of the glorious worker's paradise before he skipped out one step before the torches and pitchforks. And the last, of course, went to Mr. and Mrs. Kennedy Walker."

"You do your homework, I see, Mr. London."

"Thanks, sheriff," the detective responded honestly. Seeing no reason to help keep the animosity rolling, he added, "Honestly, I'm as willing to back off and start playing ball as you are. You guys want to know what we're up to, here's our story. Yesterday my agency gets a call from the still unseen Mr. Dennton. He offers us one million dollars to find his wife for him. Says she's been missing a week."

London pretended to need a breath, using the moment to cast his eyes about the room. Fixing everyone's expressions in his mind, he then continued, saying;

"As he explained it to us, even though he's the one that called the authorities in the first place—I'm guessing he meant fine, reasonable folks like all you people—he's considered the prime suspect in her disappearance. He cackled at that one, went on a bit about how it was the stupidest thing he'd ever heard, considering that her will left him her beach home in Malibu and that was it." The detective made a real pause that time, then added;

"I believe he was implying that would not be enough to support his life style."

"He is our prime suspect," agreed Tyrell in a weary voice, "but only because there's no one else. He isn't really under any actual suspicion."

"Agreed," added the local district attorney. "No motive, and no spine. Even if she were routinely whittling away at his salami with the fact she controlled everything, which frankly, I believe her perfectly capable of doing, he simply doesn't come across as the type who would do anything about it."

"At least," offered Goward, "anything self-destructively foolish."

"And so, if that's the case," asked London, "then I ask you, why are so many of you stressed over the fact he hired us to find his wife?"

Tyrell and the attorney general looked at each other, then turned toward London. The sheriff made a hand motion to one of his deputies while the local official replied;

"Mr. Dennton willingly offered to allow us to meet you as a gesture of good faith. If I might explain, Mr. London, there are certain elements here on this coast that were made a trifle nervous by the thought of bringing in a private investigation team before the local authorities had given up on the case. Really, there is no case ... I mean, when the media gets wind of this ... missing superstar, all her connections—"

"They're frightened, Mr. London," came a new voice, one the detective had previously only heard on the phone. "The bunch of them are simply scared that things are going to get all shook up out here."

Richard Dennton was ushered into his own living room by one of Tyrell's deputies. London scanned the man casually, but thoroughly. Kennedy Walker's husband seemed comfortable enough that the detective decided to accept the district attorney's explanation. As he noted the drink in Dennton's hand, as well, he shifted his attention back to the Attorney General.

"We've kept a lid on this about as long as we can," answered Liston. "Ms. Walker, like many of Hollywood's elite, maintains a high social profile. She is interconnected throughout the society ladder here, as well as that of local Democratic politics. Such people are expected to be at certain functions, to head committees, be seen at the right fund-raisers, you get the idea."

"It's not like the old days," sighed one of the assorted lawyers at the table. "Celebrities could vanish for a week or two, and the public wouldn't have any way to suspect. Now, with a hundred media gossip news outlets, star watch blogs, the goddamned internet rumor mill—"

"Let alone the fact her Twitter account hasn't been updated, Facebook, GetFact—"

"That's nothing," Dennton snapped. "Let's get to the real reason you're all yapping here." Turning toward the members of the London Agency, the only slightly inebriated suspect gave a sinister wink, then said;

"What's got this bunch so wired is that Kennedy's supposed to be in post-production on her new picture. Obviously the insurance has already been laid in against anything happening to her. After all, she's wrote the picture, starred in it, directed it ... feminist action/adventure flick—highbrow attitude with effects and skin for the bottom-feeders. Only my wife would be stupid enough to think you could mix the two ..."

"It's not a stupid concept," argued one of the studio lawyers, "but this whole affair, the way Mr. Dennton insists on describing it, could damage us in the public eye to the point where we would have no choice but to sue—"

"Whoa, nellie-bun," shouted Morcey. "Look—maybe you three-piece strait-jacket types can make sense of all this, but us simpler types need it laid out. Once again, the question was 'why, Mr. Dennton, did you hire us?'" While everyone stared, the balding man stretched his arms out in a pleading fashion and asked;

"I mean, I may just be an ex-maintenance engineer from Queens, but it seems to me you got everyone and his brother falling down to help you find your wife. The studio, their insurance company, the politicians, they've all got their reasons. The sheriff here seems to be the only guy who wants to find her for what I would call the 'right motivation,' mainly because she's someone who may be in need of help, but then like I said, I ain't that complicated a guy, and perhaps prone to over-simplification."

"I like your Spock, London," said Dennton, pointing toward Morcey. "He sets you up nice."

"Thanks," answered the detective. "But we would still like an answer to the question."

"Okay," responded Dennton, "the set-up phrase for this scene seems to cover getting one's cards on the table, so please, allow me to give you everybody's." Turning a bit too quickly, spilling a large dollop of his drink over the side of his glass and his fingers, Dennton steadied himself, then said;

"You want facts, here are mine. Kennedy has all the purse strings. If she's dead, I'm finished. My personal fortune, most of it's tied up in that million I offered you. That's nothing out here. If she's really gone, I'll be begging to be kept on as one of the grounds keepers. Can I spell out my situation any more clearly for anyone?"

No one asked him for any further clarification.

"You're right about the sheriff, too. Been watching too much television, he has. He's into that law and order, protect and serve crap. If I were you boys, he's the only one I'd trust."

London could not help but notice that Tyrell came close to blushing. The detective filed the emotional display away in his mind.

"The rest of this bunch, they're all just scared shitless. Why—because they don't want me telling the media what I told you. The studio, they can't afford a flop. Our officials, they don't want the embarrassment. None of them, they simply don't want to see the headline: Kennedy Walker Eaten By Her House."

The room went quiet at that point. One by one heads dropped, shaking sadly, mostly from one degree or another of self-pity. Those from the London Agency watched everyone around them intently. From what they could read in the gathered faces, there was no doubt Kennedy Walker's husband was correct. All those present were concerned about her whereabouts, but she had no friends there in her living room. Outside of the sheriff, those present were only there for reasons of their own.

"Well, I knew this was not going to be one of the good ones," thought London sourly. "But I had no idea it was going to be this much fun."

"And don't think I'm kidding," snapped Dennton. Proceeding to the bar against the far wall, he called out over his shoulder, "Because that *is* what happened to my wife. She got eaten by her own goddamned *house!*"

The man poured himself another full tumbler, downed half of it quickly, then topped it off again with a motion so smooth as to almost not be noticed. Turning back toward the others, he sipped at his tumbler casually as he walked slowly back toward them, his voice rising as he announced;

"Of course, would I believe her? Listen to her. No, I was too smart for that. I wasn't stupid enough to believe that kind of tripe. No, not me, not smart ol' Richie. I knew better. I wouldn't listen."

"Wouldn't listen to what?" asked London.

"I told you before, on the phone, she knew the house was out to get her. That it was evil. And not just the house. No, sir. No-sirre-bob. No, sir. It was all of it. Everything."

"What exactly do you mean by 'everything,' Mr. Dennton?" The detective asked his questions patiently. Quietly. "Things here in the house?"

"No, everything. Everything everywhere."

"Ms. Walker," one of the lawyers said quietly, "for some time had been making statements to the effect that she was quite, ah ... uncomfortable here in Seaside. At first she attempted to brazen it out. Nothing was going to scare her away from her paradise retreat, et cetera."

"Yeah," interrupted Dennton, "but lately, and you ask these studio scumsharks, you ask them if she wasn't saying that this place was haunted. That even the trees, and the goddamned rabbits and, and the grass, the flowers and everything else ... that every inch of this place was haunted—and that it wanted *her.*"

Many in the crowd stirred at Dennton's words, their moods darkening appreciably. The man himself started to laugh weakly, then shoved his drink to his mouth quickly to keep himself from crying. As if on cue, different voices sounded then, all fighting to gain the floor, all wanting to challenge some portion of what Kennedy Walker's husband had just said.

The sudden piercing female scream coming from upstairs trumped them all, however, sending men and women running for the stairs, the hands of those who were armed grabbing for their weapons.

# CHAPTER
# SEVEN

THE FIRST TO TRACK down the source of the terrible cry found Lai Wan stretched across the master bed in Kennedy Walker's suite, just across and down the hall from Dennton's lesser, but adequate bedroom. The psychometrist was not found in the typical sweeping, luxurious pose of a fairy tale maiden in swoon. Rather, her body lie at odd, uncomfortable angles, covered in sweat—her eyes closed, her limbs shaking, twitching uncontrollably.

Despite the disturbing moans that continued to roll forth from her lips, it was readily deduced that she was unconscious. This confused her initial examiners since there was not a mark visible anywhere upon her. Her face, however, even with her eyes shut tight remained twisted in inexplicable terror, her muscles continuing to spasm, jerking wildly.

As the crowd rolled into the room, their questions were as chaotic as their approach.

"What happened?"

"Is she all right? Is she bleeding?"

"What the hell is she doing in here?"

"Should we give her air, or something?"

"She shouldn't be in here, This room is a goddamned crime scene."

"You name the crime," snarled Morcey over his shoulder, shoving back several of the others with one hand while doing his best to control the woman's violent shaking with the other, "we'll respect the scene."

"London," snapped Tyrell, "explain this—and don't try to pretend you don't know what's going on."

"In one minute—no problem," answered the detective, moving forward as best he could through the tangle in the doorway. Pulling Goward along with him through the crowd, he moved the professor forward toward the bed, ordering, "Zack, check her pulse. See if her eyes are dilated. Check her heartbeat; check for fever, too. Just see what you can do."

"Why thank you, *Doctor* London," answered the older man gruffly. Bending over the writhing woman, he snapped, "Yes, indeed, I will see what I can accomplish now that I have the advantage of your vast medical background for guidance." Ignoring the professor's sarcasm, London turned to the others, immediately working at herding them back away from the bed as he said mainly to Tyrell;

"I don't know how extensive your notes on all of us are, or how much you shared with everyone else already, but as she told you earlier, Lai Wan is a psychometrist. That means she can sense things through touch. If she came to this room, it's a bet she felt this is the place Ms. Walker disappeared." Pushing his way through the others to the bed, the sheriff snapped at his deputies;

"Don't just stand there—earn your pay and clear this room out. Get everyone back. There shouldn't be anyone in here but her and the doctor," then, with a glance at Goward, he added, "and the funnyman, if you think you need him."

"Yes, thank you, sheriff," answered the professor honestly, adding, "And yes again, the way she's convulsing, I think it best Mr. Morcey does stay. Others laying hands on her, people she doesn't know, it could have all manner of ill effects ... considering her abilities, I mean."

As Goward turned back to his patient, Tyrell grabbed hold of London's arm, barking;

"That means you and me, too, ghostbuster. She's sensitive to vibrations and that kind of shit, you say? Okay, in the spirit of playing Halloween, let's you and me get all my nasty old negativity out of here."

Not seeing where he could do the psychometrist any good

by staying, London nodded and willingly joined the sheriff in the hallway with the others. Taking a last look over his shoulder, not seeing any change in the woman's condition, the detective turned and said;

"I can hazard a guess or two at what this's all about, but I can't tell you what's happened to her for certain, because I don't know. At least, I'm not sure."

"Oh, go ahead," answered Tyrell. "Give it a try. It's a pretty circle. See if you can tie it together without knotting it around yourself."

"What I'm saying is that I didn't give her any instructions to do anything. Remember, we weren't aware that when we got here we were going to be facing the Spanish Inquisition. Now, I'll grant you that it's been pretty much the 'comfy chair' version so far, which I do appreciate, but what I mean is, coming up here, this was her idea."

"And that idea was," asked the local district attorney, "in your enlightened opinion?"

"There was a lot of negativity being thrown around downstairs," London explained. "You all were flooding the place with it. When directed at her, that kind of thing can affect her results. One on one, you can be as negative as you want and she can still tell you anything about yourself."

"Convenient," Liston cut in, "now that she's unconscious and can't be asked to prove any of what you're saying."

"Bite me, jerkwad," snarled London. Staring down the politician, he snarled, "You dancing maidens have just about pushed my buttons as hard as I'm going to take. One of my people is down, and you lot are the cause of it. If it wasn't for your ridiculous dog and pony show, we'd have been with her when whatever happened in there happened. Now we don't know shit, and—"

"Bluster all you want," shouted one of the lawyers, "but you're just digging your hole deeper. You people latched onto Dennton in the hopes of bleeding him with your schemes, then you try and intimidate us with actresses and cheap parlor tricks, all the time putting our studio in serious jeopardy—"

"You sanctimonious toad," snapped London. As the detective turned toward the lawyer, both a state trooper and one of Tyrell's deputies unconsciously stepped in his path, fearing the worst. Not even noticing them, London snarled;

"Don't start in on a meal at my table if you can't clean your plate. Try and remember, asswipe, Mr. Dennton came to us. We're not the ones who caused any of your headaches. We haven't done anything wrong. In fact, we haven't done anything yet except get threatened by weasels in suits, and agree to try and find a missing person—the kind of job we get to do every day back on the sane coast without any hassles."

"Don't add libel to your other sins," cautioned one of the lawyers.

"You listen to me, you vampiritic little piece of shit," growled the detective, "if Lai Wan is out of this that fast, then we have no idea what we're up against here. And if you've decided now's the time to look for trouble ..."

"Let's try to stay calm, sir," said the state trooper between London and the lawyer quietly. His hand hovering unconsciously above his sidearm, he added, "no one here is looking for any trouble."

"Yah, yah, mein stormtrooper," snapped the detective, his face grim, eyes unblinking, "I can see your itchy trigger finger dragging us into a typical future already. Well, if that's your goddamned answer to everything, all I can say to the bunch of you is—watch yourselves. You want to play around with me, let's play. But I'm warning you now, whatever's actually going on here, you morons have no idea what you're dealing with."

It was, in every way, a typical threat, the kind every man in the hallway—peace officer, lawyer, or elected official—had heard before more times than they could count. But, just as they had all learned through years of practice to deflect such bravado, they had also learned to gauge the voices of those spewing it. Every single person in reach of London's voice, hearing his tone, was taken

aback in one form or another. Whether they believed the detective
could handle all of them with the ease the fierce inflection within
his voice implied or not, they all knew *he* certainly believe it.

Several of the lawyers practically fell down the stairs, so far
did they back-pedal at hearing London's orders. The officials
were not quite so frightened, but they left the deputies and
troopers plenty of room to face the detective first. Stepping into
London's direct field of vision, Tyrell offered;

"Okay, I'm thinking, there's a lot going on here, not so much
of it tied to brain power. I ain't usually in the apology business,
and getting pushed there by someone who's not even one of my
own," he sneered, looking at the state policeman in question,
"is not my idea of a good time, either. But, all I can say is, some
people fall back on their training a little too readily rather than
trying to think." Staring unblinking directly into London's eyes,
he added in a calmer tone;

"Be a shame if you were one, too, son."

The detective, realizing what the sheriff was trying to
accomplish, relaxed his pose—stood straighter, unhunched his
shoulders. Lowering his voice, shifting his tone to where it
matched Tyrell's reasonable attitude, he replied;

"I'll make an offer right now. If you people want to continue
to dither over this mess by yourselves, I'll get my people packed
up as quickly as possible and get us out of here. No charge to Mr.
Dennton. We're not here to generate headlines—anybody with
half a goddamned brain in their head should be able to figure out
that's the last thing we want."

Tyrell turned, looking over the scattered crowd in the
large hallway. He zeroed in on Dennton's face, then Liston's.
Scanning the others in turn, spending less time on each as he
whittled his way down through their levels of importance, he
finally addressed the assembly at large, asking them all;

"Anybody here really stupid enough to want these people
to leave? Don't try to calculate advantages, don't start playing
games in your head—think for a second." He gave his question

a three-count, but got no takers. Satisfied, especially as he saw a number of heads in the crowd drooping in embarrassment, Tyrell turned back to London, offering;

"Looks as if they've all realized it's better to have you here. Hell, after all, if nothing else you'll make dandy scapegoat material when this all goes to hell."

The detective smiled. The last of his apprehension about the minor players vanishing, he told Tyrell;

"There may actually be a reason they let you keep so much power around here, sheriff."

"Shucks, pard'ner," the lawman answered, affecting an outrageous cowboy accent, "I'd like to see 'em try and take it away."

"Yeah," responded London, his smile growing a trifle wider despite his concerns, "I think I'd pay money to see that myself." Taking another glance into the bedroom, the detective could see that Lai Wan, although still unconscious, at least seemed calmer. Relaxing a bit himself, he continued his previous explanation.

"But anyway, as I was saying before, my guess is Lai Wan was afraid that with so many hostile people gathered here, once their attention was focused directly on her that it might interfere with her ability to find out anything. You have to understand, leaving her home is extremely difficult for her; public transportation is her nightmare. For her to make this trip, and then be thwarted once she got here ..."

"I get the idea."

"Yeah, thought *you* might." London found himself staring at select members of the group behind the sheriff, the power of his unblinking gaze letting them know exactly what he meant.

"Anyway," he continued, "while the rest of us were grouped in one place all focusing on each other, my guess is she decided that as long as the bunch of you weren't paying any attention to her, that she might as well see if she couldn't just wrap things up on her own. And I'll tell the lot of you right now, the fact that she couldn't simply lay her hands on that bed and give us all the answers we're looking for, frankly that scares the ever-loving crap out of me."

None of the people in the hallway had wanted to hear that statement. There had been enough speculation within their ranks already. Kennedy Walker had disappeared from her home without a trace. With the entire area surrounded by guards, high walls, walking patrols comprised of men and dogs, motion sensors and numerous other state-of-the-art security devices, it was, to all intents and purposes, simply impossible for someone to come into, or get out of, Seaside without the development's deterrent net being aware of it.

Of course, that there could be something supernatural about the star's disappearance was not something any of them had wanted to accept, either. It put the answer to what had happen beyond their understanding, and put all their desires for quiet and minimal publicity in high jeopardy.

Now, worse yet, the one force all their intelligence told them might be able to deal with the problem if any could, had just announced that events as they were unfolding had just had "the ever-loving crap" scared out of it. Trying to make the best out of a bad situation, Tyrell told his deputies and the troopers to escort everyone else downstairs.

"Get everyone something to eat, drink. Try and entertain this bunch, if you would, Mr. Dennton. Maybe it would be best if we tried to find out what just happened here, so we can find out what happened to Ms. Walker."

Tyrell motioned to one of his deputies, telling her to return after everyone else was situated downstairs once more. He also told the woman to encourage as many of them to leave if possible. After that, he turned to London and said;

"So, newfound respect for each other and all that happy bugaboo aside, shall we get in there and see what happened to your lady friend?"

"Yeah," answered the detective with dark concern, "we really better."

# CHAPTER EIGHT

"I WASN'T CERTAIN YOU'D like it," said Goward, no regret accompanying his words, "but I gave her a sedative—a strong one. Understand me, Theodore, her state was growing increasingly agitated, arms swinging wildly—alternating between stark, utter calm, and then massive convulsions—violent ones. Indeed, during one of her snap-backs she caught Paul off-guard and gave him a terrible fist to the head."

"It's gonna leave a mark, boss."

"You'll live," answered London. Standing next to the bed, Tyrell to his left, the detective weighed his options. Privately, he cursed the fact Goward had sedated the psychometrist. If she were still merely unconscious, he might have easily entered her mind himself and discovered what had happened to her, even brought her back from wherever she had been dragged.

"Go ahead, smart guy," whispered a voice within his mind. "Try it. What have we got to lose?"

London cursed the thought, not so much for its recklessness, but for the position into which it placed him. Ever since his first supernatural encounter months earlier, the detective had learned more and more tricks of the occult trade, including psychometry. But, the main thing he had learned about Lai Wan's talent was that although he could accomplish things with it, when he used it on people he almost always left them scarred and broken.

"No, not in her current state," he told himself, remembering certain of his past mistakes all too clearly. "There's no telling what could go wrong."

"But we have to know what we're dealing with ..."

As the question within his mind trailed of, the detective's thoughts raced back to before the Conflagration, to when he had been merely an ordinary man. To when nothing had, as of yet, forced him to believe in vampires, in shapeless nightmares with the power to lay waste to solar systems. He had not even imagined such things as the dreamplane, the vast nothingness between all realities. He had never thought of how to combat gillmen, flying lizards, hell hounds, or any of the other horrors he had faced.

"And now," a voice from the back of his mind whispered, "we get to wonder what each new day will bring. Like today." While he stared at the psychometrist, another asked;

"Hey, you don't want to go into her mind—fine. But tell us—we're curious—just what is it now that's sniffing around here, trying to destroy us?"

"Any ideas?"

"Not really," London admitted to the sheriff. "Not that will do her or the rest of us any immediate good, anyway." Turning back to the others, he said quietly;

"Zack, stay with her. Keep a close watch. Try not to be insulted by me saying so." The older man reddened, turning his face away as he apologized for his earlier outburst. The detective acknowledged his regret, then asked;

"One more thing, you've known Lai longer than any of us. You know what she's capable of, know what she can handle. Tell me, is there anything you can think of in your mutual background that could have done this to her?"

"I'm way ahead of you on this one," answered the professor. "Sadly, the simple answer—no, there isn't. This place we're in, new as it is, no history ... hard to believe it could be haunted. Who died here? I mean, I doubt there's an Indian burial site on a mountainside. But, even if this place is possessed by some disgruntled spirit, no simple poltergeist, or any other known kind of phantasm, for that matter, nothing I've ever come across could have done this to her."

"Yeah," replied London, quietly. "That's pretty much what I was afraid of." Sucking down a great, deep breath, the detective exhaled it slowly, then indicating the sheriff, said to Morcey;

"Com'on. The three of us have got to try and get this thing right—and I think we've got to do it fast."

As the trio descended the stairs, Tyrell asked what London had meant. The detective told him;

"If you're willing to point the finger at me for the Conflagration, I'm willing to bet that means you've seen a thing or two in your time. I'm going to risk talking to you as if you're open to new ideas. Lai Wan, I'm telling you, just sitting in the same room, she can tell you the contents of your pockets, your social security and credit card numbers, how long your toe nails are, whether or not you cheat on your wife." The sheriff merely listened, a sign London found encouraging.

"I'm going to tell you something totally off the record. We figured this whole thing to be pretty much a cake walk. Truthfully, the only reason Zack is here is he wanted a free trip to California." The detective gave his words a second to sink in, then added;

"I hate to admit it, but our attitude wasn't all that different from some of the suits downstairs. We figured we'd get Lai out here, let her walk around for a few minutes soaking up whatever the hell happened to Walker, and then collect our whopping fee. It's a tight-guarded secret back East, but it's how she makes her living, and how more crimes get solved in the Big Apple than you can imagine. The lawyers, all the rest of the nonsense we found when we got here, that didn't surprise me. But this ..."

The detective stopped for a moment, looking back up the stairs. A mixture of concern and apprehension gripped him suddenly, almost making him start back up to the bedroom where Lai Wan lie. He saw her normally, tightly composed face once more within his mind, eyes fluttering madly, thin lines of drool continually oozing from both corners of her mouth.

Standing there, not wanting to share what he had to say with any of those that had been herded downstairs moments earlier, he said quietly;

"You have to understand, her powers are complete—unstoppable. No one can resist her probing. If she locks minds with you, she wins—case closed. Bring her any item, she can read its history. Hand her a book, she can not only tell you where the trees came from that went into making its pages, she can tell you things that happen within those forests."

Tyrell understood what he was being told, was willing to believe what London claimed, if only for the sake of argument if nothing else. But, if such were the case, his mind asked him, then why was the woman in the state she was in? Voicing his question, the detective told him;

"My best guess is, yes—this damn place is haunted. But by something none of us has ever seen before."

"What makes you say that?"

"Zack's major field of research is the supernatural. He's covered the world, been everywhere, seen everything in the ghost family there is to see."

"Oh, I get it," answered the sheriff, nodding his head unconsciously. "That's what you were asking him about upstairs. So, he's got no clue about this, either—right?"

"Apparently," admitted London. "And, if he doesn't even have a guess ..."

The three men stood on the stairs for a handful of seconds longer, lost in the silence interrupted on a tonal level only by the continual drone of those waiting downstairs. Finally, Tyrell offered;

"Look, I'm thinking we should go on and get downstairs. If we're gone too long, those idiots might start trying to think for themselves. And that's never a good thing."

"Gee, this guy could almost be an honorary New Yorker," offered Morcey with a grin.

"I'm really going to have to make up my mind about you,

little man," Tyrell said jokingly in response. Feeling somewhat lighter himself, London said;

"You're right about getting downstairs. Those that haven't left need to know their precious interests are being looked after. Outside of Dennton—it is his house, after all—if we could get them on their way, perhaps we can find some angle—"

"Boss," interrupted Morcey suddenly, "I'm just thinkin' ... several people said stuff about more than just the house bein' haunted. Correct me if I'm wrong, but wasn't there a mention about local animals and plants and stuff bein' weird, and complaints from workers and staff ..."

"You're thinking that maybe whatever this is runs through all the homes in Seaside," said the sheriff suddenly. "Maybe there's other stuff going on we haven't been told about by some of the other households. Rich people, as you might guess, do not like to feel, let alone look, foolish."

"You're kiddin'. Rich people, easy to embarrass? Oh, say it ain't so."

"You must have been one funny janitor."

"Hey, you know it," Morcey answered Tyrell. Displaying a wide smile, he told the lawman, "what with all the clever stuff you're constantly cleanin' off the walls, you can't help but turn into a great comedian."

"Sheriff," asked London, various parts of his brain all shouting at one another, "you probably didn't tax the other residents too greatly, did you? No real pressure; probably weren't really looking for a kidnapper or killer within the community—right?"

"No, not really," admitted Tyrell. "Didn't seem too plausible that any of her neighbors could have had anything to do with her disappearance. Especially since Seaside's security is run through an independent contractor all five estates pay jointly. Four different security measures all confirm the Walker mansion was entered that night by Walker, and that was it. No one else entered, nobody left. Wherever Kennedy Walker is, she never left this pile of glass."

"So, how hard would it be to round up some representatives from all the other shacks around here?" Just as London asked his question, the deputy Tyrell had ordered to return after those escorted downstairs had been settled came around the bend. Seeing the woman;

"If I was to put someone right on the case," answered Tyrell with a degree of self-satisfaction, "I would think no time at all."

# CHAPTER NINE

**W**ALLACE BEARDSLY WAS NOT amused.

"This is, Sheriff Tyrell, as they used to say when people understood more than single syllable words, an outrage—one of Biblical proportions!"

"Ain't he cute," asked Morcey, chuckling, rolling his eyes. "Just everybody out here acts like they wanta be in movies, don't they?"

"Who is this worm?" Beardsly's glare burned a path toward the balding man, an expression which only brought forth only a louder guffaw from their target. London, frowning at his partner despite his personal amusement, offered;

"Sorry, sir—but this situation is perhaps more complicated than you were lead to believe earlier."

"So what? You're the police, aren't you? It's your job to handle these things and report to the citizenry, not harass them as if they were the villains. I won't stand for this. Do you hear me?!"

The owner of the P7 Organizer, as well as all the subsidiary products which had rolled forth from it over the last few years, had been practically removed from his palatial estate by force along with a large number of his staff. The Walker home, with Dennton's consent, had been turned into an interrogation facility, and interviews of all those brought in had been running for hours.

"Your complaint has been noted, sir," answered Tyrell with a long sigh, one indicating both his physical weariness as well as his growing exasperation with the wealthy. "But as you so correctly pointed out, we are the police, and this is a police investigation, and unless you want to be considered someone with something to hide, I recommend you calm down and just answer the questions we need to ask you."

Tyrell squeezed at his closed eyes, wishing he could stop the burning feeling tearing through them, making every moment he held them open more agonizing than the one previous. Returning to pain, he told Beardsly;

"Try and understand, a woman's life may depend on it, sir. And, for that matter, so might that of everyone else who lives here in Seaside."

Beardsly took the news that his own life might also be in danger with little show of emotion, as if the words had not actually registered within his brain. The arrogant glare he chose to cast about at all concerned spoke volumes, letting anyone who cared know that he was also completely uninterested in the idea that his time was needed if a woman's life was to be saved. Still, for whatever reason clicked within his mind, the tycoon stopped arguing and moved along in the direction in which the sheriff pointed, which at that moment was all Tyrell wanted from the man.

"Rich people are fun, ain't they?"

The sheriff turned to find Morcey at his elbow. The balding man was removing the cap from a plastic water bottle. Tyrell watched, intrigued as the balding man put the mouth of the bottle directly against his eye and then tipped it upward, forcing a splash of water across the eye alone. As he did the other, the sheriff said with admiration;

"I'm going to have to remember that trick."

"Yeah, it refreshes, doesn't waste water, and keeps ya from spillin' it all over the front of yourself. Works especially well when you're drivin'."

As they spoke, one of the state troopers emerged from the maze of back rooms with several members of the staff from the Dalton home. It seemed Mr. Dalton himself had not been in the area for several weeks. To him Seaside was but an occasional weekend retreat to be saved for whenever the grind of being the next great movie producer became too much for him. His staff conspiratorially admitted that they rarely saw him, which made them much the envy of their colleagues.

"Get anything interesting," asked Tyrell as the officer walked past. Waving the maid, grounds-keeper and maintenance man along, thanking them for their help, the trooper turned to the sheriff and answered;

"Either I got a bunch of gibberish, or ..."

The man paused, not able to find the words with which to make a comparison. After a few seconds, Morcey finished screwing the cap back on his water bottle, saying;

"Oh yeah, I know what you mean. But hey, just wait, it gets better."

"You mean this is all going to start making sense?"

"That depends on just how much of a free thinker you are." When the officer's face went a shade dark with annoyance, Morcey shrugged, telling him;

"Let me just say that you should cross your fingers and hope it's gibberish, but don't be too surprised when shit starts poppin' outta the darkness and tryin' ta eat ya."

Those members of the Beretella family the authorities had found at home had been cooperative in every way, something Tyrell had attributed simply to "practice." The entire household had come in quite voluntarily with their entire staff, and had given voluminously long answers which upset their interviewers exceedingly. All of them, from the family's matriarchal grandmother to the chauffeur hired only two weeks earlier had felt strange eyes upon them, and made many complaints about the area similar to those reported by Dennton as having been made by his wife.

"Tell me something, Morcey," said a practically exhausted Tyrell, "and for once, don't show me the baboon's butt, okay?"

"You got it, sheriff," answered the balding man earnestly.

Tyrell took a long look into Morcey's eyes, sighed slightly, then finally asked;

"You really do believe in all this supernatural crap? I mean ... really?"

"Yeah, I do. And I'll clue ya, this thing's got all the smell of one'a the worst of 'em. You want my honest opinion ... this is gonna turn bad—and soon. I'm speakin' from experience here, you and yours better be ready for some crap that'll put your heads on backwards."

The two men stared at each other for a moment, Tyrell searching Morcey's face, Morcey letting him see all that he wanted. Finally, the sheriff sighed, then tapped the water bottle the balding man was holding, telling him;

"You come across anything stronger than that, I'll join you for a double."

"*After*, sheriff," answered Morcey, his face grimly sincere. Holding up a cautionary finger, he added, "Trust me, always *after*."

Tyrell was about to make a comment in return, when the deputy who had been dispatched to the Polimar Grenzenki residence came in the front door with only two people, neither of them Grenzenki from the look of them. One, a black female was immediately ruled out. The other was a white male, but far too young to be the former Soviet block politico. When the sheriff asked for an explanation, the deputy told him;

"Better talk to these two yourself, sir."

"Why's that, Cody?"

"Because they claim they haven't seen their employer in over a week."

"And that," asked the sheriff, "I take it, is not normal?"

"No, sir," answered the black woman. "I'm the maid. Mr. Grenzenki, he liked things a certain way, you know? He made a plan, set a schedule—you kept to it, surely. Or else."

"It's true," added the man. "I'm Belden, the, for lack of a better word, the butler. The cook, too, sheriff. Mr. Grenzenki might have been well off, but he didn't waste a penny. I prepared what he wanted, and like Melody said, everything was on a schedule."

The man paused for a moment. His eyes looked frightened. Tyrell did not get the sense that the butler/cook had something to hide—rather that he was apprehensive about telling something he knew. The sheriff made a few coaxing comments, to which the man responded;

"I know this isn't much to get upset over, but ... you see, I ordered food for the household as per the menus he set. I ordered food two weeks ago for this entire month. We haven't seen Mr. Grenzenki in nine days now."

"Yes," snapped Melody, her voice shaking. "We just haven't known what to do. There's no relatives, no one to call. And, at first ... to be honest ... we, you know ... we kind of, just didn't want to."

Tyrell and Morcey both thought her statement over for a moment, then decided it was harmless. Grenzenki was a tyrant. Bad boss leaves, who asks questions? As she went on, they accepted their initial assessments completely.

"Mr. Grenzenki is not an easy man to work for," offered Belden. "It's not like we found like, signs of a break-in, or bloody handprints, or anything. One day, he was just ... gone. We didn't worry. I mean, the boss is allowed to do what he wants—you know. I mean, sure, it seemed odd—off for him, spending money for food, planning meals, then not being there. But, food keeps, emergencies come up."

"We thought about the fact that he didn't even leave us a note," said Melody, "but we're not talking no kind of considerate person. It just didn't seem out of place for him to just go off without saying anything. What I mean is, yeah, it seemed odd because he's usually so on top of everything, but it didn't seem odd that he wouldn't give two cents about us."

When neither of her interrogators said anything, the woman drew a few inches closer, then lowered her voice as she added,

"But, after a while, you know, when we finally started to really talk about it ... it just didn't make no sense. He never did anything like that before—ever."

"It's true," added the butler/cook. "For that first one, two days—it was like a vacation for us. But then, we began to wonder. After a week ... well, we finally asked security when he had left, if he had told them when he would be back. They, they didn't have any records ... then, Ms. Walker ..."

Tyrell and Morcey stood silent for a moment, considering everything they had just heard. Finally, the sheriff told his deputy to take the two Grenzenki employees to one of the back rooms for a few more questions. He assured the pair that they were not under suspicion of anything, and that he had the feeling what they had already told him was of some importance. As the pair went off with the deputy looking somewhat relieved, Tyrell asked;

"So, my funny friend, is it just my imagination, or is my head already starting to turn backwards?"

"Sheriff, let me put it like this," answered Morcey, his face completely serious. Pointing down the hallway back toward the main living room, he said, "If I remember correctly, the bar is down that way."

Tyrell fell in line behind the balding man as they both headed for the large room where they first met. As they approached the bar, the sheriff said;

"Hey, so what happened to doing one's drinking 'after?'"

"My friend," answered Morcey, already pouring a large cognac for himself, "*after* what I just heard, I'm thinkin' I'm ready for a jolt." Pouring a second quickly, he scooped the tumbler up and handed it to Tyrell, asking;

"Join me?"

The sheriff looked at the amber liquid for a moment, then grabbed the glass answering;

"Why the hell not?"

The two men both sucked down several fingers worth

from their glasses. Tyrell exhaled heavily while Morcey wiped his mouth on his sleeve. The two looked at each other, said nothing, and then turned back to their drinks, each draining their tumblers.

"What do you think," asked the lawman as he set his glass down on the bar. "Should we have another?"

"*After*, sheriff. *After*."

# CHAPTER
# TEN

"**A**LL RIGHT NOW, EVERYBODY," announced Liston, his voice showing a decidedly weary strain, but still strong enough to be heard over a crowd. "If we all co-operate I think we can get through this—for this evening, at any rate—fairly quickly."

It had been a difficult day on everyone. Progress had been made, however, and as the sun began to set, the number of people still on the Walker estate had greatly diminished. All of the cooks and maids and chauffeurs, the security people and groundskeepers, and all the others who had been gathered had been questioned, had their statements notarized, and then released.

All of the members of the London Agency that had arrived in the morning were still there—London and Morcey downstairs with the others, Lai Wan still indisposed with Goward watching over her. Sheriff Tyrell and his two deputies had also remained, as well as the two state troopers. But outside of the State Attorney General, all of the other politicians and lawyers had been sent on their way. Of course, the mansion being his home, Richard Dennton had remained as well.

"It's getting kind of late," the sheriff said to London. "What about my people? Think they could leave?"

"I'd put it to them," answered the detective. "I myself would feel better with a few sets of professional hands around here. Can't say why exactly. And no, I'm not holding anything back— call it a hunch." Tyrell nodded, indicating he knew what London meant. Staring back at him, the detective added;

"You could always call for more men, but like our troopers here, anyone who's been on-site all day, they've gotten a feel for this that can't possibly be explained. I mean, well ... how exactly would you bring someone new up to speed on what's been going on out here?"

"Considerin'" offered Morcey, "we don't actually *know* what's been goin' on out here yet."

"Without sounding as if I'm personally buying into all this crazy," interjected Tyrell's female deputy with a knowing smile, "It would be pretty hard, chief."

"Yeah," growled the sheriff. "That's just because you enjoy crazy shit like this."

"Awww com'on, Sheriff," said his other deputy with a tired laugh. "Can you see Edwards face if you tried to get him to understand this place? Or Montoya? 'You see, we think the house ate it's owner ...'"

As even the troopers chuckled, Tyrell worried his lower lip with his teeth, then waved his hand to bring a halt to the officers' chatter as he said;

"Okay—I can't argue with people making sense. But, everyone here's put in too long a day already. Choose between you now—two of you catch a nap. Get an hour. I got the feeling we'll be going for a while after that. The other two, you'll grab an hour when they're done."

"Don't tell me you expect to keep me here another two hours," blustered Beardsly suddenly. "I've got rights."

"You've got yourself a community with something very wrong happening within it, sir," retorted London. "And if you don't sit down, shut up, and tell us what you know, it is only going to get worse."

"Who is this man," demanded the programming genius. "Who does he think he is, talking to me that way. I'm Wallace P. Beardsly, goddamnit. I ..."

"Need to sit down and just listen!" Tyrell's growl was so unexpected it shocked Beardsly into cooperating for the moment.

Jumping on the opportunity to get things started, Liston barked, too quickly and too loudly;

"Okay—let's get underway." Only slightly embarrassed, the state attorney general slowed himself down and went on in a quieter voice. "And for the sake of Mr. Beardsly, if nothing else, let's try and keep this concise, shall we? Mr. London ..."

"There is definitely something going on in Seaside. We can rule out mass hysteria for two reasons. One, most of those interviewed do not know each other. For hysteria to spread, there has to be contact, and the residents and staff of this community do not get much of a chance to talk to each other."

"And two ..."

"And two, sheriff, is the fact that we now know that another person has disappeared besides Ms. Walker. Polimar Grenzenki is also mysteriously missing."

Only Morcey, London, Tyrell and one of his deputies had been privy to that bit of news. The sudden announcement of it left the room finally quiet. Once more taking advantage of the moment, Liston pushed forward, even while his mind reeled over the idea of another vanished multi-millionaire for the media to slobber over. Putting the thought aside for the moment, he said;

"If we can keep moving, there is much more to cover. The interviews we conducted all afternoon have brought quite striking, perhaps one might even say, disturbing results. Mr. London, might I call upon you to give us a summation?"

"Why not," answered the detective. Standing, he stretched his arms out as far as they would go, relieving some crimp or another in his back. Stretching his neck first to the left, then the right, he let out a small sigh of relief, then began, saying;

"Let's start with the little things. First off, let me say that the responses I'm going to be discussing were culled from three sources: private staff employed here in Seaside, the community's outside security force, and the various homeowners as well."

"Not me," Beardsly offered gruffly. "I haven't seen anything or heard anything ..."

"That's why we're having this pow-wow," said Tyrell, "to bring you up to speed. Go ahead, Mr. London." The detective, noting the professional courtesy, understood that the sheriff was now clearly working in tandem with him. Giving Tyrell the slightest of nods, he continued coolly, saying;

"Nearly a hundred percent of those interviewed mentioned a shift in the atmosphere here in Seaside over the past year. Those willing to name a date pinpoint the beginning of building here at the Walker estate."

"Oh now, there you go," Beardsly interrupted once more. "When I first came to this area, twenty years ago, when I would come out and climb the cliff faces, explore the caves, this is the very land I liked the best, because it was so peaceful, so calm."

"Geez, if I could ask," interrupted Morcey. "Why'd you build way down from here if this is the area you liked best?"

"Simple matter, really. I built where I did because when I first bought the land, even I couldn't afford to tear into the terrain in this area. It was contrary to all practical building practices. We had to reshape this parcel incredibly to make it stable enough to support a home of this size, and still, half the thing hangs over the ocean as it is."

"Sorry, for the distraction, sir," said London. "But to return to the topic, it was at the time of all that work people began feeling uncomfortable. Granted, many of them had to be cajoled into finally picking a time period, but it's the one nearly everyone settled on. And nobody picked one preceding it."

"Try this one on," said Tyrell. Staring harshly at the programmer, he added, "that's just the general feeling that's been playing over everyone. There are numerous specific complaints as well. Did you know that sixteen household animals—dogs, cats, exotic birds, reptiles, two horses—have all died since people moved in here? Ten of them since ground was broken for the Walker estate?"

"I, ah ..." Beardsly struggled to retort, then finally answered simply, "No. No, I didn't."

London continued.

"Many of those interviewed said the wild animals in this area, raccoons, gulls, rabbits, you know them, you live here—they say that the animals are watching them. Sitting in their yards, staring at their houses."

"A couple of people sent servants out to chase the animals off," one of the state troopers added. "These people claim they were actually met with resistance. From rabbits."

"People have heard all manner of weird noises since work stopped on this place, as well," said Morcey. "They've had problems with their electric and with the plumbing, oddly enough, only after dark."

"These folks all had trouble getting some of this out," chimed in one of Tyrell's deputies. "They felt silly, or uncomfortable, because they knew how what they were saying sounded, but ..."

"Thank God they knew how it sounded," answered Beardsly. Standing himself, spreading his hands before him in a placating gesture, the industrialist said, "Gentlemen, I can't believe we're here taking this seriously. Threatening rabbits, evil trees, intelligent grass ... people have trouble with their toilets and light switches and it's time to call the in the Catholics to get hold of their exorcism squad? Honestly, how much more of this am I supposed to sit for?"

"Two people have disappeared," said London, "without a trace. From your little perfect community. Don't you understand, when word of that gets out, this place is going to be a circus? Is that what you want? Why wouldn't you want to help us figure out what's going on around here?"

"Listen, Mr. London, is it," Beardsly responded, "it's not my job to figure these things out. That's what I pay a security force for. That's what I pay taxes for. That's what Dennton here is paying you for. So a commie dictator and an empty-headed twinkie disappeared—so what exactly is that to me?"

While the rest of those assembled merely watched in silence,

Wallace Beardsly slammed his fist against his palm, demanding, "You all listen to me—I do not care about any of this. If someone is trying to hold me responsible for any of this, say it now, and be done with it. Otherwise, I have an empire to—"

"Excuse me ..."

All eyes turned to the doorway. Zachery Goward, looking quite worn out stood leaning against one side of the jam, smiling through his exhaustion.

"Pardon my fatigue—jet lag I suppose. Anyway, I thought you all might want to know, Lai Wan is awake."

# CHAPTER
# ELEVEN

L ONDON BOLTED FROM THE room so quickly there were those who wondered if he had actually taken any steps toward the door, or simply disappeared. Whatever the case, he found himself inside the master bedroom long before any of the others had made their way past Goward and through the door.

"Are you all right?" asked the detective, kneeling next to the bed. Keeping his voice low, straining to not immediately betray all they had learned, he blurted;

"You look a lot better—that's good. But, what can you tell us? I mean, can you comment, are you too weak, did you see something, did some ..."

And then, suddenly, as full memory returned to him as to with whom exactly he was dealing, London laughed softly, feeling foolish for trying to keep anything from her. Rolling his eyes to indicate exactly how stupid he was feeling, he said;

"All right, perhaps I should just be quiet now and let you do the talking."

"Do not reproach yourself," the psychometrist responded in a raw voice, one sounding thick with some sort of coating. "I am actually quite touched at your concern. Zachery tells me I was unconscious for a number of hours now."

"Most of the day. Do you remember anything?"

"Some. But first, allow me to see for myself what has happened so far." So saying, the psychometrist reached out and touched London on the arm. Instantly her eyes glazed over slightly as she relived each moment of the day since she had first blacked out. Seconds later, her fingers released their grip, her eyes snapping back to their normal distinct wariness quite quickly.

"This is not the simple case you thought it was." Lai Wan's eyes narrowed sharply, filling with accusation. "Is it?"

"No," answered London, not quite yet understanding the psychometrist's comment. "Sorry about that."

"Yes, you have done it again," she said, forcing herself upward off the pillows. Her face draining of color, the strength rushing from her body, still she shouted at him, "you've dragged me down into the middle of some miserable nightmare again—*again*—have you not? You arrogant, you ..."

Exhausted by the outburst, short as it had been, Lai Wan fell back into the mound of pillows Goward had arranged for her, perspiration bursting forth from every pore. As she gasped for breath, her hand fumbling toward the water on the table next to her, London moved the glass into her fingers as he said;

"Listen, you know I thought I was doing you a favor. You were in for half the proceeds. That was clocking at half a mill for a day's work. We all thought this was going to be easy, a simple haunting of some sort ..."

"Yes," she gasped, sipping at the lukewarm water, half of each sip dribbling over her chin. "And once again, we thought wrong, did we not?"

As footsteps finally sounded outside in the hallway, London asked the psychometrist quietly, "Listen, is there anything you want to say privately?"

"Not especially, but I must confess that I will ... need a moment to gather my strength." Letting her know he understood, London halted the human tide preparing to spill into the room, announcing that outside of Goward, Morcey and Tyrell, their patient would most likely do better if the others constrained themselves to the hallway.

"If no one minds," Lai Wan explained in a weak voice, "I am feeling quite done in, and would prefer as much air as I can get."

No one voiced any complaint, no matter what they believed the woman's real reasons to be. Finally getting all the others to either return to the first floor or at least listen in from out in the hallway, London pressed the psychometrist to tell them all what had happened. At that point, Goward arrived with a iced glass of ginger ale, with a straw, which he thought would prove beneficial. Lai Wan accepted it gratefully. After getting down several deep pulls, she thanked the professor once more and then asked him to set the glass aside.

"I should tell you all what happened before, from the beginning, I mean. Our Mr. London guessed correctly. Growing increasingly uncomfortable with the mounting tension downstairs earlier, I excused myself in the hopes of solving the mystery of Ms. Walker's disappearance before the hostility running rampant began to interfere with my abilities."

The woman coughed suddenly, and was forced to not only take another drink of soda, but to slow her rate of speech even more than she already had.

"Forgive me," she said, somewhat embarrassed to have to apologize. Beginning again, she told the others, "After my ruse enabled me to leave the room, I waited a beat, listening in to the surface thoughts of all gathered, checking to see if anyone found my departure suspicious. Several wondered about my leaving, but I merely nudged the idea off to the side, whispering within their minds that they need not be concerned about me."

One of those standing within the doorway to the master bedroom, Liston remembered the moment, remembered the voice within his head gently suggesting he pay attention to more important matters. As the blood drained from his cheeks, and his eyes went wide, Morcey caught his expression, commenting dryly;

"Yeah, 'these aren't the droids you're looking for.' Now maybe you guys will get on board here."

London gave his partner a wave of his hand indicating that they had no time for foolishness. Struggling hard enough to tell her story, Lai Wan ignored them both, saying;

"What you first must understand is that I had no doubt we were dealing with some sort of haunting. That death was present in the walls of this home was as obvious to me as the wallpaper. I will admit to overconfidence. I knew there was a ghost or specter of some sort here somewhere. I assumed, foolishly, that all I had to do was search around for a moment and find it."

The woman coughed again, but the attack was shorter and less vocal than the last one. After another few sips from her cold drink, she continued, saying;

"Throwing my powers outward, I simply allowed myself to be drawn to the last place Kennedy Walker had been within her home. That, as you must realize, brought me here."

The psychometrist had found herself in the master bedroom, but she had been confused upon her arrival there. She could feel the actress' presence in every corner, in the floor and carpet and each object with which she came in contact, as well as that of the ghostly presence she had felt throughout the house, but none of these impressions told her the story of Kennedy Walker's disappearance. Finally, she touched the bed.

"And what happened then?"

"At first, I barely noticed the change. The bed, as I touched it, the fabric, the very *feel* of it hinted to me, lured me, let me know the memories I wished were just about ready to reveal themselves to me ..."

London said nothing; did not even know how to begin to say anything—had no idea what to say. No other description the psychometrist had ever made to him had been so vague, so confusing. Morcey and Goward were equally puzzled. Those in the hall had not the slightest comprehension of what they were hearing. Finally, the detective asked;

"Did this seem, ah, normal to you? Has this ever happened before?"

"Only once," she said. "In your office. When you asked me to tell you about Arthur Bonn." Cold dread passed through the members of the London Agency. Noting the change in the detective and his companions, and not especially liking it, Tyrell asked;

"Whose this Arthur Bonn character, and do I really want to know?"

"We fought a creature," London answered absently. "Killed it. Had Lai Wan check the remains. Turned out to have been a normal man who gave himself over to a force from beyond our universe. He was a traitor to humanity, gave up being human for wings and claws. Trying to get a reading from him almost pulled Lai into ... almost gave her over to that force."

London held back the rest of the story from the others, that the force in question was the horror which had devastated so much of the Eastern seaboard, that had killed millions on the night now known as the Conflagration. The detective could not help remember the nightmare of it, or the parade of others he had known since then, similar in power to that first terrible, faceless thing. In truth, the idea that some manner of hideous power could be back once more in yet another form left him shaking.

"This is not good news," asked Liston. "Is it?"

"Not hardly," answered Morcey, no trace of humor in his voice. As the balding man stared unblinking at his partner, trying to keep the dread panic rising through his nervous system in check, the detective asked Lai Wan;

"But, what happened? What caused you to black out? How'd you get back? Is this thing close? Wha—"

The psychometrist raised her hand to stop the flood of London's questions. Gulping air in desperately, Lai Wan cleared her system as best she could, blinked her eyes hard several times, then sat completely up in the bed, telling the assembly;

"To make this story as brief as possible, I fought the force I could feel actually dragging me into the bed with all the power I had. This is what happened to Ms. Walker."

"You mean, she's in the bed?"

"No," Lai Wan told the sheriff, "she was absorbed into it,

into the house, into something in the very land here, which is what we all face now."

"So you fought it, yes ... then?"

"No. I was not sufficiently strong to fight it. At best I was able to shield myself from it, but only at a cost. I had to reduce my life force to a minimum. By making contact with the bed I had given this thing access to me. To cut it off I had to cut myself off from the world. It was merely a stalemate, I had escaped it, but only by retreating to where it could not reach me, and I could not reach any of you."

"Then, I mean," asked Morcey, his voice quiet, concerned, "how ... how'd you get away from it?"

"As best I can tell," answered the woman after another deep breath, "You distracted it for me."

At that point all in the room and the hallway merely looked at each other in confusion. Not knowing what else to tell them, the psychometrist tried to explain herself another way.

"The force of the thing, that part buried here somewhere, that kept digging, searching, slavering over what few traces I had left behind, looking for me, wanting to add my power to that which it already had acquired—somehow, you caught it's attention."

"We distracted it?" Liston's words were vacant things, voiced more to the entire assembly than Lai Wan herself.

"But, ma'am," offered Tyrell, "ain't no one here seen any monsters. I mean, all we were doing when the professor here came and told us you were awake ..."

An electric flash ran through most everyone present at the same moment. More out of foolish hope than any real expectation, London asked if Wallace Beardsly was there in the hallway. The answer that the tycoon had not accompanied them upstairs did not come as any great surprise to the detective.

# CHAPTER
# TWELVE

"FIND THE SON'VA BITCH, goddamnit," ordered Tyrell, his one hand crashing against the palm of the other for emphasis. "Contact his own damn Seaside security people. Have them tune up all that hot shit motion sensor equipment of theirs—just find him before he gets away!"

"I don't think he's going outside, sheriff," offered London. Standing up, he told his associates, "Lai's a threat to this thing, whatever it is. Paul, Zack, stay with her. Keep her safe."

The detective pulled his gun from his shoulder holster, a old and worn .38 he affectionately referred to as "Betty." Reflexively, London checked it for cartridges despite the fact he knew he had loaded the weapon immediately after removing it from his luggage. Closing the chamber once more, he said;

"Everyone keeps mentioning the underground, things being deep, or buried ... I don't think Beardsly will be outside. I think our best bet is to head for the basement."

"Boss," shouted Morcey as London began to leave the room, following the others. "Do you really think it's safe here? Maybe Zack should just drive Lai outta here."

"If whatever the hell this thing is we're up against can really control the trees, the animals ... the people too, apparently ... I'm thinking there could be a lot of bullets out there waiting for anyone who makes a run for it. Lot of guards out there, lot of guns. We're a heap better off barricading this place first."

"And that's why he's in charge of the company," said the balding man to Goward. The professor nodded, escorting Lai Wan to a chair on the other side of the room. His main thinking was that if Kennedy Walker really had been absorbed into the bed, their foe might have some easier access to that particular piece of furniture than any other. His secondary idea was that the bed would make a much better bit of blockage for the door than the chair.

Even as he and Morcey began securing the master bedroom against a possible siege, however, London caught up to the others at the base of the stairs. As they began to look around for the route to the basement, one of the troopers called out for someone to find Dennton on the assumption he would know where the stairways were in his own home. Only a few seconds brought the group to another unwelcome conclusion.

"What in all the bloody hells, you mean he's disappeared on us, too?"

"Yeah, looks like, sheriff," answered the reporting deputy. "But, he did come upstairs with us, didn't he?"

"He did," Tyrell confirmed. "I remember him there."

"So where'd he get to?"

Liston held up his hands, hoping to get the small group organized. Catching everyone's attention, he said;

"Listen—I'm not saying we should be shooting on sight, but it's probably a good idea to consider Mr. Dennton a risk, at this point, that is. I mean, after all, if we're ready to be ... to be ... considering Wallace Beardsly ... a ..." And then, the State Attorney General turned to London, asking;

"Good Lord, almighty ... what? What is it we're considering Beardsly to be?" And then, before the detective could answer, Liston suddenly started off in a different direction, asking the room in general;

"We came here today, to, to *stop* a witch hunt. To stop the idea there was anything—any thing, what—abnormal, out of the way ... oh my God, oh my dear God in Heaven ..."

"Liston," asked London cautiously. "Are you all right?"

"Ghosts," the man let the word escape his lips softly. Trembling, his eyes staring at the detective as if he had no idea who he was, he said, "Ghosts. Demons and, and ... and I don't know what ... we're talking about real, honest to God ghosts. Ghosts and demonic possession ... we're standing here, in the twenty-first century ... acting as if such things are *real.*"

"Yes, sir," answered London quietly. Touching the trembling man gently on the arm, the detective continued, saying, "We are. Are you going to be able to handle that?"

The State Attorney General stood motionless for a long moment, his eyes blinking rapidly, beads of sweat forcing themselves to the surface of his forehead. Straining to compose himself, he asked;

"Is that what we're going to find? With Walker and Beardsly? Dennton? Grenzenki? That they're under the control of spirits from beyond? Is that what's become of them?"

London made to answer, but before he could, one of the state troopers, his voice hesitant and cautious, asked;

"Can I point out something?" When everyone merely turned to stare at the man with questioning eyes, he offered;

"Can I just say that we all seem to be jumping into something rather blindly here. We're talking about who to shoot and who not to shoot, about ghosts, and now possession, and ... and all I'd like to ask is ... uummm, do we actually know what's happened here? What's going on—really?"

"No, son," answered Tyrell, feeling almost sheepish. "We don't have any hard proof yet. It's a good point ..."

"But I mean, we're talking ghosts. Ghosts! Haunted houses eating people—possession. How can we ..."

Moving forward, London assumed his most disarming stance, made his voice as placating and friendly as possible as he held his arms wide and said;

"You're absolutely right to question these things. It's good for us all to remember that at this point we merely want to find Mr. Beardsly for further questioning."

"No, no you don't want that at all." The man's tone grew shakier, wilder. Taking several backward steps, his voice rose in volume, cracking as he shouted, "you're going to kill him. You've all gone crazy."

"Now, try and take it easy," London said calmly. He moved on the man cautiously, taking only half-steps, closing on him so slowly he barely seemed to be moving at all. "Really, we actually do have a pretty good idea of what's happening here."

"You," the trooper snarled at London. "Especially you. It's all your fault. Mr. Beardsly's a great man, but you want everyone to distrust him. You brought these ideas here." The detective noted the officer's hand reaching for his sidearm, his fingers appearing as if moving of their own volition.

"You're the one—you're the *danger!*"

London flashed forward as the trooper's weapon left its holster. The detective's arm slamming out at a blurring speed, he knocked the lawman's hand sideways even as he pulled the trigger of his .45. The slug fired, but ended buried in the wall. London's other hand followed the first quickly, driving deep into the man's mid-section. The detective followed that blow with two others, one to the neck, the last to the side of the trooper's head. The man bounced off the wall, toppled to the floor and stayed there.

Taking the officer's weapon up from his now open fingers, London handed it to Liston, asking;

"All right, your honor—pardon me asking, but are you sober again. You playing with a full deck—yes? No?"

"Full enough to see this game through to the end—one way or the other." The politician was badly shaken by all he had seen, but not defeated. Coming up to London's side, Tyrell spoke to the detective, but loudly enough for everyone else to hear.

"I don't think what we just saw with that boy was normal." Pointing to the fallen trooper, he suggested the man's partner handcuff him to something solid, then said;

"You jump in and contradict me if you have a mind—you're the expert on these things—but I don't think that was just the jitters, or anything any of us have ever seen before. That woman upstairs, what she was saying is the real deal—ain't it? Cause if it is, then this house *is* grabbing people, changing them, twisting them ..."

"I don't think it's actually the house, but something ..." London's voice trailed off for a moment, then offered;

"I'll tell you one thing, I think whatever it is we're up against feeds on doubt. Dennton told us Kennedy had doubts about her new film, Dennton himself had doubts about his future, Lai Wan has been known to have doubts about her safety when working with my agency ... what I'm trying to say is, that doubt could be the doorway whatever we're up against uses to get into people's minds."

"So, what do we do?" asked one of Tyrell's deputies. "Stop doubting?"

"Be nice if things could be turned off and on that easily, officer," London answered. "But it isn't as hard as you think. I mean, you now know something supernatural is going on here. That's what you have to remember—you now know something extraworldy is up in this house. You *know* it. You know it's true. If you keep that in mind you won't be able to doubt it, and you should be all right, at least as far as possession is concerned."

Everyone nodded soberly. Without realizing it, all present had filled their hand with a weapon. After a few minutes searching, the doorway to the basement was located. Before descending, London suggested they look for flashlights. The sheriff handled that problem by sending his men to their cars for the heavy duty lanterns stored in their trunks.

"Might want to bring in our shotguns and extra shells, oh, and riot vests, too—hell, just grab anything that looks handy." The man and woman nodded, disappearing out the front door without a word. As they did, the sheriff asked why London wanted flashlights. Checking his revolver absently, the detective explained;

"I was just thinking, if this thing can play with the water and the electric, it might cut out the lights on us when we need them most."

"If we live through this son'va bitchin' night," Tyrell promised, "I am definitely going to buy you a beer."

"Sheriff," answered London, "we live through this night, I will definitely drink it."

Then, as the front door opened and Tyrell's people returned, London took his first step into the basement. For a few moments, at least, nothing happened.

# CHAPTER THIRTEEN

B Y THE TIME HIS foot had found the third step, London knew something was wrong somewhere ahead of him. He could literally sense it, a thickening wrongness in the air, a hostility he could feel through his shoes—one that swelled more strongly with each downward pace.

"What in the name of God is down here," he wondered to himself. Already his nose caught the scent of something off-kilter. The stench of ancient putrescence came to the detective, a rotting aroma that threatened to pull his lunch, meager and bland as it had been, violently up and out of his bowels. Gritting his teeth, London swallowed whatever saliva and mucus he could pull forth to coat his throat and then continued downward into the basement.

Fourth step.

Fifth step.

Sixth ...

The detective paused again, straining to determine if he was really hearing something or not. Listening intently, his senses focused on a noise—a sound both distant, and nearly rhythmic, which London could not identify. What was it, he wondered. Was it merely machinery—water pipes, air conditioning or recirculating units, something simple—easily explainable? Or was it something creeping, sliding across the floor, skittering up the walls, hanging from the ceiling? Waiting for them, waiting for him—waiting for him to reach the landing, to take just one more step—waiting to fall on him, to pounce, to drive its fangs, its claws, tendrils, extractors—

"Stop it!"

"Stop what?" Tyrell, following directly behind London did not have the slightest idea as to what the detective was referring. Sheepishly, the detective explained that his imagination was running away with him and that he had merely been talking to himself.

"You can stop doing that anytime you want," the sheriff offered, "And it wouldn't bother me in the least."

"I'll see what I can do," London replied. Both men stared at one another for a moment. Finally, the detective nodded slightly, indicating he was ready to move forward. Although admittedly shaken, he had shattered the panic that had been clawing at him, and did feel ready to begin making his way toward the bottom once more.

The Walker home was all modern angles and spacious areas, and the basement was no different. The stairs did not simply descend straight to the basement floor as in most mid-American homes. Instead it angled around a central area twice, dropping some twenty feet. The greater than usual depth had been created to allow the home's massive party area better acoustics, and to accommodate Ms. Walker's personal screening room.

Hitting the first landing, London made his way quickly to the next set of stairs and took them rapidly to the second landing, two, three at a time. From there, he could see much of the layout below. The area could not be properly called a cellar or basement, the words were too provincial. Too confining. To most the area would seem to be practically a theme park.

Great over-sized couches sat everywhere. From his vantage the detective could see two fully stocked bars, including everything from recreational drugs to oxygen tanks. Pointing the cylinders especially out to Tyrell, the sheriff nodded, whispering back;

"See that a lot out here. These types have trained themselves to handle all manner of problems they don't want in the papers. Wonders what a bit of pure oxygen will do for hangovers, drug highs, you name it."

London rolled his eyes, then cautioned the sheriff and the others, using hand signals only, to follow him forward slowly. With a nod of understanding from Tyrell, he then took the stairs to the bottom of the basement rapidly, exposing himself as a target to anything that might be waiting. Once all the way to the basement floor, the detective found the answer to at least one of their questions.

"I found Dennton."

Richard Dennton lie twisted and broken on the ivory-colored tiles stretching away from the landing. The thought ran through London's mind that even if Dennton's body were to become possessed, so much damage had been done to it that it was useless as a tool to anyone or anything.

"Found what's left of him, anyway," said Tyrell quietly, descending the steps behind the detective. Both men stared for a moment at the mistreated body. The man's legs and arms were shattered in several places each, his head caved in, turned backwards on his shoulders, ribs crunched into little pieces. Much of his spine lay here and there across the floor, separate vertebrae scattered everywhere.

"You think Beardsly did this?"

"I don't think there is a Beardsly anymore," London told the sheriff. By this time, the others had turned the last corner. They stood ranging up along the last flight of stairs, all staring at the body, engrossed by the arresting sight—distracted ...

"*Move!*"

London's command came seconds before three long, rope-like tendrils came smashing forward, grabbing at the small party of invaders. The detective's mind had begun to think about the positioning of Dennton's body, so obviously placed as it was for some purpose of the other. Whatever was after them had wanted them to come to it, had wanted them to pause where they had, still and thoughtful, easier to capture—

"Get it off me!"

The state trooper had blocked one of the grasping lengths from ensnaring Liston, but had then become ensnared himself. Tyrell's deputies, both carrying shotguns, twisted around and blasted at the enormous strand, severing it in several places. The stump retreated, as did the other two appendages. As the others shouted, checking the state trooper for injuries, strained to see if another attack was coming their way, et cetera, London bent to examine the corded length left behind. What he found astonished him.

"This isn't flesh," he announced. He shouted to be heard, knowing everyone's heads would be ringing with the explosive reverberations of the gunfire. Even in a space as dramatically large as the Walker basement, the shotgun blasts were far more than the average human ear could absorb instantly.

"What do you mean?"

London held out a piece of the tendril so Liston and the others could see what he had. So they might examine it, focus their minds on something practical to distract them from the fantastic.

"It's made up of vines, and electrical wire," said the politician with amazement. "And grass, and thread ..."

"There's human hair in there, too," said the detective, "and God knows what else. But this makes sense. I think I'm beginning to get what's going on here."

"Care to share?"

"Sure, sheriff," answered London. "There's the remains of something under the house, probably in the land when building started. Whatever it is, it's not human—that's why this isn't like a normal haunting, why Goward couldn't recognize it as a ghost right off the bat, why Lai Wan had trouble with it ... it's up to something, and it needs people to make whatever it's doing work. It's pretty damn intelligent, too."

"You think so?"

"Well, it left Dennton there for whoever came down next to see. Set a trap. We survived only because there were more of us than it expected."

"But what the hell is this all about," asked Liston, shaking the bit of pseudo-flesh he was holding.

"It's just like Walker said, but no one believed her—this thing has possessed the house, the grounds as well. It's trying to live again, to piece itself together from whatever it can find, bend to its will."

"What the ..." stammered one of the deputies. "What is it?"

"I don't know, but I have an idea. I want the bunch of you to get on the phone, get through to Seaside security, have them get through to each house and get everyone out of here."

"But what about possession, the way it can just—"

The detective cut Liston off. With almost a snarl, he ordered;

"Listen to me, this thing has invaded human minds. It's catching on to how we think, what we can do. But, I'm banking on the hope we can confuse it, overtax it. If we've got people running all over the place, cars headed in every direction, everyone consciously thinking of nothing but getting out of here, you can get everyone to safety before it can get its hands on anyone else."

"But why us," snapped Tyrell. "What are you going to do?"

"While you keep it busy in this world, I'm going to keep it busy in the next."

"What are you talking about?"

"If I tell you, I tell it. You guys, all of you, get going. Get upstairs and get the others, get security, get to the other houses, and get everyone out of Seaside. Move—do it, while we still have a chance."

Then, just as the others began to move back up the stairs, the voice of Wallace Beardsly sounded in the massive basement. Calling to them all, it commanded;

"You will not leave."

And, so saying, Beardsly walked into view, or more correctly, his body was manipulated into view. As the party on the stairs watched in unbelieving horror, the tycoon was puppeted across the floor by the same tendrils which had attacked them moments earlier. Wrapped around his waist, slithering up underneath his pant legs, they reappeared through his very shoulders, one twined around his neck, moving his lower jaw, the other draped over the top of his head, grotesquely working his eyes in a series of horrid pantomimes of human expression.

"You will stay and understand."

"They will leave," barked London. "I will stay. I'm all you need. You have no use for them. Their power is nothing compared to mine."

The Beardsly-thing considered for a moment, then it raised its arm. As it did, a thin length spun out from the palm of the hand, an appendage made of telephone wire and flesh, of bone and tree bark and a dozen other elements. Approaching London gently, non-threateningly, it licked at the edges of his aura, gauging his personal energy. Finding something within London it recognized as far more powerful than the average human being, the Beardsly-thing recalled its extension and waved the detective forward.

"Come. I will explain why you can not resist."

As the meat puppet staggered away on legs which did not actually touch the ground, London turned to the others and hissed;

"Go—while you still can."

Then the detective turned and followed Beardsly's corpse, while the sound of rapidly retreating footfalls clattered up the stairs behind him.

# CHAPTER FOURTEEN

L ONDON FOLLOWED THE TENDRILED automaton back into the Walker mansion's lavishly appointed screening room. Down through the luxurious theater the zombified body moved, finally stopping near the thirteenth row. Pointing to the lounge chair directly in the middle, it said;

"King's seat, if you please."

The detective entered the aisle and sat down where indicated. Hoping to distract his host, encouraging the thing to believe he was falling under its spell, London slid Betty back into her holster. Then once the detective had made himself comfortable, the lights dimmed, and what appeared to be a motion picture began to play. The screen illuminated slowly, bits of darkness appearing within the light. Scattered at first, they finally began to congeal into a recognizable image.

"Beardsly ..."

"More or less," Beardsly's voice agreed, bubbling forth from the theater's speakers. "Consider this image my stand-in, as it were. Are we communicating effectively enough?" When London nodded, taken somewhat aback by the fact the face on the screen was hearing him, responding to him, the image said;

"It has taken me some time to accomplish ... but I believe this display will be most effective ... I was sent to this world a great many of your years ago ... as a gift ..."

"A gift?"

"Yes ... the master ... wanted certain tasks performed ... before he arrived ..."

As London stared, the image of Beardsly broke down, then

reformed into a formless shape, a black tide of fetid goo which seemed more to boil than actually live. Myriad eyes and tendrils formed, dissipated and reformed within the bursting greenish pustules of the rolling creature on the screen.

"I was sent with servants ... shoggoths we called them ... foul things ... rebellious ... surly ... but creations only ... brewed from parts ... made to order ..."

As London continued to watch in cautious fascination, the image on the screen shifted once more, this time reforming itself into a rigid, barrel-shaped life form. Thin, horizontal arms radiated from its body—spoke-like—outward from a central ring of cabled skin. Various vertical knobs or bulbs hung from both the head and base of the barrel. Each of these bulbs was the central hub of a system of five long, flat, triangularly tapering arms arranged symmetrically around the thing in much the manner of the arms of a starfish.

"My race ... before we were destroyed by the master ... on great membranous wings we flew the currents of space ... several billion years ago ... we ruled this world ... might have created your kind accidentally—no real way to be certain ... what now would it matter ..."

As the Beardsly voice droned on, the images continued to change on the screen, depicting each new topic. His mind continually shouting warning to him, London kept a part of his attention on the screen, but focused most of his senses on his surroundings.

"Great wars stole our power in this sector ... degeneration followed ... rebellion of the slave population ... little remains ... but then ... that is the past ... long gone ... forgotten ... useless ..."

As the detective watched, the screen went black once more, then shifted to the sight of three of the star-headed aliens gliding through space.

"The master took us from slumber ... revived ... sent us here to ... amuse him ... but dread mistake ... our approach incorrect ...

terrible meteor shower struck us ... Earth we reached ... but not alive ... not alive as you understand it ..."

As the odd lights continued to flicker, London sat quietly, part of his mind paying attention, most of it straining to watch his perimeter, making certain no more of the slithering appendages which had attacked earlier as well as motivated Beardsly's corpse, were not approaching his position.

"Hard we hit ... my companions burned ... destroyed ... but not destroyed ... master's work does not die ... ever ..."

"What," wondered London, hoping his thoughts were his own, "is this master? And when's he going to show up?"

"Long I remained buried ... dead but not gone ... could reach minds ... draw life ... but could not reach enough power at one time to revitalize ... not under Beardsly."

The images continued to change. London had been somehow shown the space flight of the alien advance party, had witnessed their run-in with a meteor shower, watched them burn and crash to the surface. He saw the one which was obviously speaking to him now die, slam into the surface, and be buried by debris. Years went by, hundreds in a second, until the scene became that of the Seaside area a number of years previous, before the bulldozers had known it.

As the detective watched, a young rock climber entered the wildly dangerous area, laughing at the prospect anything could happen to him. Reckless but confident, he made his way to the heart of the shattered, tangled landscape. Triumphant, but exhausted, the youth stretched out to nap.

"I felt him immediately ... sent my mind to his ... strained to know him ... control him ... own him ... like a shoggoth ... I entered the building blocks of his brain ... simple construct ... looking for what I could use to control him ... I found it ..."

Images of wealth, floating dollars, cascading rivers of golden coins, fountains of gemstones, spraying in the air, then trickling downward, all of it showering the sleeping youth. London understood he was seeing into the rock climber's dream, a vision supplied by the spirit of the long dead alien thing. As the youth agreed that he would do anything for the riches he had been shown, the never-ending stream of wealth changed into a flood of figures, vast lines of computer coding, endless formulas and electronic data, until the detective murmured in surprise;

"Beardsly, he said he always loved this area. You, you gave him the secrets of the P7, taught him how to take over the world's computer market."

London's mind streamed ahead quickly. The alien had possessed Beardsly on that day, turning an unknown into a genius with but a fraction of its star-spanning knowledge. Then, it had brought him back to the area, using him to shape the area to where it might attract more people to the region.

"More than that ..." The detective was somewhat startled that the ghostly creature could hear his thoughts, but only slightly. Making no comment, he instead simply continued to watch the screen, listening to the alien narration.

"Already Beardsly mine ... made him invite others I could use ... Grenzenki perfect ... ruthless ... efficient ... organized ... knew this new world and all its weakness ... perfect ..."

As the screen showed London the night the former Soviet leader was captured by the walls of his own garage, dragged down into the very foundation, the voice over droned;

"Walker ... an intricate part ... Grenzenki teach me to think in this world ... Kennedy teach me to act within it ... to dazzle ... to emote ... after all ... Mr. London ... what matters power ... without personality?"

And then, the screen the detective had been watching began to pull upward into the ceiling. Standing behind it, London saw three figures. Two were oversized lumps, like boiling sofas, but the one in the center the detective recognized.

"Ms. Walker, I presume?"

"Not yet ..." the alluring form said in its near toneless voice, "but soon ... very soon ... and now ... I thank you for your attention ... Mr. London ... but it is time for our finale ... Dennton and

Beardsly ... their energy powers me ... their bodies have been thrown over the cliff into the sea ... Beardsly's will leave all to Kennedy ... he loved her ... that is the story ..."

"You're just nuts," laughed the detective. Unfazed, the replica of Kennedy Walker moved toward the edge of the stage. Looking down at London, it smiled, telling him;

"I have learned from my human teachers ... the media loves tragedy ... her husband fighting jealous lover to the death ... it will be perceived as fair she receive Beardsly fortune as recompense ... no one will miss Grenzenki ... will take Dalton soon ... he will throw his family fortunes into making movies with Kennedy ... for Kennedy ... will absorb all members of Beretella family ... will bring family together here ... absorb all ... will have wealth ... armies ... politically astute knowledge of how business and power works here ... has taken time ... planning ... much struggle to learn bipedal locomotion ... but worthwhile endeavor ... don't you think?"

"Are you telling me," London asked, his voice boarding on the incredulous, "That you did all this to become a movie star?"

"No ..." answered the Kennedy-thing. "to disrupt ... to please master of all ... this country had no problem electing a male actor president ... now the race sense of right ... wonderfully ... amusingly misguided ... seeks insane balance by looking for a female to elect president ..."

As London stared, the shape of Kennedy Walker stood erect, then spun around, its hands balancing the movement, the single pair almost replacing the five its brain still expected to find.

"I almost have all components I need ..." said the Walker-thing. "All required now is the human energy to keep this body from decomposing ... and ... as we both understand ... there is no human on Earth more powerful than the man who began the Conflagration ..."

And then, in respond to a piping whistle the Kennedy-thing made, the pair of the Shoggoth creatures there on the stage began to slide quickly forward toward the detective.

# CHAPTER FIFTEEN

WITHOUT HESITATION, LONDON THREW himself up and out of his seat, pulling Betty from her holster. He fired directly into the center of the nearest creature, but found his bullets had no effect on the whistling, screeching thing that he could detect. Undeterred by such a minimal attack, both the shoggoths rolled forward over the edge of the stage, contact with their skin actually melting everything in their path. Knowing he could not reach the aisle in time, the detective reholstered his .38, then stepped up onto the back of his seat instead. Running for the rear of the auditorium over the backs of the chairs, he cursed;

"Damn. Some days it just doesn't pay to get out of bed."

Behind London the shoggoths rolled onward relentlessly, dissolving the rows of seats, churning their way toward their target. As he strained to reach the back of the theater before the creatures, the detective combed through his ancestor memories, searching for anything that might help him. As he expected, he found nothing there to help him against such monstrosities.

Stepping onto the top of the back row while the creatures trailing him were still less than three-quarters of the way to the door, London leapt down, heading for the single door. Throwing himself onto the other side, the detective used his back to slam the door closed while grabbing a set of half-moon clips from their compartments on the back of his belt. Even as he used them to instantly reload his revolver, Kennedy's voice came to him through hidden speakers.

"Ah, Mr. London, so wonderfully defiant—a real life action

hero to the end. Yes?"

Noting something shifting within the Kennedy-thing's speech pattern, the detective answered;

"You want the big bucks, you got take the big jobs."

"Sorrowfully small creature," it answered, "you still don't actually understand, do you? You believe me distracted, think your friends will spread the word, that your valiant sacrifice will not be in vain—but you are wrong."

London locked the door behind him, gasping for breath. He thought for a moment to throw things against the barrier to brace it, then remembered that the creatures pursuing him could simply burn their way through the walls. Looking for some other means to turn the monsters, he suddenly realized;

"Oh, Christ—it's her voice ... it's shifted to human. That thing's almost got this together—almost brought itself back. I've got to think!" His mind racing, the Kennedy-thing continued to taunt him through the theater's speaker system.

"Those you sent forth, they run from home to home, gathering people who can not escape. Can you not understand it yet, I am Seaside—I control everything. When their vehicles reach the gates, they will not open."

Racing for the nearest bar, London dove inside it. Grabbing bottle after bottle, he threw them at the door from which he had just emerged, shattering them, spilling their contents everywhere. Then, as the wall began to dissolve, first in one spot, then another, he ran back to the bar and grabbed the two oxygen tanks he had spotted there earlier by the shielding top grips.

"They will all be consumed. But, admittedly, that which I will gain from them is nothing compared to that which I shall gain once you are a part of me as well."

The strain of dragging the two tanks off their shelves at the same time was practically crippling. London grit his teeth against the harsh pain pulsing through his arms, but finally managed to wrench them both down.

"I will create a chaos untold ..."

The heavy tanks smashed the ivory tile floor, shattering it. His arms throbbing, London kicked the tanks, getting them both rolling toward the wall. As he reached his objective the detective got down on his hands and knees, struggling the tanks into place—one near the first burning spot, the second beneath the other. After that, he threw their valves open wide, then retreated back to the steps.

"The master will be pleased ..."

As the spots on the wall grew larger, hotter, London pulled Betty forth once more, then set the revolver beside him as he worked frantically with several other things he had taken from the bar. From the speakers, Kennedy's voice mocked him.

"Oh, foolish Mr. London, oxygen tanks, your gun to the ready—you're thinking to remake 'Jaws.' Didn't you know, you can never trust Hollywood. That was just a movie."

As London stared, Betty in one hand, a liquor bottle in the other, the rich female voice purred;

"You can fire bullets at those tanks all day, all you'll do is put holes in them."

The melting spots on the wall fell through almost simultaneously. As they did, the doorway flew open as well. The Kennedy-thing strode forth into the room even as its shoggoths burned their way through the walls. Its demon monsters sliding into the room, the thing pulled its face into a hideous sneer, then barked at the detective;

"They won't explode."

"I know," he answered, lighting the tapered fuse of his Molotov cocktail. "But man, when you open them up, all that oxygen sure can help set one hell of a fire."

As the bottle flew through the air, the Kennedy-thing screamed as London pumped six bullets directly into its brain.

# CHAPTER
## SIXTEEN

"**I** KNOW I MUST sound a little crazy, since I was there, and have eyes and all, but I still don't know if I'll ever believe all of this or not."

It was two days after the destruction by fire of not only the home of Kennedy Walker, but of most of the seacoast community known as Seaside. The speaker was Sheriff Michael Tyrell. He was sitting in a very dark corner of one of the many bars offered to the travelers moving through the Los Angeles International Airport. With him in the curved corner booth were the four members of the London Agency. As best the lawman could tell, all of them seemed quite ready to head for home.

"Don't know what to tell you on that one," answered Morcey. "Except that I do understand. I mean, the bunch of us, we ain't been at this all that long, but I've already seen so many things beyond me comprehension, I've given up worrin' about it."

"How about you, ma'am," the sheriff asked of Lai Wan. "After the wringer you got put through. You going to be okay?"

"Yes, Mr. Tyrell. Thank you for asking. It was a difficult experience, yes ... but ultimately my strain was mental only. The type of wounds I suffered ... sadly, I have become proficient in healing." Raising her glass, the psychometrist tilted it toward the others, adding;

"And, if Mr. Dennton's promised funds actually reach us, I will have no problem recovering completely."

"Spoken like a real woman," joked Morcey as he tilted his tumbler in Lai Wan's direction.

"Spoken like a Chinese woman, anyway," scoffed Goward,

giving the psychometrist a challenging glance. Taking into account the fact the professor was already on his fourth drink, Lai Wan merely nodded in his direction, smiling demurely.

"How about you, me and the deep blue sea," asked London of the sheriff. "We going to be all right?"

"It's covered," Tyrell said with assurance. "Arson squad found things just like you said they would. But, they gave in their report just like I told them to. They were two of my boys, know the score. No one else has got permission to be on the scene."

"Very convenient."

"Yeah, surprise, surprise, the state police didn't want any part of it, and the locals, well, after word came down from the Attorney General's desk that my office was to have complete autonomy, that pretty much cinched things."

London nodded, his mind flashing back to the recent past, again watching the nearly human head exploding once more under his hail of bullets. The creature had forgotten—had been a part of the land for so many centuries, had been intertwined with all about it for so very long—that when it took on a living form once more it would no longer be in immediate contact with its vast array of underlings. When it had finally relinquished the last vestiges of its former self, moved completely into the Kennedy Walker body it had fashioned for its occupancy, slipped its feet into her high heels and broken its connection with the ground, it had left behind its alien existence and become completely and utterly human.

Thus it was that simple lead pellets were enough to extinguish its consciousness. Without its guiding instructions, its shoggoth servants became confused—disoriented. Seconds afterward, the lumbering horrors were covered in fire, the oxygen rushing from the tanks eager to find places to race, the lapping flames quickly spreading everywhere. The Walker mansion burned to the ground, collapsing on the twin nightmares, crushing them beyond their ability to adapt.

Tyrell let those present know Liston had already pulled in, and cut a deal with, Beardsly's people as well as everyone necessary from the studio holding Walker's picture. Much to the overwhelming relief of Beardsly's board of directors, the CEO's new will would be quietly forgotten. The corporation would expand or contract on its own merits without the alien-inspired genius of its creator. The studio would cut Walker's picture however it wanted. Her fans would mourn, life would go on.

"What about Grenzenki," asked Goward. "I haven't heard any mention of him."

"Oh, that's my favorite," answered Tyrell. Smiling widely, he told the others, "Old Polimar, he and Beardsly both are being listed as heroes who tried heroically to save their neighbors but perished in the blaze. Liston also 'discovered' the paperwork leaving all his holdings to his servants."

"Amazing," said London drily.

"Yeah, ain't it, though," answered the sheriff with a wry chuckle. Taking a last pull on his glass, Tyrell smacked his lips, then extended his hand, shaking those of everyone around the table one after another.

"Pleasure meeting you folks. I know I played you hard when you first arrived, but ... you proved me wrong about you, and fast, and I guess I'm just hoping I made up for it eventually."

Everyone made polite noises. Lai Wan brightened considerably when the sheriff assured her one last time that the state of California would make certain the London Agency received its payment from the Dennton estate. Only seconds after that, an announcement came over the bar's speakers that the next flight to New Jersey's Newark Airport was about to start boarding. As London signalled for the check, Tyrell caught the waitress's eye and point to his chest.

"Hey now, New York boy, I do owe you a drink, remember?" London smiled, admitting;

"Yes, actually—I do. Thanks, sheriff. Maybe someday I'll get to return the favor."

As the detective threw his carry-on bag over his shoulder, Tyrell smiled ruefully, adding;

"If I got to earn it the way you earned yours, no offense, son, but I think I'll switch to water."

The men shook hands once more, then London headed to join the others. The sheriff watched the four board the plane, watched the door close from the inside. Then, he stood in the window and not only remained for the plane to begin its taxi run, but waited and watched until it was given clearance, took off from its runway, and then disappeared miles away overhead.

After that, the lawman stood just a bit longer to make certain the detective and his crew were truly gone before he turned and headed for his vehicle. Along the way, he wondered, as he had asked earlier, if he would ever finally believe all he had seen and been forced to accept two days earlier or not.

The question would recur within his mind for the remainder of his days. Though it would plague him, keeping him awake at night, he would never answer it to his complete satisfaction. Still, that was good enough for Tyrell. His part in the affair, after all, was over.

For London and his friends, however, it had barely begun.

# CHAPTER
# SEVENTEEN

L ONDON LEANED ON THE heavy metal bars, staring forward. He did not lean against them for support. The detective was, after all, a strong man in his early thirties who had merely stopped for a moment to relax and, not wishing to draw attention to himself, had decided to blend in with his surroundings. Thus he had left the Brooklyn sidewalk and stepped close to the old iron fence running around the park which had caught his eye, staring into its green as if he had not a care in the world.

*"Think the kid can go higher?"*

*"Which one?"*

London waited for the first voice in his mind to answer the second. This was not a reaction to an internal monologue as most would understand it. Due to circumstances which had occurred for no other mortal being since the time of Solomon, Theodore London was in direct contact with the entirety of his racial memory, meaning that communication with every ancestor in his direct line, running as far back as humanity had known conscious thought, was open to him.

*"The one already going the highest."*

If he desired, London could converse with any of them, ask their opinions, use their memories as his own, utilize any of their abilities. This left him with the capacity to speak some fifty-eight current languages, although the further back he went the more regional, and sometimes unintelligibly colloquial, the dialects became.

*"Oh, yes—he's going quite high."*

Because of this, the detective could also shoe a horse, chip flint into weapons and tools, deliver a baby, brew a passably drinkable ale, handle both foils and sabres as well as quarterstaffs, throwing knives, axes and the bolo. He was brilliant with the bow and arrow, and he could also skin an animal, bleed it, dress it, and then prepare it in a score of different ways. His rapid introduction to his linage had also left him with the ability to sew, make turpentine, walk a high wire, bake all manner of breads, perform somersaults, tend to the growing of grapes, make paper from scratch, tend a kiln, dig a well-considered ditch, illuminate texts among scores of others.

All of his new-found talents and abilities were, however, by-products, as it were—inconsequential and minor when compared with the main gift which fate had cursed him with some seven months earlier.

*"I don't know ... can he?"*

*"I think he can."*

*"You would."*

London listened to the voices. On the one hand, they were always present within his mind. Most of the time he ignored them, the way one does conversations at another table when one is dining. That day, however, he was grateful for the distraction. Only seven months previous he had run the best one-man operation in New York City. Then, a gateway to another dimension had opened and Fate had moved him across Destiny's play board to stop such from happening. During this moment in time he acquired all of his new abilities—some minor, others extraordinary—and lost his best friend. If he had not also found the love of his life at the same instant, the detective would have considered the trade most unfair and cruel.

*"He's gonna do it—"*

Watching the competing children on the swings with one eye, he scanned the rest of the park with the other, letting his peripheral vision take in all the sights laid out before him. There was nothing out of the ordinary present, mothers with strollers, children playing, old men walking old dogs, merely life—normal and simple. Of course, to be certain, London had not been looking for anything unusual. Indeed, after what he and the others had been through in California, even the thought of finding something unusual, something bizarre, unexplainable—dangerous, cruel, deadly, voracious, whatever—would not have been pleasing. Then again, he was certain that, no matter what he might or might not find pleasing, that something of that nature was going to find its way to him, regardless—

*"Yes ... the master ... wanted certain tasks performed ... before he arrived..."*

Soon.

The words of the Kennedy-thing had continued to haunt him over the ten days since he had returned to New York. No matter how much attention he tried to pay to the various ancestor voices within his mind, or anything else for that matter, London had found it impossible to distract himself for very long from the disturbing memory of what the creature had told him back in the basement.

*"The master took us from slumber ... sent us here to ... amuse him..."*

The creature had not meant to deliver a warning to the detective or his world, but nonetheless, it had done so. Leaving London with a head filled with questions he could not answer.

"This thing," he thought, staring through the bars, seeing nothing, "with all its powers, the ability to create those shoggoth things to be its servants, and it wasn't the menace—"

*"The master will be pleased..."*

"Powerful as it was, and it was just the flunky. What in the name of God is headed toward us? What am I supposed to do this time?"

Again the detective thought of his meeting with Zarnak. Of the overwhelming power of the thing behind the door. Was it something like that which was headed their way—or something worse? London had taken Guicet to 13 China Alley, finding there two servants. The one was a young black man, barely out of his teens. The other was so elderly the detective could scarcely believe he still had duties. The older caretaker, a Hindu named Ram Singh, had recognized Guicet instantly, and had wept at the sight of him. Charging the younger man with taking the doctor to a room and making him comfortable, Singh had then entertained London, sharing a pot of tea with the detective and answering questions about Zarnak. The old man had told him endless stories of horrors which Guicet and Zarnak both had stopped in their time. Sighing, London blinked, then asked of the clear sky above him;

"Just one day, you know? Just one day. That's all I'm asking. One day without some mindless evil from beyond." His tone had almost been joking, but then he added the sharp challenge;

"Is that actually too much to ask?"

*"Measuring out your life in coffee spoons beginning to look pretty good to you, eh?"*

London ignore the poet's voice from the back of his mind. Suddenly wanting nothing that might remind him of all that had been thrust upon him in evidence, he shoved his ancestors from his conscious mind, turning off his ability to hear their chatter. Right then he did not want to concern himself with being the defender of the universe. It was a thankless task which had given him only heartache.

"And Lisa," he reminded himself.

London smiled, his grip on the bars relaxing considerably. Lisa Hutchinson, the woman he loved so dearly—it had been her plight that had placed the detective within Fate's path, and it had been for her sake he had faced and conquered the evils he had. Nodding his head in defeat, he admitted to himself that, yes, there was one thing connected to his awakening that he never wished to forget for even the slightest moment.

"That admission made, however," he thought, "could I please now just enjoy the scenery?"

The back of his brain properly chastised, the detective stared into the park, letting the simple human sights wash over him once more. Here he could see a stand of wind-formed pines, stooped and twisted from decades of continual gales forced forever in a straight line from the ocean two miles away down the canyon path of Stillwell Avenue. There a short, rotund grandmother, slowly pushed a baby carriage past the dog run, listening to her daughter's son's delight over the frantic barking just beyond the safety of his stroller.

"Ahh, just one of those days," he thought, smiling softly. "Just a nice, simple Brooklyn day surrounded by people without a care in the world."

In one direction his eyes caught the legion of old men with the scatter of younger faces, all of them gathered around three cement game tables—each of them watching the park's chess masters take on all comers. In the other direction, a large open area played host to scores of children. They were on bicycles and tricycles, scooters and skateboards. They were jumping rope and playing hopscotch and busying themselves with a hundred other age-old activities—one of the carefree even bouncing along on a pogo stick.

"Now where," wondered London honestly, "did he ever find that antique?"

The detective marveled at the sight, pleased that in the era of the omnipresent video game industry there were still children who delighted in such simple pleasures as throwing balls and dressing dolls.

Sighing, London forced clinging fatigue away from himself with the intake of each new lungful of air. The afternoon was a mild one, the sun above soft, but surprisingly gentle, the air bright—feeling warm, smelling clean. By rights the detective should have been in his office in Manhattan, but for once he had not felt like working. The confrontation in California had left him tired and angry, and a trifle nervous.

"The master," whoever or whatever he or it might be, was headed toward the Earth. When he arrived, London wondered, what exactly would he want? And what exactly would the detective's responsibilities be when he arrived?

That was the part of what had happened to London which disturbed him the most. Yes, he had been given the power to protect humanity. But, how long was he supposed to do so? And who or what was doing the supposing? The detective had no idea if he had just been a random piece on the board, buffeted by circumstance, or if there was such a thing as Destiny and he had actually been picked for the role.

For a while, he had held hope that eventually the insanity would stop finding its way to his doorstep. That he would be able to escape the responsibilities somehow thrust upon him. After meeting Zarnak, and then Ram Singh, however, he was now beginning to believe that such would never happen. That the rest of his days would be spent battling the forces of Hell.

And worse.

*"I don't think anyone's going to beat him—"*

*"Think you're right—"*

*"Kid's a winner ..."*

London reacted with mild surprise at the return of his ancestors' voices within his mind. Realizing his control over them was slipping as he relaxed, he smiled slightly, giving his shoulders a slight "what-the-hell" shrug as he allowed them to ramble on about the exuberant boy on the swing. Why not, he asked himself. Anything to help him forget the nightmare that had just gone by.

Or any of the others.

*"I use to love to swing ..."*

*"Didn't have such things when I was a girl—"*

*"Didn't have books when you were a girl ..."*

London hung his head, the face of Timothy Bodenfelt, commonly known when alive as "the Spud," flashing through his mind. The man who had been his best friend, the man the detective had been forced to destroy to save all of existence from the slavering evil just beyond the ken of normal man's consciousness. The sacrifice demanded of him to return everything to normal.

At least, he had *believed* when it was all over his life would return to normal. Oh, not the previous "normal" he had once known, of course. That he had realized was gone forever. But still, at least, he had supposed, some form of it nearly as good. He had, while recovering in his hospital bed, expected to be able to simply run his agency once more, to read the newspaper casually over breakfast and worry over to whom he should give his vote, to go bowling, enjoy the occasional movie—

*Didn't work out that way, did it, kid?*

"No," London answered the voice, angered at its intrusion. "No, it didn't."

Instead of normalcy, chaos had followed. Hideous things of every stripe had begun to surface, all of them somehow his responsibility. The destruction of Elizabeth, New Jersey and much of lower Manhattan had only been the beginning. Before long Geneva, Switzerland had sunk into the ground and burned, almost taking him with it. Chernobyl—site of the former Soviet Union's nuclear disaster—that nightmare had arrived only moments after Geneva.

*"Now, don't forget what we did to the Grand Canyon ... that wasn't so bad."*

London snarled; his grip tightened. All his ancestors went instantly silent. A thin wisp of gray cloud drifted in front of the sun then, dancing a slight grey pattern across the playground. None of the children, none of the chess players, neither grandmother or grandson or any of the dogs in attendance of their stroll noted its passing. It was but a single cloud on an otherwise glorious day, and not one person in fifty million would pay it the slightest mind. London saw it, however, and the slight touch of darkness made him cringe.

He knew looking for omens in everyday life was a fool's game, and yet, just as the cloud had covered as much of the sun's face as it was going to be able to eclipse, the phone clipped to London's belt vibrated. The detective's hand went to it automatically, reflex unclipping and answering it before his conscious mind could debate the matter. His eyes moving from branch to branch among the pines, counting the cones and birds to be found there, his soul enjoying making such simple lists, he asked;

"What's up, Paul?"

"Customers, boss."

London knew that if whoever was in their office wanted some simple assistance—a cheating spouse followed, a security detail for their workplace, employee background checks run, whathaveyou—there would have been no need to call him. Since his partner had called him, however, the detective swallowed hard. London had told both Paul and Lisa he needed a day for his head and that he would call them when he was coming in. For Morcey to buzz him—

"This can't wait?"

"I hate to say it, but if these guys are on the level ... it might already be too late."

*"Yes ... the master ... wanted certain tasks performed ... before he arrived ..."*

London looked back to the pines and watched as all the birds took flight at the approach of his eyes. Across the way, the assembly of dogs in the run began to howl, setting off their audience of one grandson as well. Knowing with certainty that any further indecision on his part would soon be felt by everyone around him, the detective answered;

"I'm on my way."

"Don't take the train. Catch a cab."

London assured his partner he would hurry. Releasing his grip on the old iron fence rail, the detective noted that his palm was covered with flecks of paint and rust. Brushing the decay against his pant leg, he thought;

"Well, at least I broke off having a good time before I caused that kid to go flying off his swing."

Accepting the slight moral victory, London fastened his cell phone back into the holder on his belt even as he moved away from the park. Looking for a cab, he blinked at the slight pooling of moisture in his left eye.

"Not even one day," he snarled deep within himself. "I can't even have just one goddamned day."

The streets of New York City's outer boroughs were not packed with taxis the way those in Manhattan were, but the park was situated at a major Brooklyn crossroads—Stillwell Avenue and Bay Parkway—and the detective managed to find a ride in only a few moments. Getting into the back, he said;

"Manhattan—132 West 31st—between 6th and 7th. And, I'll double the fare if you can make it in less than half an hour."

The cabbie smiled. London closed the cab door, noting as he did so that even though the sky's lone cloud had moved on, no birds had returned to the pines.

# CHAPTER
# EIGHTEEN

GETTING OUT AT HIS floor, London walked the fifteen paces to the front door of his office. "Theodore London, Private Investigations"—the words stared back at him from the wire-meshed glass of the door's window as he stood in the hallway for an extra moment, fortifying himself before entering.

*"Once more into the breech, dear friends ..."*

The detective growled within his head, letting his ancestors know that he had endured enough for one day. London had not asked his partner what was so important; in all honesty, he had not wanted to know. Truthfully, he still did not want to know. Indeed, as his hesitation continued, part of his mind whispered in a low voice wet with self-interest, urging him to turn away—to simply ignore whatever awaited.

"Ahhhh, get thee behind me," he muttered to himself without conviction. Then, he reached out and, sighing in frustration, grasped the knob to his door and let himself into his outer office.

In his waiting room, both his partners sat with their eyes glued to the front entrance. Seeing his own office door closed, but with the lights on, told him where the agency's potential clients were waiting. Upon the detective's entrance, Morcey crossed the room as he blurted;

"Boss, sweet bride a'da night, but we got a doozy cookin' this time."

"He's not joking, Teddy," added Lisa. "The story these people told ... it, it's unbelievable."

London stared at the woman, soaking her in for a loving split-second as he always did—her striking eyes and cheekbones, her wealth of chestnut curls. He had bent the laws of time and space to rescue her without a second thought. Indeed, if he had stopped to think about what he had been doing, he would not have been able to do it.

"More unbelievable that all the stuff we've already lived through?"

The half-joking tone in the detective's voice fizzled quickly. The looks in his partners' eyes, their body language, everything about them told him they were serious. As much as he hated the thought, something else incredible, some new unfathomable had surfaced, thrown itself onto the beach and dragged its way to his doorstep.

"*Ah, isn't it wonderful to be popular?*"

Ignoring the antagonizing voice in his head, London asked if there was anything else he should know before he met their guests. Morcey told him;

"This is really one of those time-is-of-da-essence things, if ya know what I mean." Nodding his head unconsciously, the one-time maintenance man added, "Honestly, boss, I'm really thinkin' it's best you just get in there."

London made a whatever-you-say gesture, then pointed Lisa toward the phones giving her a certain nod. Knowing their routine, she moved to her desk where she turned off the recording devices which had been monitoring their guests. Even in the short time since the detective had acquired his new abilities, their offices had been visited, and invaded, by such a variety of phenomena, that London had installed listening and video devices, as well as mechanisms to record sudden changes in temperature, air and foot pressure, and others even more exotic.

Lisa gave the detective a high sign as he moved toward his office, indicating that everything within seemed normal. She and Morcey had studied the results of their recording devices while their guests had been sequestered. None of them had displayed any type of abnormality the detective needed to be informed about. London nodded, then turned the knob to his inner office so he could find out just what had brought those inside to him.

As he entered the room, the detective was greeted by five individuals—three men, two women. All of them rose at the same time, moving forward toward London. Narrowing his eyes, the detective took them all in with a glance.

The closest man was an Indian, specifically a Hindu—close to sixty, balding, gray eyes, very lean, no more than 4'8". Next to him was his near polar opposite—a black woman in her early twenties, her hair thick and full, her ebony eyes and the tilt of her head giving London to believe she was from the African mainland. She stood slightly over six feet tall and the detective noted that even the powerful amount of fear shining within her eyes could not stoop the pride with which she carried herself.

"Neither of them Americans," he thought as he eyes moved on, "and yet here they are."

Next to the tall woman was another bald man, this one a Chinese of average height. He was the oldest of them all—well past 70, London was certain—possibly a monk. He did not wear any specific religious garb, but he gave the detective a certain feeling of serenity and order, as did the man next to him. Also older, but most likely only in his early fifties, the last man in the group struck London as a Native American, and also a religious leader.

"I have to admit," he thought, reaching out to shake hands with the gray-bearded Hindu, "they're keeping it interesting."

The last figure in his office was another woman—late thirties, early forties, green eyes, red hair stranding to gray, medium height, slightly plump—the detective placed her as British, Irish, perhaps, or some other variant. She had the smell of the North Atlantic to his senses, although he could not say why for certain. After all, people with red hair could live anywhere they chose. But still, he was as positive about that hunch as he was all of the others.

His half-second of studying those assembled passing, however, he finished extending his hand, taking that of the Hindu and shaking it firmly as he announced;

"Hello, I'm Theodore London. How may I help you?"

"Our names are unimportant," announced the gray-bearded gentleman. "Our mission is, however. To help us, you must listen to us, and then you must act as you see fit. Already too much of our time has gone rushing away."

"Mr. Penjii," said the older woman, her accent confirming London's guess of an Irish residency, "is our spokesman. He not only speaks English, but he best understands our concern." Unconsciously moving her hands as she continued to speak, she indicated to the others that they should return to their seats as she added, "I say to you, though, please, Mr. London, you must listen to him as there's precious little time left to us now, this bein' the day and all."

"*The day?*"

London felt his left eyebrow raise as he responded to the woman's phrase. Her emphasis on the word "day," as if there were something dreadful about that one day in particular.

"What could she mean," he wondered. Nodding to her to indicate that he would listen to her Mr. Penjii, the detective also motioned to the assembly to take their seats once more. As the five began to sit back down, London moved to his usual place behind his massive desk. Dropping into his leather chair, he pressed his spine against the tight slats of its back, moving his shoulders just so, digging his way into the seat. As he did, he said;

"It's my job to listen. We'll find out what your problem is, discuss what might be done, by myself, my organization, et cetera, we'll go over all aspects of your case, set up a time schedule, a payment rate, every—"

"Are you a fool?" All eyes turned to the Native American man as he rose from his seat.

"I've been called one in my time," the detective admitted,

only the slightest of edges in his voice. "That and worse."

"I did not ask what you have been called, Mr. London. I asked what you are." The older man's face went hard as he spoke, its deep lines cracking further as he spoke.

"Wasting precious time when your senses must be telling you how urgent is our burden, your noise makes my mind burn. Thus, I will ask again. Are you a fool?"

While the detective searched for a response, others in the visiting party spoke in varying tones to the Native American, but he snapped back at them all without facing any of them, keeping the entirety of his energy focused on London. Crossing the room until he was directly before the detective's desk, he said;

"My name is Dies On The Right Day, Mr. London. I am shaman, not for my family, or village, but for my entire nation. I have drunk the light of the moon, eaten the holy root that sends a man to the purple mountains." As the detective's face revealed that he understood the older man's reference to the dreamplane, the shaman pointed a hand at him, adding;

"Yes, I have walked in the mountains of lightning. And I have done more. I have made peace with coyote, wrestled with ghost souls, and cleansed the windigo. To those who know me clearly, I am a man of great power."

The older man put both his palms on the wide desk top then, leaning down and in upon them to force his face closer to the detective's. Staring into London's eyes, the shaman dropped his voice a note lower as he said;

"But, we both know that yours is a far more powerful spirit than mine." As the detective merely continued to listen, Dies On The Right Day continued.

"You do not seem to understand what gravity pulled us to you, how it has whispered to us, making it clear that you are our only hope. Everyone's only hope."

"I've heard that before," answered London.

"We know this. That is why we are here. The end of all things is coming, when men and birds, fish and insects and every piece of creation under the sun's warm light will face extinction." Reaching for something strapped to his belt, hidden from London's sight by his jacket, the shaman asked;

"Mr. London, the shape of your spirit light as I see it all about you tells me you believe in vampires. That you have seen them, wrestled with them—that you know how to collect energies as they do. I am correct?"

Seeing no reason to be disingenuous, the detective admitted; "I wouldn't give you too great an argument on any of that—no."

"Then, listen as I say that you must, here and now, stop thinking like a man of the false world, the civilized facade of venal nonsense, and step beyond into the real world—the true world. We are not here with a 'case,' nor can we be bothered with any kind of 'payment' your banker might understand."

"What were you planning to pay with then?"

His eyes still locked with London's, the shaman answered; "You will need great power for the battle ahead of you. Here is our down payment."

And, so saying, Dies On The Right Day pulled free the horn-handled hunting knife his father had given to him and buried it within his heart.

# INTERLUDE

NOW LET ME THINK ...

The tall, slender man with the knowing eyes and the sinister grin walked across the red plane, scarlet dust billowing all about him as he moved. Behind him in the distance, purple mountains rang with the echoes of thick, golden lightning. It crashed throughout the pulsing rocks, cracking open dimensions and resealing them just as quickly.

*How long shall I give them?*

The clean-shaven man with the yellow hair and the antique spectacles was in The Between, navigating the everlasting trails of the dreamplane, the last stepping stone to the beginning of everything. He was, as he was nearly every day, back in the Dreamlands, that anchored, yet insubstantial strand of plasma which connected all dimensional doorways, lead to all places— the only common ground of Most of the Many.

*After all ...*

There were times in his past, as he walked into a new plane of existence, his precisely clipped march beating his gait into the rhythm of this or that world, that he had not cared to play by his own rules. It was such an amusement, he recalled, when he had found primitives whom he could make cower with ease, not as *a* god, but as *the* God.

*How many times ...*

He began to ask himself for a specific answer to the question, but gave off the thought. He had come across such beginning civilizations more times than he could remember. Taking hold of them at that moment of budding social intelligence, guiding them through as a race to linear thought, on to abstract thought, and further and further, he would mold and cherish them until finally he could crush and slaughter and scatter them—certainly not as equals, but as a species which should have known better.

*I should be sporting about this.*

But those were the exceptions—those times when he was tired, or bored, or giddy. Normally, the rules did apply. They had to, or where was the fun, after all. He would find yet another new dimension, one which as of yet had not been graced by his presence, and he would find its finest, most advanced world—its greatest civilization—and then he would see how much chaos he could bring it during one of its standard days.

Sometimes he would allow himself numerous of his lesser abilities. But, most often he would simply attune himself to the vibrations of his latest target, adjust his metabolism to breath the atmosphere found there, gift himself with sufficient communication skills to be able to converse with the natives, et cetera, and then he would go amongst those he found and set them to destroying themselves.

Within one of their own standard days. However long it took their particular world to revolve once upon its own axis, that was all the time he was allowed to bring them low, to grind their proud spirits as they deserved.

*Now, when was it I left exactly?*

The slender man paused for a moment, bringing his home dimension into focus within his mind. Flipping through the millennia of its existence, he closed his eyes as he fingered along its rambling centuries until he felt a familiar tug, the unmistakable odor of home.

*Ahh, this feels right.*

Bringing his attention sharply into focus on a particular cluster of decades, he sifted reality back and forth until he found the one single moment when his essence had first departed from his home world. The moment made him positively sentimental, a fact which hit him as almost unbelievable. That he could have missed anything about the confining narrows of his former existence stunned him into a sort of awed amusement.

The moment passed quickly, however, and the man returned to work, searching his memory for those beliefs and points of reference which had been his on the day of his enlightenment. For a handful of seconds, the grinning man was stunned at the sheer volume of his former ignorance.

So simple he had been back then. So typical, so ordinary.

*Just a man.*

It was true. At one time, though he had forgotten the fact ages earlier, he had once been nothing more than a simple human being. Two legs, two eyes, two arms and ears, a mere sack of symmetrical flesh, a thing that gasped for oxygen, a beast in need of daily nourishment—an automaton in constant need of slaughtered flesh and harvested fibers, grains and organs and anything else a bellyful of acid could break down into fuel.

*Just a man.*

The weight of the formidable truth slammed into the man's brain and for an instant he felt weak. Paralyzed. Keying in on the exact moment of his ascension, he stood between the joy of his ascendence and the nearly overwhelming terror of his cast-off humanity. Reliving the monumental joy of accepting godhood, he was forced to remember what made the moment so joyful to him in the first place.

*Pain,* he thought, fascinated and frightened at the same time. *I remember pain.*

For a delicious moment, he allowed the alarming sensations to flood over him. He remembered bruises—skin discoloring, flesh throbbing. And cuts, slices of all manner, from shaving to the kitchen to laboratory mishaps—thin lines appearing on skin, the second or two of hesitation, and then the inevitable separation as the walls of flesh slid away from one another and the crimson would begin to flow.

The slender man's normally sharp grin softened dramatically as he dove into the memory of each and every pain he had ever experienced throughout his former life, the one dependent on flesh and blood. And then, once he had tasted everything from the terrorizing horror of being ripped away from his mother's body—feeding cord slashed, their bond mindlessly rent asunder—upward in time through each and every other instance of suffering, including that felt during his several deaths, he spoke aloud to his surroundings, his voice dark with bitter memory.

"Oh, yes—I remember pain ever so well."

He would make his return to his particular Earth an event to warm his heart over the following ten thousand years. As he continued to stare into his past, it occurred to him that for far too long he had been merely wasting his time. Yes, worlds had perished, entire universes had been collapsed. But not as they should have, not with any real form or style.

The slender man realized suddenly that for far too long he had been simply going through the motions. Too often he had merely taken the path of least resistance, finding a few perfect subjects that would allow him to satisfy his own rules and then bringing down another world in gore and ruin. He had allowed himself to grow sloppy, careless—his efforts ultimately as pointless as those of the creatures he despised.

"Well," he told himself critically, "that will all be changing."

Refreshing himself with the world as it had been when he had left it, he shuddered to move forward in time. No one would be able to stand against him then. Oh, they had cobbled together a slight form of nuclear power, but that was all. If he remember correctly, during the last great conflict before his departure some of the combatants had still been riding into battle on horseback.

*That will never do.*

Skipping ahead, he watched as he saw chemical and biological weapons being tested, used with abandon and without concern. He saw the growth of underwater launch pads for nuclear missiles, the creation of bombs using hydrogen, and then neutrons. Things were looking better.

Getting a feel for other layers surrounding his former existence, the man watched the concept of television grow from a novelty some thirty years before he left the Earth behind into a sinister mechanical succubus, draining souls while actually charging a fee to do so. The symbiotic horror of it made him smile, but he let this development pass as well, and many more.

He waited for weapons of all size and stature to be created, for space travel and instantaneous global communications to come into being. He had decided to abandon all his powers, to bring his world low with nothing but that one overwhelmingly fabulous invention of his which had made him the equal of all the powers that were anywhere in existence.

And then, he felt it.

*What's this?*

Suddenly there was an occurrence which threw all his notions right out the window. There, on his Earth, was another mortal with powers and abilities to rival his own. Less than a century after he had pulled God's crown down out of the Heavens and slung it around his own incomparable brow, here came another to claim the power cosmic as theirs.

The thin smile which had softened somewhat, suddenly expanded into a thing capable of releasing the most joyous of laughs. Unbelievably, the Earth, his little backwater ditch of a world, had a champion—a native son who understood the laws of creation better than most of his fellows comprehended the laws governing traffic.

And then, the slender man witnessed the champion's first encounter, and the laughter stopped. His jaw hanging open, he realized that the figure he had decided to make his opponent was quite possibly powerful enough to destroy worlds himself. Remembering of a sudden the gift he had sent to the Earth in advance of his arrival, the blonde man searched the ether for his servants. His hunt was met with an answer he had not expected.

The creatures he had flung home in a fit of mischief had been destroyed. By the same champion.

"Still," he pondered, "what could it matter?"

A glee flooding his heart, the clean-shaven man could actually feel his blood pumping within his veins. Unable to restrain himself for another moment, he stepped forward, shedding the hold of the dreamplane, moving into the still familiar existence of his youth. The man with the sinister eyes and fast-paced gait had returned to the Earth he had left so long ago, and the idea charged him with excitement.

Dropping himself into his old home town, he shuddered as his immortal, invincible body shed its vast and varied immunities to take on the appearance of being fully human once more. The claws of gravity pierced him immediately, and he was forced to compensate. Breathing hard, gasping, he sat down on a nearby bench and caught his breath, the first actual one he had taken in longer than he could remember. Then, reaching backward out of singular reality, he felt for the pages of time to discern exactly how long his opponent had held his powers.

*Seven months ...*

The thin man reviewed the handful of months, marveling at the massive and terrible destructions the planet's defender had caused. Then, rising from his seat, he said to no one in particular;

"Yes, I think that's long enough for you to get a handle on your abilities. Best we meet now, I think, before I give you too much time and you destroy this world all by yourself without any help from me."

That said, the thin man slid his hands into his pocket and walked forward into his old home town, thinking all the while on exactly how he would destroy Theodore London.

# CHAPTER NINETEEN

THE DETECTIVE'S HANDS SHOT forward after the knife, the gushing arcs of blood it was releasing splattering across his fingers. As the others in the room gasped, either bolting from their seats with concern or driven back into them by surprise, scarlet ribbons pumped with violent speed from the chest of Dies On The Right Day.

"Paul!"

Even as London's conscious mind caused him to cry out for his partner, his subconscious leapt body-to-body, throwing itself into the mind of the dying shaman at twice the speed of light. The detective's spirit plunged into Dies On The Right Day's consciousness, soaking up information. He did not try to process any of it. Indeed, stopping to understand any single fragment as it flowed to him would have been a disastrous waste of time.

"Boss! Wha-oohh, oy ge'velt!"

Dies On The Right Day twisted his bone-handled blade into his heart with savage intent even as London's hands finally came down atop the shaman's own. As Morcey fought his way into the office, life energy began to leak away from the Native American, thrown violently from his body by the knife thrust, like water from a puddle reacting to a passing car tire. London's senses reached out and snagged every iota of it easily enough, but when the detective tried to return it to its owner he received surprising resistance.

"Take what is given," the dying man's consciousness snapped at London. "Accept this life—it is the payment you demanded. And you will need it. Every drop."

"Take it back," demanded the detective, his mind screaming

the words within Dies On The Right Day's flickering consciousness. "Live. For God's sake — help me with whatever it is you fear instead of running away from it."

The two mens' mental conversation raced by at a fantastic speed. Their sentences compressed into hundredths of a second, those around them seemed to be moving at a comically slow rate in comparison.

"I can be of help in no other way. I am giving you all my strength—all my tricks—and you must take them."

"It's not right," snapped London.

"Nor is what approaches. But this is what must be," answered the dying shaman solemnly. Continuing to resist the detective, he added, "And what is more, trust me in this, my son, my sacrifice is but the first."

As the two men argued, their physical bodies continuing to struggle, bits of understanding came to London. Shocked as a part of his mind was at what he had witnessed seconds earlier, as his subconscious merged with the brain he had invaded, the detective began to get the sense that as far as Dies On The Right Day was concerned, what he had done had been practically inevitable.

"You begin to understand ..."

"You didn't have to—"

"Yes," answered the dying man, "*I did. You had to be awakened at the primal level. You needed to know instantly what we have been trained our entire lives to understand.*"

"*'We?' 'Trained?' What—*"

"*You will learn ...*"

"*But ...*"

As the two men continued both their physical and mental struggles—London still hoping to rescue the dying man from his suicide, Dies On The Right Day determined to thwart him—the others in the room began to move in a matching time, coming close to entering the confrontation. Penjii and the Irish woman held to their seats, forcing themselves to resist the temptation to interfere. The African woman and the monk were on their feet, however, their arms outstretched, both reaching for the contest of hands before them.

"Boss, what should I do?"

Dies On The Right Day's fingers began to twist the blade within his heart back in the other direction. Flesh ripped, muscle tore, arteries collapsed and more blood pounded forth, crashing in thick splatters against not only London, but those others approaching as well. Their hands headed toward the confrontation since the instant it had begun, the four agonizing seconds since the knife tip tasted flesh, they reached it at the same moment. First the woman's hands came down upon London's, then the monk's wrapped atop hers.

"*What are you doing?*"

The detective's question was answered only with a surprising force. Rather than working to assist London, both of the newcomers to the struggle threw themselves into helping Dies On The Right Day overwhelm the detective's resistance. As the quartet thrashed, the dying man's heart pumped once again and another quart of blood splashed freely from the grave rent in his chest. It washed over the tangle of quarreling hands, sluicing through their fingers, painting all the same shade of scarlet.

"*There's no need for this man to die.*"

Locking eyes with London, the old monk smiled at him serenely, then thought, "*Your entire sentence should have been, there is no need for this man to die alone.*"

And, so saying, the monk looked into his companion's eyes. As she nodded, the old man tripped a long ago prepared mental switch which allowed the release of his own life energies as well as the woman's. As London reeled in horror, the life forces of the two began to simply ooze from their bodies, joining the flood already gushing from Dies On The Right Day.

"Take what is offered," said Penjii softly.

The detective could have easily rejected the two newcomers if he wanted to do so. Indeed, it was not beyond his capabilities to restore them both with a thought while forcing life back into the shaman as well. Even after the horribly long flow of seconds, he could have returned all their lives to the state they had been in a scant moment earlier before Dies On The Right Day had pulled his weapon. But, as knowledge of the situation flooded into his mind, he found himself accepting the scene all about him.

"Boss," called out Morcey, "what'll I do?"

"Stay back, Paul," London snapped, surprising himself nearly as much as he did his partner.

Yes, he realized, he could play God, use his powers any way he liked. But acting thusly created consequences, and he had learned all too well how painfully quick such tallies could mount when he did as he liked without regard for what might come of it.

"They all think this is fine," he thought, trembling at the notion of not stopping what was happening, "that this is what has to be ... well, then so be it."

The detective could not explain any of what was happening, but everything coming to him in the chaotic jumble of memories and personalities told him he was a part of the fate of the trio struggling with him. And, with that decision, London relaxed, setting himself the task of accepting what had been thrown at him so unexpectedly. Steeling himself against the rush to come, he stopped trying to force Dies On The Right Day's soul back into his body.

"It is for the best," he heard the shaman's consciousness whisper within his mind.

Nodding, the detective not only began allowing the dying man's essence to flee his body, but he pulled it free, snapping up every speck of it for himself. As the spirits of the monk and the woman began to slip loose from their moorings, he accepted them as well. Pink and golden sprays of life spiralled through the air, reaching out for London's own aura, wrapping themselves around it, moving within it, merging smoothly.

"Teddy?"

Lisa called from the doorway. She had finally reached the scene and her mind reeled at what she saw. There before her were two clients sitting calmly in their seats as three others and the man she loved struggled over a knife buried in the heart of one of that trio. Blood was everywhere, even dripping from the ceiling, but that was not the sight that made her gasp, that caused her to skid to a halt in stammering confusion.

As she watched, the confrontation before her calmed. Suddenly London was not so much trying to pull the knife from Dies On The Right Day's chest as he was holding the man upright— his companions as well. While the others watched, it became apparent that the horrific rush of blood had been stanched. In fact, not only had it ceased to flow from the shaman, but it had begun to dissipate as well. First the warmth rose from the scarlet smears and blobs, the energy of it heading for London, then the cooled atoms of it began to separate, following along with the rest.

From throughout the room, all of the blood began to break down to its simplest level, the resulting life essences merging with the detective's. That was not all. The marrow within all three of the bodies locked with London's began to boil within its bones. The trio's flesh began to peel as well, splitting along wrinkles, falling away as drops of fat and flecks of leather, all of it fading into basic atoms as it dribbled out of physical existence.

Lisa moved forward, not understanding, not wanting to understand, but Penjii stood and barred her path. Seeing the Indian meant her no harm, Morcey joined him.

"It's okay," the balding man said, trying to be reassuring. "It's what the boss wants, so ... like it's gotta be okay."

"Does it?"

Along with Penjii and his companion, Lisa and Morcey watched as the bodies of the three, suddenly completely cleansed of blood, began to disintegrate. Hair wisped away into nothingness, eyes and organs mushed into a chowdered liquid which boiled up into steam, all of it breaking down into particles of energy which London pulled to himself almost greedily. The clothing of the three unraveled as well—buttons and zippers and other hard bits, nails in shoe heels, belt buckles, et cetera, melting a touch slower, but rendering down nonetheless.

And, in less than a minute from the initial moment when Dies On The Right Day had lived up to his name, the confrontation concluded. Theodore London, eyes wild and glowing, chest heaving, hair crackling, mind exploding with additional power, stood behind his desk, his outstretched hands grasping nothing. Even the bone-handled knife had faded from existence, each atom of it reconfigured and digested at the request of its former owner. Where there had been four people, now there was but one.

And before him, the companions of the three now departed sat with their hands folded in their laps as if this were the most natural thing in the world. Morcey and Lisa held onto each other, neither quite certain what they had actually witnessed.

"T-Teddy ..."

London ignored Lisa's call, his expression clearly showing he had not actually heard her. Instead, trying to get his bearings once more, slowly, deliberately, the detective quietly returned to his seat. He was surprised to find his heart rate steady, his pulse normal. Needing to calm his mind as well, however, he scanned through the knowledge he had absorbed from the three people who had so recently thrown their lives at him. He was not surprised to find that all three of them believed a bizarre, incredible idea to be true. Realizing his partners might not share in all his newly acquired knowledge, and that he quite likely was not in possession of all of the story yet himself, he said;

"Well, perhaps those of us who are still alive should have a talk. What do you think, Mr. Penjii?"

"What shall we talk about, Mr. London, sir?" Scowling, the detective pulled a name he had received from the memories of the suicidal trio and answered drily;

"How about 'the Life-A-Day Man?' Do you think that would be good for starters?"

"Oh yes," responded Penjii, nodding gravely. "I think that would be most appropriate."

# CHAPTER
# TWENTY

"TEDDY," LISA INTERRUPTED, HER voice on the edge of shattering into hysteria, "what happened? To those people—what ... what did, did you ..."

"What you think you saw is what happened," he told her calmly. "I just broke three human beings down into their essential building blocks and then had them for lunch. Not something I normally do, but it was at their insistence. Now," he growled, his eyes narrowing at he turned toward the remaining two clients;

"I'm hoping to find out why they wanted me to do so. Care to shed some goddamned light on that subject, Mr. Penjii?"

"It is why I am here."

"Well, jump and down, and bully for you. So, spill it. I don't intent to trust what I think I unscrambled from your friends' minds—I want it from your lips—give me the story—now. Who's this Life-A-Day man, and what in Hell has he got to do with me?"

"Since the beginning of time," the gray-eyed man said quietly, "he has been a part of our universe. Or, more specifically, he has been a part of all universes."

"All universes?" asked Morcey.

"Yes, good sir. This dimension of ours is but one of an infinite series of universes. I know you are familiar with this concept, as you yourself have dealt with various creatures from realms beyond our own—have you not?"

Morcey looked to London for a high sign as to how he should answer the Hindu. There were those times when the Agency put its cards on the table and others where they kept information close to their vests. The detective moved his eyes in one direction while nodding in another, signaling Morcey to go ahead and talk, but to keep his questions, and especially his answers, from revealing too much. When the balding man agreed it was possible that the London Agency had indeed had its share of occult run-ins, Penjii nodded sagely, then continued.

"The Life-A-Day Man is simply that, a man who spends but one day alive on any one world. 'Man,' of course, is no word to describe this thing, for its power is truly staggering. It is a god-creature of some sort—oh, yes. But, for whatever reason it might have for doing so, it takes the form of a man wherever it goes—yes, a human man. No matter where it is, it looks like a human man."

London stared at Penjii evenly. As he listened, the man's story, the words he heard seemed to make no sense. But, the detective could sense that the trio of lives he had just ingested had believed the same story with the same unshakable conviction which the Hindu's voice displayed.

"Whatever it is, however, is not important. What can be agreed upon is what it does."

"And what's dat?"

"What it does, Mr. Morcey," answered Penjii, "is to spend its one day on the world it has chosen trying to find a way to destroy that world, or ..." the Hindu paused, considered his words, then added, "perhaps more correctly would be to say, he spends that day trying to find a way to convince the inhabitants of that world to destroy it for him."

"You said that this thing's a god," interrupted London. "I mean, even a low rent god, can't it just snap its fingers and wipe out anything it wants to?"

"Oh, it could. Yes, certainly," agreed Penjii. "But like many beings from our own world's various mythologies, it has its own code, ah, set of rules ... hummmm, I mean ..."

"It likes to play games." All heads turned toward the red-haired woman.

"What kind of games?"

"Games of its own devising," she answered. "It's made a sport of going from world to world and getting those what live there to destroy themselves."

"Jeez, I hate to seem rude, an' all," Morcey threw in, "but if no one minds me askin', how come you people know all this stuff about what this god-thing's been doin' in other dimensions and the such since the beginning of time?"

"Because," the woman answered, "he has told us."

"Sporting devil," whispered Lisa. Her nerves getting the better of her, the third partner of the London Agency retired to her desk in the outer office. She would be able to hear everything that was said within London's office if she desired, but at the moment whether she was going to listen further or not, she wanted to do it sitting down. In her own chair. Behind her own desk. Where the world was still, at least in some small way, familiar. Seemingly less fragile.

In the meantime, not nearly as bothered by what he was hearing as Lisa, London continued his questioning.

"Well, that's awful convenient. And pray tell me, why would he do that? What makes you folks so special?"

"I told you," the woman hissed. "It's not us—it's that ..." her voice froze for a second, the feeling in her pause one of trying to get across a lifetime of nightmares in a single sentence. "It's that bloody thing—can you not understand? It's a gamester, a trickster. That's the fun of it for this thing, don't you see? It enjoys seeing worlds destroy themselves. Like the favored champion in a competition spotting the other team points."

"And you are ..." London asked, "Miss, Ms., Mrs. ...?"

"Maura McNeil, of the clan McNeil," she announced in a proud voice, "and the only title I recognize is priestess. I've been raised such since birth, since I first displayed the gift. There's always been one of us born in the same region, as it was for Ling and Na'ruma and, and ..."

"And Dies On The Right Day?" McNeil nodded in response

to London's suggestion. As her until-then stormy eyes suddenly quieted and grew moist, the detective diverted his attention to the Hindu once more and asked, "And yourself, Mr. Penjii?"

The older man nodded quietly.

"Interesting," said London. "All right, well then, here's a serious question. If you and yours have had all this inside information for however many centuries, why did you wait until now to tell anyone? Why isn't the urban legend of the Life-A-Day Man a story we all know, something we can find by clicking over to Hellthings.com, or at least Wickipedia? I mean, I've heard of Satan, and Loki, and the Monkey King. How'd this particular trickster miss the roster?"

"It calls us the Cassandras," answered Penjii. "It selects beings in all realities and tells them of itself. Then, it makes certain no one will believe the story. Like the Greek seer who could predict the future, people could hear what she said, but no one would believe her."

"But," said Morcey, one eyebrow arched in puzzlement. "I'm pretty sure that I'm believin' ya ... so like, wha'das that mean?"

"It means, my friend," Penjii said sadly, "that he has arrived. That somewhere on the face of our world, the Life-A-Day man is taking his first steps."

London leaned back in his chair. His hands knotted one within the other, he rested them on his desk, his head down, eyes closed to the thinnest of slits. He withdrew himself from the current instance in time without apology or permission, retreating into his own head for the moment to sort things out.

Five people had come to him with a fantastic tale, one for which they seemed to have no proof except their own word and rather unshakable belief. Indeed, so convinced they were of the truth of what they had to tell that the majority of them had sacrificed their lives there in his office just to prove their point.

The detective had read the life energies of the three as he absorbed them. The act had allowed him to know everything there was to know about the trio—to experience the entirety of their lives. London knew that every word they had said beforehand, as well as every word Penjii and McNeil had said afterwards, all three of them had believed completely and without reservation.

"Yeah," thought the detective, "but people jump off roofs believing absolutely that they can fly, that still doesn't make them super."

"Is that really what those people believe?"

The voice from the back of the detective's mind caught him off guard. Although he did not want to admit it, he knew what his mind was trying to tell him. People who did such things might allow depression or drugs or whatever to rattle them, to convince a part, some section of their brain, maybe even most of it, that they could do something they otherwise knew they could not. But, deep down somewhere in the recesses of their consciousness there rested a part of them which knew the truth. And because of that one sliver of resistance to breaking with conventional wisdom, they fell when they jumped.

"But not you," the back of his mind whispered. "Oh, no. When you jumped, you soared, because you've got a god-complex all your own, don't you?"

London shut his eyes completely, squeezing the self-doubt away from his mind. What was done was done. Fate had offered him a choice—accept responsibility for the universe, or watch the woman you love die. Without hesitation, without a second thought, he had accepted the power cosmic and used it instantly.

*"Don't do the crime if you can't do the time."*

London sighed as the voices within his head chuckled amongst themselves. As the others in the room simply stared, the detective debated his next move within his head. He decided to trust his partner's instincts. If Morcey felt he believed the story of the Life-A-Day Man, then he would as well. Three people had given their lives to catch his attention—they deserved at least twenty-some hours of respect.

"But," the detective wondered, "where do we go from here? A

god is supposed to simply appear here on the Earth. Somewhere. Anywhere. Only he's going to look like a normal human being. And the only thing we know about him is that he's going to try and get the world to somehow destroy itself."

London moved his head back and forth, stretching the muscles in his neck. Starting a nuclear war would most likely be the easiest way to get the deed done, but that seemed too easy, and didn't this thing like a challenge?

What did they know about this monster—really? That it limited itself to a single day; that it tricked worlds into destroying themselves; that it allowed these worlds to know of its coming ...

And then, it hit him. Sitting forward, eyes open, brow furrowed, mind working, London asked;

"Maura, you said this thing called you 'the Cassandras,' right?" When the woman agreed, the detective asked;

"Now, what do you mean by that? I mean, is that the term it uses everywhere, or is it just a reference meant for this world, just for our Earth?"

"No," the woman said matter-of-factly, "we're all given visions of other places the Life-A-Day Man has visited. I've heard him talk within my head in a thousand different tongues. No matter where he is, or how he communicates on that world, he always calls those he's cursed with the sight as 'the Cassandras.' Right, Mr. Penjii?"

"Oh, yes indeed. This is a true thing, sir. I have heard it in my dreams as well. So had those who now dwell within you. Ask them."

London nodded slightly, mulling the information over within his head. For close to a minute he sat quietly, head bobbing slightly, up and down, until suddenly he sat back in his chair, the faintest beginnings of a grin spreading across his face.

"Boss," said Morcey, the knot in his stomach relaxing as he drank in London's expression, "you gettin' an idea?"

"I think so," answered the detective. Reaching into his side drawer, he pulled out his shoulder holster. In it rested his .38, Betty. Grabbing up its companion, the blade he thought of as Veronica, he said;

"Yeah. I think our god may have made a mistake." Slapping his knee, the balding man chuckled;

"Oh, don't they always. Shall we proceed to kick this one's haloed ass?"

"Get a call off to Pa'sha and the professor," answered London. "And Lai Wan, too. Let's get the team together and see what we can do to whip up a 'welcome to Earth' party for this son of a bitch."

# INTERLUDE

*H, HOME, SWEET HOME ...*
The tall, slender man with the knowing eyes and the sinister grin strolled down the quiet, New England avenue, taking in the streets and buildings and peoples of his native home. So many years had gone by since he had left it, so many hundreds of billions of years, and yet, the town which had seemed elderly when he had been a boy appeared hardly changed.

Everywhere he looked he saw sights he remembered. Nearly a hundred years later, and yet so much remained exactly as he had left it. His pale blue eyes marveled to see so many of the diamond panes in so many of the windows all across the town still intact. Here and there he spotted replacements, of course, bright and shining pieces of modern, thinner glass taking the place of some long-ago shattered cousin, but for the most part, unlike what he could sense from so much of the rest of the country, his hometown was much the provincial center it had always been.

"Simply amazing ..."

Wherever he wandered throughout the ceaseless maze of colonial houses with their ancient vanes and antediluvian gables, he studied each pocket of musty, moss and ivy-covered houses, looking to see which ones he could actually remember. He marveled at the contentment he felt in the people he passed by, at their relaxed harmony with the universe, felt simply because of their, for lack of a better phrase, "home town spirit." Pride swelling breasts over nothing more that the fact that all about them here one structure in five still stood with one foot as firmly in the sixteenth century as in the twenty-first. And well, of course, if you included the seventeenth century, then half the town still belonged to the past, different neighborhoods clinging to their own different versions of the long-gone-by—as always.

"Arkham ..." the slender man said, "really, it is a perfectly lovely little town."

"Isn't it, though?"

The question came at the man's arm, and a more delightful surprise he had not had in a very long time. No. Not since they would have measured the passage of it as "a coon's age."

She was a small thing, old but kind and sociable. Especially to nice young gentlemen. And, if the slender man with the quick gait had ever been anything, he had always been a nice, young, gentleman. Perhaps a tad stiff, awkward with the ladies, but always willing to please within the boundaries of the socially acceptable.

"Yes; it actually is."

He bowed slightly, tipping a non-existent hat politely. The woman smiled at his simple curtesy, so rare in someone so young. Willing to be charmed for a moment, she asked;

"What do you like best about it?"

"I like the coziness. The privacy."

"You think you've got privacy here in Arkham?" The old woman tittered, laughing gently until she coughed, stopped herself, and began laughing once more. Apologizing, she explained;

"It's just that the thought of this town as being 'private,' Heavens, it just made me think about how who knows what about everything in everybody else's business ... oh, it just made me think of some old times—fun times."

"Really?" The Life-A-Day Man smiled widely. "Tell me about one of them."

"You wouldn't want to hear me ..."

And with a wave of a finger and a smile as generous as the

bounty of Zeus, he told her;

"We are, human beings, all of us, wonderfully multi-talented creatures. We can be scum and vermin and degenerates; we can. It's true."

The old woman shook her head sadly as she thought to what low levels mankind could sink, knowing the splendid young man next to her was correct, wanting to believe he was right once more as well when he added;

"But we can be a great many more things, as well. Each and every one of us has moments we remember fondly that make us happy, just because we were there. And these moments of pure happiness rival any joy possible, even those felt by the gods themselves."

He was the most impulsively wonderful young man she had ever met. The various pains of age which she carried with her throughout each of her days left her for the moment, his very presence making life suddenly bearable, making her feel so warmly special. Even more so when he added, "That's what I want to hear about. You tell me one of yours, and I'll tell you one of mine."

The elderly woman stared into the young man's pale blue eyes, and she saw an intelligence so deep it had no bottom. She felt a true and honest fascination in whatever she was going to say, the way one felt when a friend asked for advice, and the air fairly rang with their interest in their words.

In some ways she was taken slightly aback at the stranger's intensity, surprised that he could feel such interest—in her. In what she might have to say. Maybe the young man had some sort of decision to make, and he was gathering opinions without telling people he was, so he would get their honest first reaction. Maybe he was just friendly.

"Choose one you remember especially," he told her. "One that means a great deal to you."

And so she told him a story of a summer when she was a counselor at an all girl's camp. Just a ramble of remembrances of several months teaching art classes, tucking the children in at night, helping to ride herd on the boys—keeping them from wandering down the road to the "sister" campground after hours—frolics and silliness and one fondly, long-remembered romance. When she finished, she blushed at the amount of time that had passed.

"I had a rewarding college year summer once myself," the slender man mused.

"Did you?"

"Indeed, madame," he responded. "It was the summer when I as well did some teaching, and ..." he snickered, his hand rushing across his clean-shaven chin as he burst out laughing.

"And yes, there was some tucking in of the 'children' at night," his laughter came under control, but his smile was giddy. "And there was a 'campground' down the road a bit, and yes, there were frolics, and ..." And suddenly, the slender man's eyes went quite mischievous as he admitted;

"Yes, I must confess to having indulged in a few bits of silliness, as well."

The old woman blossomed to meet such a wonderful person—one so young who could understand the joy of simple things—who could relate to her despite the apparent vast difference in their ages. To meet someone his age who would even take the time to talk to someone of her years, it made her feel so ... special. It made her feel as if so many pointless days of wasted existence had suddenly had a purpose if only to get her to this one special moment in time. Not wanting it to end, she asked;

"What was your summer like?"

"It was the moment I had waited for all my life." His eyes gleaming, honest pride swelled his entire being as he told his companion, "It was the moment when I discovered that I could reanimate dead tissue, and it lead to, my getting into ... goodness, just all sorts of shenanigans."

"Excuse me ...?"

The wonder of those exciting times rushed back to him, the danger of it, the thrills, that a mere fly speck of life could show such nerve; after all, he had been just a man—*only a man*—and yet the things he had found the will to accomplish, stealing bodies, animal, human, oh the joy—

"A dear friend, it's been so long, you know, I can't remember his name, but he and I worked until we had it perfect, carved in stone. We could, if we reached a corpse quickly enough, reanimate it—return it to a mobile state, if it were ..."

As the old woman blanched, hands trembling, her hearing confirmed, the young man adjusted his spectacles and rambled on himself for a moment, telling of the exuberance of those passionate months, experimenting on various segments of human torsos, linking parts from various bodies together, then the menagerie, Greek myths brought to life, animals join to men, parts of human bodies joined to animals, and things ...

"Then, then I would take three of four hands, and I'd make a fish ..." the memory left the slender man in a giggling panic. In a true moment of honest happy reenactment, he mimed the actions he spoke of as he described how he might take a number of human hands and carve them and rearrange the muscles and connections of them until his resultant living beast made of hands and buttocks flesh would slap around across the floor like a fish flopping about in the bottom of a boat.

"It was the funniest sight," he told her, giggling hysterically, a tear actually rolling down his cheek. "Oh, yes, those were the days."

The old woman could feel her heart racing, her nerves flashing warnings such as she had not felt in untold decades. The young man, he was crazy. He had to be. The things he said, they did not make sense. He spoke of happenings at nearby Miskatonic University which simply horrified her.

As he smiled at her, all the old woman could think to do was to flee. She had to get away from the stranger. Abruptly, not caring for once if she was being rude, forgetting manners and common Christian decency, she turned away and began to move herself at her best pace in the opposite direction. She threw a hasty goodbye over her shoulder, not slowing as she did so. Watching her feeble departure, the Life-A-Day Man called out;

"Before, when I said Arkham was a great place for privacy, I meant what I said. Yes, I agree, everyone knows everyone else's business here, but the wonderful thing is that despite what people in this town know, they might gossip about the usual things, but that unique to Arkham, that they keep to themselves. All the dark and slithering happenings this twisted plague of a town has known it has kept marvelously quiet about. But I'm thinking it never forgets."

Something in the man's voice caught the woman's attention. Feeling her mind being tugged along, her consciousness being directed toward some long ago sealed-up wall, she heard the slender man's voice tell her, "You remember ... back when you were a little girl, maybe about six, that was my wonderful summer. Com'on now, Louise, think back—surely, you remember ..."

The woman slowed her pace, not noticing that the stranger had called her by name although she had not offered it to him, and then suddenly, her mind caught. Something in her memory nagged at her, a secret always wondered about—never clear, but always remembered. A terrible, mind-numbing memory strapped away in the furthest reaches of her subconscious which the Life-A-Day man pulled out and shook like an old rug to refresh it within her mind.

"My God!"

It was him. That man ... when she was a little girl—

"Oh, my God; my God!"

The funeral parlor, they had gone to see an uncle, a brother of her father's, but she had not cared about the chatter of the adults come to view the dead and she had snuck away, and she had opened a door and seen a thing—

"Oh, I'm noticing a hint of happy remembrance in the corners of those old eyes ..."

There had been no lights in the room, just that which crept around her and thinly wandered into the room of caskets and other containers, a place a tiny young girl should not have been—

"You remember ..."

She saw him, ninety years in her past, the same small, slender man, the same pale blue eyes, the head of yellow hair, the soft voice, that arrogant, smug, holier-than-thou tone, standing behind the thing she saw in the darkness, a dwarf, a creature, too many arms, mouth in the strangest place—

"You ..." the old woman sputtered, nearly swooning ... "I do remember you ... you're, you're that, that *monster!*"

"Monster?" The Life-A-Day Man rolled the word over, as if he had never before heard it, his face draped in false puzzlement. Then, snapping the fingers of one hand, he said;

"No matter, for having such an excellent memory, let's find you ... a gift."

Because Louise had once had a sweet love she had never consummated, that same summer the blonde man had learned his first trick on the road to immortality, he decided to reanimate her fantasy lover, some eighteen years in his grave. With but a thought he summoned the moldering remains to his presence, then reintroduced the old friends, stepping back to watch them rekindle their long-interrupted romance there on the Thursday morning sidewalk.

The drooling thing, mind gone, arms flailing, stinking of the grave and decay, stood motionless, waiting for someone to give it some kind of idea of what was expected of it. And then something started its motors turning once more, and the shambling horror moved on the woman it had cared about in an ancient time. She tried to fend it off, but her arms were too weak to resist.

Its touch all bones and leather, its architect gave it voice enough to intone;

"Louise ... Louise ... Louise ..."

The abomination grabbed at the woman, stroking her hair, running its cracked and decaying hands over her arms, shredding her skin with the sharp snags of its own. Blood dribbled down her arms, soaking into her clothes, slipping on the sidewalk.

"Louise ... Louise ..."

The woman screamed finally, and yet those few passers-by on the streets of Arkham that morning heard nothing from her lips, saw nothing of her plight. Eventually she died on the quiet corner, her body sinking to the wide slab of flagstone, her life horribly strangled away from her by the hideous caricature of the man she had loved secretly until the day he had died and beyond.

The Life-A-Day Man watched the entire spectacle with something akin to amusement. He remembered the day in the funeral home, remembered his servant, Topsy. He had stitched the marvelous little horror together on a whim, and he had been obedient as a pup, as loyal a dog as any man had ever known. And young Louise had come stumbling in on them, pointing and screaming about monsters, and he had been forced to flee once more, and poor, poor Topsy, the beloved hound simply had not been able to keep up.

Staring at the piles of flesh on the ground before him, the freshly dead one, bleeding, glazed eyes staring blankly to the sky, and the other one, dead so much longer, vainly thrusting its long decayed stump into the lifeless sack beneath it, the Life-A-Day Man sneered;

"You see, Louise. That's what happens to rude little girls who point."

And then, the slender young man turned and began to walk off in the direction of Meadow Hill, to discover whether or not the old Chapman farmhouse could still be standing, and to see what other old friends he might be able to dig up.

# CHAPTER
# TWENTY-ONE

"TEDDY," LISA ASKED, RUBBING her eyes as she turned from her monitor, "once again, what exactly should I be looking for?"

"Everything," he answered. "Anything."

Immediately realizing what an insane statement he had just made, the detective stopped what he was doing and said; "I know what I'm asking is impossible. But we've got to search for some kind of clue as to who this guy is, was, whatever."

As the others that had been gathered turned toward London, he continued, telling all of them, "The one thing, hell, the only thing we have to go on is that this guy almost certainly must have been a human being at one time—one born right here on Earth, the old fashioned way."

"What makes you think this, little brother?" The speaker was a large black man, heavy-set but well-muscled. His name was Pa'sha Lowe. He was a black market weaponeer, and a friend of the detective's from further back in time than any other man. His hair as expansive as his voice, he added, "From what you told me on the phone of this creature, well, I ..."

"He, it, whatever—he uses a reference from human history, from our past, no matter where he goes in the universe. He calls prophets whom people refuse to believe 'Cassandras,' after the woman who told the citizens of Troy to beware Greeks bearing gifts."

"I see," said Goward. "Clever, Theodore. But how does the fact that he was once one of us help us discover precisely which one of us he might have happened to be?"

"I won't have any idea until we have the answer, professor."

"It is sounding as if t'ings are of the most desperate variety—yes, no, my brother?"

"Well, I could just ask 'when aren't they,'" answered the detective, "but look, I figure it this way. This Life-A-Day Man bozo, it stands to reason that he must have had to start somewhere along the line like I did."

"You mean that there had to have been some moment when he was still a normal human being?"

"Yes, sweetheart," agreed London. "Now, maybe that moment was a thousand years ago when he disappeared from the world and completely useless information to us—who knows? But, Lisa, if you could just keep going through the Internet, searching around, and Paul, if you could help the Doc with those books he brought, if everyone could just keep searching for some clue—some kind of strange event, bizarre disappearance, whatever—something that might lead us to this guy's roots ..."

The detective paused for a moment, using one hand to squeeze the crown of his nose while he closed his eyes. Rubbing at them, he added;

"Then maybe we can get some kind of a handle on him."

"Any advantage being better than no advantage," offered Pa'sha. "A true thing?"

"All too true," agreed London. "Which brings us to the inevitable discussion of what we can use to take this guy down."

"As you know, I have limited supplies of firepower for throwing against gods," answered the weaponeer. "Truly, you saw the best we had to offer when we attempted to stop those hounds."

London's mind instantly sprang to the moment to which Pa'sha was referring. They had been presented with the problem of one of their own being tracked by a thing from beyond. With all the time in the world, they had prepared a trap for the stalker, one utilizing all the high tech weaponry and sophisticated firepower they could find. Everything they had put together had been used up and it had barely been enough to stop the first wave of the ocean that came at them.

"Could we even try that again?" asked London, to which Pa'sha shook his head sadly;

"I t'ink such would be impossible, my brother. You knew exactly where the Tindalosi would arrive, and thus we were able to construct our trap around that spot. A spot, you will remember, which we tore apart to its basic building blocks." The weaponeer shrugged sadly, adding;

"I'm afraid the games you play these days are too rough for my simple toys ..."

Pa'sha spread his hands in a gesture of futility. London did the same in response, his shrug making his old friend laugh softly in frustration. When he finished chuckling, the weaponeer asked;

"This is not a good thing, this inability of ours to prepare for what is coming—no?"

"No," admitted London. "Not really. Still, if you have any new tricks up your sleeves—either one of them—I'm willing to listen."

Again the large man shrugged. As the detective looked over toward his partner, the balding man made the same gesture of helplessness, an act which started Pa'sha laughing once more.

"Oh, what a fine bunch we are this day."

"Yeah," agreed London in frustration. "Look, I know this is a thankless task, but let's keep at it. Elsewise the only other option we have is waiting for this thing to come to us."

Throughout the suite, everyone kept searching. In Morcey's office, Maura McNeil scanned the news channels. She flipped from one station to the other, watching for anything—the slightest strange broadcast that might give them a clue as to where the Life-A-Day man had arrived on the planet.

At her desk, Lisa kept jumping from website to website, trying to find some mention somewhere in the world's popular folklore which might give them a clue as to their enemy's background. Also there in the outer office was Goward, combing through the various reference texts he had brought from the university in the hopes he might find something in print that had not found its way to the web as of yet.

Sitting there in the other office with Lisa and the professor was Penjii, using his cell phone to call in every member of his loose organization of prophets. Each one he managed to contact was told to call another, and all were urged to head for New York City as quickly as possible. They were also told to consider the notion that the Life-A-Day Man had been a mortal man at one time, and to try and think of whom that mortal could have been.

Morcey was in his own office, using the telephone, calling various London Agency friends, informants and confidants around the world. With each he spent as little time as possible, explaining the situation and asking each outpost contacted to keep theirs eyes and ears open for at least the next twenty-four hours, staying alert for anything that might signify the coming of this incredible new menace.

As for London, he and Pa'sha sat in the detective's office trying to come up with some type of man-made destructive power they might turn against the Life-A-Day Man once his whereabouts had been discovered. While they continued to get nowhere with their task, their attention was diverted to the doorway to the outer hall as the doorknob gently rattled for a moment. All eyes turned in that direction, everyone relieved at the sight of the Asian woman in the doorway.

"Lai Wan," called Lisa cheerfully, glad if for no other reason that to have another female present to thin the mix, "come in. Join the latest little London Agency party."

The woman nodded slight to acknowledge Lisa's words, then carefully moved into the room, her measured gait careful to not allow even the slightest hem of her floor length skirt or the draping shawl she wore over her head and shoulders to come in touch with anything. Rising, Lisa met the woman halfway, careful not to greet her in any overly physical manner, and quickly introduced her to McNeil and Penjii. After telling Lai Wan about the "Cassandras," she apologized for the term, then introduced her friend by saying;

"And this is Lai Wan. She is a psychometrist."

"Ahhh," said Penjii, recognizing the term, "do you read objects or people—the past or the future?"

"When I received my powers," she answered the older man, "I was given all these abilities. I can tell a person their past and sometimes their future. With objects, I can tell where they have been, and when." The Hindu made a loud whistling noise, then slapped his leg.

"No one in our sect has ever been able to do all these things. This is a great deal of power."

"'Great' has never been my word for it," answered the woman quietly. Turning to Lisa, the psychometrist asked if she knew what London required of her. Before Lisa could answer, the doorknob rattled once more.

"This place is Grand Central Station today," said Lisa, crossing to the door. She turned the knob just as whomever was on the other side had gotten it completely turned, thus they both ended up opening the door at the same moment. The effect was that of comedy—Lisa stumbling backwards slightly and the person coming in falling along in her wake. They both caught themselves before there were any mishaps, however, leaving everyone who saw the moment smiling.

The man who had entered the office adjusted his spectacles, then asked Lisa;

"Pardon me, but could I see a ... Mr. Theodore London?"

"He's in his office right now," she answered. "He is in there with someone at the moment. But, if I could ask your name, sir, and what this is in reference to ...?"

"Oh, of course," the slender man responded. Brushing aside a lock of his yellow hair, he grinned slightly as he added, "Tell him Dr. Herbert West is here to see him."

Then, the Life-A-Day Man's grin widened into a full blown smile as he added, "You can let him know it's in reference to the end of the world."

# CHAPTER
# TWENTY-TWO

MAURA MCNEIL SCREAMED, HER hands flying to her face, fleshy fists trying to hold back the escaping terror. Penjii merely stood, his phone slipping from his hand, his other pointing forward—hand trembling, entire arm shaking. Lisa backed far into the side office; Lai Wan followed her. Dr. Goward looked up, removed his glasses and wiped them clean, then looked again. During the same time, both Morcey and Pa'sha pulled weapons and aimed them at the newcomer.

"My, my, what a dramatic greeting," said West with a chuckle. "I mean, really—is this any way to treat a doctor who still makes house calls?"

"Nobody sick here," responded Morcey. Closing one eye, he held his Auto-Mag leveled directly at the bridge of the Life-A-Day Man's nose, adding, "I guarantee it."

"Ummmmmmmm, I'm not so certain," responded West with mock seriousness. "I mean, you all certainly seem quite the excitable bunch."

"Poor upbringing," came London's voice from behind Pa'sha's large frame. Squeezing around his friend, the detective stepped into the waiting area of his office. "You know how it is, some people find themselves around a celebrity and they can't help but go all to pieces."

"A celebrity?" West rolled the phrase across his tongue, repeating it several times with mock humility. Finally he put his hand to his chest, giving himself the gentlest of shoves as he asked, "Who? Me? Oh, no. I don't think so."

"Now, don't be so modest, doctor," London said expansively

as he moved forward, arms held open. "An inter-dimensionally well known fellow such as yourself. Ravager of worlds, murderer of untold trillions, self-made god ... that is, I suppose I'm only assuming that you're a self-made god. Any other hands at work in there, eh? Some secret elder architect your bio sheet isn't telling the rest of us about—*hummmmmmmm?*"

West gave the detective a queer look for a moment, then smiled expansively. Lowering his chin to his chest to acknowledge that he had caught on to London's burst of humor, he lifted his head once more, then fussed with his hands, almost as if he were entertaining the idea of applauding. As his fingers rattled against one another, he said;

"I see, I see, marvelous. Fishing for information, aren't you? Quite clever—I'll give you that. But then, I should have expected such. We are in your office, after all. What else would we do here but play your game—the de'tec'tive game—yes?"

"So, are you going to answer the question?"

"Oh my, but what a scamp you are," West said back to London. Moving forward toward the detective, acting as if the weapons pointed at him meant nothing to him at all, he added, "I must admit that I really should have expected nothing less. After all, what with all I know of your vast string of successes, why ... you'd have to be good at your work—"

"Jeez, my'knees, boss," blurted Morcey. "Should we send some lead his way or what?"

London took a millisecond to read the man-shaped being before him. He could tell instantly that the thing calling itself Dr. Herbert West was possessed of remarkable levels of power, that it held scores of strange and horrible capabilities the detective could barely comprehend. Darkening his eyes, he warned his partner away from such activity, saying aloud;

"Oh, I don't know, maybe later, Paul." Then, London turned to their visitor, apologizing as he offered, "Unless, of course, I'm being rude. I mean, if you'd like them to shower you with lead ..."

"Come now, Mr. London, let's not be boorish." West tone was sharp, brittle—almost hurt. "After all, I think it quite sporting of me to come here at all."

"Please, doctor," answered the detective, "you're as much of a sportsman as the Trojans were. You're here because you want something. Self-absorbed as it might sound, my guess is you want it from me. So, why don't the two of us get down to business. All right, Dr. West, or should I call you 'Herbert?'"

"Yesssss," The slender man drawled his word, giving himself a scrap of time to search the atmosphere for bits of information about London. He read the concern of the others, learning what they thought of the detective, how much of that emotional attachment was taken on faith, how much was deserved without question. Impressed with what he learned, he answered quietly, his words chosen with care.

"I believe I see a great danger in learning to like you, Mr. London. So, I'm thinking formality might be our best route. If you don't mind?"

"Oh no, not at all," answered the detective. London moved his left arm just to make certain he could still feel Betty hanging under it where she belonged. The Life-A-Day Man's sudden arrival there at his offices had rattled the detective slightly, and he needed to tally his options within his head. An innocent brushing of his leg against Lisa's desk let him know Veronica was in her sheath where she belonged as well. Comforted by the simple weapons, understanding how illogical such peace was, he asked;

"What did you have in mind?"

"I thought we should get to know each other somewhat before the inevitable. What do you think?"

"I think it's a swell idea. We could take a cruise. You can learn a lot about a man from his shuffleboard game. Oh, yes—I think we should do something together right now."

London, despite his jest, was not humoring West. If some sort of cosmic free-for-all was inevitable between the two of them, the detective certainly did not want it to start in the middle of nearly all the people he cared about in the world.

"You do?" West did not seem as surprised as his tone indicated. "Why is that?"

London took another millisecond to throw all his powers of observation into sizing up his opponent. The being before him was powerful beyond measure. He was highly intelligent, ruthless and more confident than any logical creature deserved to be. There would be no tricking him without a great deal of thought and preparation, neither of which the detective had had the time for as of yet. Not seeing any other option open to him at the moment, London told the truth.

"Well, it's like this, doc, if I get you out of here, that will give my staff time to try and learn things about you that I can use against you later. And hey, if you and I do spend some time together, who knows, I may find a weakness here or there myself, some chink in your armor you yourself haven't noticed."

"You think you can best me, Mr. London?" The words came softly, but in clipped precision, gently hissed from between West's thin lips. Smiling, acting as if he had not noticed the challenge implied in the doctor's words, London answered;

"Oh well, yeah—sure. I mean, there's no doubt of that. The problem is just how to do it. For instance, I'm thinking that if I was to take you to lunch, and we were to talk a while, that—hey, you never know—my boyish charm could so delight you that you'll just be on your way and we won't have to bother getting our suits all mussed up."

Dr. Herbert West stood and stared at his chosen adversary. All around the pair, people were shrinking back, giving the two of them room in case the situation suddenly exploded. Pa'sha and Morcey had both taken up defensive positions behind the nearest door jambs, their weapons moved out of sight, but still at the ready.

"I mean," offered London, "it is a lovely day here in the big city. Lots of fine eateries. Good time to be had by all."

The detective stood before the Life-A-Day Man, tall, but loose. He did not attempt to use his larger frame to intimidate; neither did he take a servile posture. His stance said that he was merely waiting to take a business associate to lunch—nothing more. The self-assured courage of it impressed West as had no other thing he had ever seen outside of his own accomplishments. Bowing slightly, West tipped a non-existent hat politely to the ladies, and said;

"I agree, sir. It is quite a lovely day at that, Mr. London. I think stopping somewhere for a fine nibble of this or that might be just the very thing needed. Shall we all go?"

"No, I think we should leave the others here."

"Oh, but no," responded West, the slightest of sinister curls turning one side of his mouth. "I can't have that. I think we should all go and have a wonderful meal. In fact, I insist upon it."

"Doctor," countered London, "we're not all gay travelers like yourself. It must be great to have been able to retire at an early age, but some of us have to work for a living. If I just let all these lackeys of mine run off to lunch, well, I mean ... who would look up all the facts about you I need so desperately, so I can destroy you later?"

London spread his hands before him in a gesture of guileless futility, adding, "You see my predicament, don't you?"

West smiled fully. The sight of it made most in the office tremble slightly.

"Yes, too true, too true, I forgot. You have your ulterior motives as I do mine. Very well, send your drones back to work. You and I shall repair to some fine establishment for our luncheon while they do the necessary research. Agreed?"

"Agreed."

Then, just as London took a forward step, West reached out sharply to his left, his hand going through the wall of Morcey's office, fingers wrapping around the wrist of Maura McNeil. With the slightest of efforts he pulled her through the wall undamaged, then slipped his arm through hers, saying;

"It dawned on me that we couldn't go out without at least a bit of feminine companionship. And, since this dear rose seemed the shyest bud on the vine, I thought it best we take her along with us. Don't you agree, Mr. London?"

The voices within the detective's mind all spilled over, shouting scores of contradictory bits of advice. Before he could speak, however, McNeil answered for him, saying;

"Ach, now—and isn't ... isn't that charming of the good doctor to worry so about me poor self? Why, I'd be ... happy to accompany you both to lunch."

"Would you now?" The words crawled out of West's sinisterly curled mouth and stung the woman one after another. As she tried to maintain her fragile smile, the doctor announced, "Why then, good—it's settled."

Turning his back on the assembly, West started for the hallway door, gently pulling McNeil along as he said;

"Shall we, Mr. London?"

The detective gave Lisa a long look, throwing his eyes into hers, reaching into her, holding her, squeezing her as tightly as possible from several feet away, letting her know that he would be all right.

Somehow.

Then, he turned and answered;

"Certainly, Dr. West."

# CHAPTER TWENTY-THREE

THEODORE LONDON STOOD NEXT to the most dangerous being in all creation and his captive as they all descended in his building's elevator to the lobby. McNeil had ended standing between the antagonists, unable to mask her discomfort at being arm in arm with the Life-A-Day Man. The detective could tell the woman was working hard to keep her true feelings hidden.

London was a touch uncomfortable himself, but his unease was being generated by the tune coming through the elevator's speakers. The Muzak selection was annoying some section of the back of the detective's mind, not only because of the triviality of its arrangement, but because it was certain it knew the real number. By the time the elevator had reached the fifth floor London suddenly realized he was listening to a frolickingly mediocre rendition of Black Sabbath's "Fairies Wear Boots."

"Oh yeah, there's a great way to spend your time with this maniac," a voice from within the detective's mind sneered bitterly. "Earth's got a great chance with you leading the troops."

London spat a chastisement toward the back of his brain with anger, then noted West staring at him and nodded to the doctor. As the steel doors slid open to reveal the lobby, the others in the car with them exited quickly, leaving the detective and his guests behind without a second thought. As the trio made its way forward more slowly, Dr. West observed;

"This twenty-first century of yours. I don't know ... people certainly are in a much greater hurry these days, aren't they?"

"Could be, I suppose," answered London. "Understand, I'm

not trying to be coy, but since I don't really know anything about you, I can only assume you're referring to some date in our past that would make your statement true."

"Oh, you know things about me, Mr. London. I smell a particularly keen brain within that well-shaped head of yours. Come now, admit it; what I just said, none of that actually took you by surprise—did it?"

When the detective admitted that West was correct, the doctor pressed him, asking how he knew. London related his deduction over the 'Cassandra' label, then added a bit more.

"There's your speech pattern, of course. You've standardized your grammar, but there are nuances that tell me 'New England,' and none of them are modern. No more so than your haircut or your clothing. Either could be traced back fifty years—easily. Probably more like seventy, eighty. Of course, the styles of both such things constantly come and go, but you don't strike me as a man whose daily life was consumed by fashion."

The three passed through the building's revolving door. Once out on the sidewalk, West gulped down a huge, deep breath, exhaling loudly as he answered;

"Yes, I have to admit to never having been much of a fashion plate. Not much use for such silliness. More Miss McNeil's kind of worry, I would imagine."

"And what makes you imagine that?"

McNeil's first words since the trio had left the office caught both the men somewhat by surprise. Impressed by her ability to throw even a small bit of emotion at him when he was so obviously trying to make her cower, West turned to her, gracing the priestess with his warmest smile.

"It was a generalization, to be sure, my dear lady, but one I believe to be grounded in something like fact. Even in this modern age of women with shaved heads, wearing men's clothing, smoking cigars, driving automobiles, and so on, still, the female of the species is the more vain, the more flighty, more interested in the shape of their shoes than the shape of their future."

McNeil fumed, wanting to snap back at West as she would any other man. She held herself back, however, for the simple fact that the tall, slender man with the pale blue eyes and the unconsciously sinister grin was not any other man—or even any kind of man at all. London, however, did not share her reserve.

"Oh, come on, doctor," he said, off-handedly. "I know you've been away for a while, but you must know a little bit more about things male and female than that."

"What do you mean, Mr. London?"

"Go for it," the detective told himself, "engage him, keep him talking, distracted. Off-balance. Keep his mind occupied."

"Well, you know, human history has had its periods where both sexes have played the peacock. And, the recent world wars, when women around the world were pulled out of the homes, put into the factories ... anyway, we've learned a lot about how women's roles might be more a thing of tradition than mental conditioning. I mean, com'on, you're a doctor. Don't you think, really, that it's just more about hormones and who has how much testosterone, and how much estrogen?"

The Life-A-Day Man stopped walking abruptly, his halt coming so unexpectedly that McNeil was jerked so roughly she nearly toppled to the ground. London noted the power of the moment, tucking away the fact that West had become an immovable object simply by stopping his forward motion.

No concentration, the detective realized. No summoning of power, no thinking. He wasn't trying to prove anything. He merely stopped moving and everything near him had to stop as well.

And, in that moment, London froze. He had assumed his opponent was formidable, could tell the man had power to spare simply by reading the heat signature surrounding him. But, until that instant he had been given no real gauge by which to measure West's abilities. Now suddenly the doctor's casual action had told the detective more than his faculties could easily process. Not noticing London's internal struggle, however, West stroked his chin several times, then said;

"Do you really think so, Mr. London? Women, actually equal to men? Tell me, have you met any female gods yet?"

"Hey," answered the detective, spitting his words out in an effort to make his mouth work, "I'm not one of these guys who thinks every woman can do anything any man can do. Nothing is ever so black and white. I just think that in a world with lady wrestlers and male strippers that, well, the lines just aren't as clear as they used to be."

"So, you haven't met any female gods yet," West sneered in a tone almost sinister, "have you?"

"I've met a few women who thought they deserved the title," London responded, "but let's just say they might have been a little generous when they filled out their scorecards."

West began moving again and the other two fell back into step along with him. The time already past noon, well into lunch hour, and the streets of Manhattan were over-flowing with people bustling in all directions. London prayed that no one bumped into West, that no one stared at him, or made a comment about his manner of dress, or in any way, shape or form drew the Life-A-Day Man's attention away from himself and McNeil.

So far the doctor had played his role as meekly as possible for a creature used to commanding the fear of entire galaxies. Sooner or later the facade was going to be cast away, however, and the detective wanted to make certain that moment came as far in the future as possible.

"I must say, you're a very cagey individual, Mr. London."

"Is that a good thing or a bad thing?"

"I think as far as you're concerned it's a good thing."

"And," asked McNeil, the sound of her unasked for voice once again surprising both men, "why do you think would that be, Dr. West?"

"Good girl," thought London, loving the priestess at that moment. "Get him talking, keep him full of himself, that's the only way we have to make this nonsense work to our advantage."

"Oh, our Mr. London here plays games very well. Look at

him, attempting to act calm and dignified. 'Normal,' I suppose would be the word these days. Inside, you know he's a turmoil, wondering just what I'm going to do, when I'll do it, how I'll do it—that's all churning his guts, and yet—look at him. Not sweating, no jerking motions, cool and collected."

"But why is that good for us?"

"Don't you see it, my dear? Unlike yourself, he's ever so good at making his opinions clear without hurting anyone else's feelings. You'd make an excellent dictator, you know, Mr. London. Or referee."

"Hummmm," mused the detective. "Both career choices I'd never given much thought."

"Too bad," responded West. "And, too late now to do so."

"Why, doctor," London replied, "haven't you heard—it's never too late."

"I suppose that is what this day will tell us, eh, Miss McNeil?"

The woman nodded weakly in answer to West's question. Needing to take command of the situation, even if just for a moment, both to give McNeil a moment's rest, and to prove to the doctor that he was not completely in charge, London raised a finger to signal a second halt in their walk. As the others turned to him, he said;

"Since we're supposed to be going to lunch, perhaps we should decide on where we're going. I mean, what is it that everyone wants? Italian, Chinese, French ..."

"I don't care where we go," answered McNeil, "as long as they have a bar."

As West considered the question, London, himself usually not much of a drinker, thought;

"Yeah, you and me both, sweetheart."

# CHAPTER
# TWENTY-FOUR

AFTER ONLY A SHORT walk and a bit of discussion, the trio ended up in an All-You-Can-Eat Chinese buffet, one of several chains that had become quite popular throughout the New York City area at that time. Of course, such a place did not really feature authentic Chinese food. Even though when most Americans were introduced to the real thing they usually enjoyed it, still the conventional wisdom in the restaurant business was that what Americans really wanted was something that looked exotic but with no more taste or flavor than a hamburger or pizza.

London was certain that West no longer needed to eat to sustain life. In truth, the detective wondered if the doctor would actually even be able to taste what he did eat, or if his body could still digest solids properly.

"Did he recreate himself especially for this visit home," London wondered, "or has he travelled the cosmos in his original body since he first left? Will he have to restart the old systems, or is he the kind that never turned them off? Maybe he can still taste and smell. After all, if he has been eating the local cuisine on all these worlds he's destroyed, gone native long enough for a snack before he wipes everyone out—"

*"You really got time for crap like this?"*

*"Yeah, wondering about his diet ain't going to give you any clues on how to kick this creep's ass."*

"Good point," London admitted to the rest of his mind.

The detective pulled his thoughts clear, refocusing his attention on what he was doing. While West and McNeil left the table to make their first pass at the buffet, London stayed behind—holding their spaces, watching McNeil's bag. He had suggested the action to the others, not because he wanted to abandon the priestess, but because he needed a moment to catch his breath, to think about all that had happened, was happening, and was going to happen—most likely far sooner than anyone would want. The detective also did not want West to be left alone for too long—at all, really. The doctor was too much of an unknown quantity.

*"That's putting it mildly."*

London sighed. Try as he may, the detective simply could not find a course of action. The Life-A-Day Man was too good at playing his role—had had far too long to perfect his act. The realistic segment of London's nature was already certain that no matter how long he searched, he would find no cracks in the doctor's armor, no flaws which he might exploit. The cynical side of his mind laughed at him. Making reference to a television character he had enjoyed in his youth, it reminded him;

"Captain Kirk would figure a way out of this. He could beat West at his own game ... with ease—and he doesn't have super-powers, like some people around here."

"Yeah," thought London wryly, "and he would have done it all in an hour, less commercials and credit sequences."

As the detective's stomach grumbled, reminding him that he had not eaten yet that day, he found himself scanning the restaurant for a sign of either of his companions. Spotting McNeil on her way back, he rose, then waited for her to reach the table before going off to fill his own first plate. As she neared the table, the woman whispered;

"What are you going to do?"

"Get my lunch—why?"

"I mean about that goddamned lunatic," snapped the priestess. "He's just bloody toying with us, you know. He's having a grand day out. This is all just so much larking about to him, but we're running ourselves into a tizzy, tripping over each other to wipe his damn nose, and getting precious little more done from all I can see."

"You're damn right that's all we're doing," snapped the detective. His eyes darting, making certain West was not yet on his own way back, London told the woman, "what the Hell else did you expect? Did you think I was just going to snap my fingers and he'd go away, or that I had cans of God Repellant or something in a back closet for these kinds of things?"

The detective rubbed at his eyes with one hand, muttering under his breath, "Hell, I don't even know how *you* people found me, for Christ's sake."

Dropping his hand, London squinted, catching sight of West loading a bowl at the salad bar. Unusually moved by the sight of the monster of monsters quietly deciding between blue cheese or oil & vinegar, he told McNeil;

"Look, you have to understand that, yes—I've done this before. But what that really means is that I've been lucky a few times with problems beyond the understanding of most individuals—including myself. But this, this ... I don't know ..." Then, seeing the mad fever of panic rising in the woman's eyes, he added softly;

"Yet. It is true that I often do my best work over lunch, so ... let's keep wiping his nose for the moment and just see what happens." McNeil nodded, then added hurriedly;

"I understand. Please, go fill your plate and hurry back ... if you could. I, I don't think I can bear to be alone with him too long."

London nodded and left for the buffet. He met West at the counter, puzzling over the various metal tubs of unfamiliar food.

"Don't know what you want?"

"Don't know if I can bear to eat this way," West responded absently. "It's all pretty much like a pig farm, isn't it? Trough after trough laden with slop for all the fat, pink flesh. I noticed when one gets nearly empty someone comes out with another tub of vittles and slides it into place so the hordes can continue to consume uninterrupted."

"It's just called good service," answered London absently, pretending to be interested in picking out his lunch.

The Life-A-Day man simply glanced sideways at the detective for a moment, then began asking questions about a number of unfamiliar dishes he was inspecting under the sneeze guard. After a few moments the blonde man had filled his plate and turned to make his way back to their table. London gave him only a few seconds head start so as not to appear obvious, then headed back himself so McNeil would not find herself alone with West too long.

*"Too long,"* questioned one of his more immediate ancestors, *"At all is more like it. This chick ain't gonna last."*

London agreed with himself, sadly, then caught up to the doctor as if they were old friends. The men settled in and soon all three were quietly enjoying their meal. West commented on each new delicacy with a growing rapture and fondness that almost began to put his companions at ease. During his previous time on Earth, he told them, he had never had a chance to try Oriental food. There had been opportunities, of course, but the idea had never appealed to him.

"Over the years since I left, though, I must admit some of my horizons have broadened somewhat."

"That's interesting," answered London. Holding a curried shrimp in his chop sticks, he delayed biting into it long enough to ask, "So tell me, do you eat often? Regularly, I mean? In other words, do you have to, or do you want to? Or, come to think of it, do you actually like to? Eat, I mean." As the doctor simply stared, the detective explained;

"There's an old quote, can't remember who said it now, but it goes, 'I don't eat to live, I live to eat.' My partner's a live-to-eat-guy; I guess I'm pretty much the opposite. Anyway, I was just wondering how it works for you, if you can still taste things? That kind of stuff."

"It's interesting, actually, Mr. London," West answered, cleaning the corners of his mouth with a paper napkin. "I can go, most likely, I believe, forever if necessary—without eating. And usually, I must admit, I don't bother."

"Oh, why not?" asked McNeil, sounding genuinely interested. "Don't you enjoy it?"

"No, I never did."

The words came from West's mouth slowly, as if he were just realizing the truth of them for himself for the first time. Looking at the various rices and meats and filled-pastries on his plate, the Life-A-Day Man stared at it all, working to see if he had overstated his position. Stabbing a miniature egg roll with his fork, he held it aloft and stared at it.

"Food," West said, his eyes examining the egg roll with an increasing intensity. "It's only fuel—just hay to keep the cows mooing. I never much enjoyed shoving it down my throat. Now that I actually think about it, I believe I resented the necessity of it all."

"Resented it?" McNeil was taken aback. "Eating? I've never thought there were very many things that are better."

"Be that as it may, though," responded the doctor, his voice lowering into a slight growl. "It wasn't the enjoyment of eating, but the *necessity* of it that I resented. The God-imposed dictate that we have our three squares a day, that mankind must partake from all the food groups—or die. Now, I ask you, does that seem fair?"

"Well," answered London, "I suppose we should have to put some effort forward."

"My, my, now there's your good, old-fashioned Christian work ethic solidly in place," sneered West. Setting his fork with its still-speared egg roll onto his plate, he asked;

"So, tell me—slight change of subject—do you think there's a god out there, Mr. London? One who sent his only begotten son to die for our sins? Were you thinking that there's actually something to that asinine story?"

The doctor's hand hovered over the table for a moment, then before the detective could answer, it suddenly slammed down hard enough to make the food jump from West's plate. McNeil winced. London stayed remarkably calm.

"I have to admit this notion makes me lose a touch of respect for you, sir."

"Jumping the gun a little, aren't we ... doctor? After all, I haven't gone on the record about God yet one way or the other."

West sat back against his chair, lips tight, head tilted. He stared unblinking for a moment, then smiled slightly, pulling his control back to the surface. Lifting his fork to his mouth, he swallowed his egg roll whole, then speared a meatball that had rolled away from his plate, saying;

"Very good, Mr. London. I have to admit my ability with people seems to be somewhat lacking."

"Well, maybe it's more difficult to be a god one day and a regular guy the next than you thought. That respect-for-others thing, it's hard to keep in place when you think the universe revolves around you alone. Puts you on a par with rock stars, or some of the old popes."

"Touche," answered the Life-A-Day Man. Picking up his tumbler, he took a long pull on his iced tea, then set it back down with a great deal of fussing. Noting the uneaten meatball still at the end of his fork, he returned it to his plate, then looked up toward the ceiling as he spoke.

"I suppose it's a personal thing. I can accept evolution pushing our hairy-backed selves sweating and puking up out of the primordial ooze. That I have no problem with, but the idea of God? A God who creates us in his own image, but forces us to feed every day—or else. A God immortal, all-knowing, all-seeing, all-powerful, who shapes us in his own likeness, but then only gives us a finite handful of years, who births us into the world empty and weak—what good is there to find in such cruelty?"

London sat quietly. He had no answer for his adversary. McNeil lowered her eyes, having an answer but not daring to voice it. Hearing her fear, West dropped his head slowly, then fixed his vision on the priestess. Tilting his head back upward slightly, he told her;

"You believe in God, don't you?"

"I, I ..."

"It's true. You buy into the whole Creator nonsense, the omnipotent bully, watching us batter each other into submission, keeping a tally sheet in the clouds. Tell me, does the thief who steals a loaf of bread go to Hell?"

McNeil sat petrified. She could not speak, could not turn her head, could barely breathe.

"What if he steals it to feed his family? Or because he's hungry? Does he? Does he merit everlasting damnation? Or what if he's merely lazy?"

West was out of his seat at this point. Moving to the next chair over, he stared cruelly at McNeil, shouting at her;

"What if he steals a loaf of bread every day because he's just too lazy to work? Does he go to Hell then?"

Tears rolled down McNeil's face. London watched the doctor as he inched his chair closer to the woman. The detective was concerned for the priestess, but more he began to worry that West was about to make his move. The question of God had agitated him to the point where London could no longer even begin to predict what he might do next.

"Tell me, strumpet—give me an answer. You actually *believe* in this God of yours; tell me what he would do. Is his mercy boundless or not? Does he turn the other cheek or just expect you to? Is the sinner blessed? Tell me. *Tell me!"*

"Oh, Mr. London," McNeil cried out, turning to the detective, grabbing his arm gently, "I'm so sorry."

The detective stared without understanding for a moment, then looked into West's eyes, and understood all too well.

# CHAPTER
# TWENTY-FIVE

ALL AROUND THE RESTAURANT, people began to turn and stare. A number of those closest to London and the others had been listening uncomfortably ever since the argument over an Almighty Creator had started. Now, some had actually begun nervously shuffling their feet, considering moving to another table, or even leaving altogether.

"Maura," the detective implored, "hang on. Everything is going to be all right."

"And what makes you say that, Mr. London?" asked West. Changing to the kind of patronizing voice one might use to insult a child, he asked, "How could you know such a thing—with such certainty? Tell us, do you believe God is going to make everything better?"

"Look, you freak," snapped the detective, "back it off. That's enough."

The Life-A-Day Man smiled. All around him people began to stand. Some felt a disturbing call of self-preservation that sent them looking for their packages, bags, whatever—grabbing their checks, heading for the door. Others, most of those who had noticed anything at all, pressed closer to see what was about to happen. As they watched, Dr. Herbert West pushed his chair back a few inches with his feet.

"So, the veneer finally cracks."

"I'm sorry, Mr. London. I couldn't ... I can't ..."

The detective was standing, his arms protectively hugging McNeil's shoulders. Inside his head, ten score voices shouted suggestions, wailed in fear, or babbled uncontrollably. London silenced them all, not wanting to hear from any of them—not having the time for them. No one from his past or anyone else's was going to have any information or ideas that were going to help him. No one from his past—no one anywhere, at any time—had ever faced anything like he was facing at that frozen moment in time.

"So what do you think, Mr. London," the doctor asked. "Is God going to intervene here? Is he going to stop me? Will his infinite mercy force him to smite me before I do whatever it is that I shall do next?"

The detective stared hard. His hands remained gentle, protective, continuing to shield the woman in front of him. His eyes, however, generated sparks of furious anger. Without blinking, without moving, he kept West fixed with his gaze as he growled his answer.

"I don't believe it works that way."

"No," answered the Life-A-Day Man. His voice a contempt-laden sneer, he spewed, "It doesn't. I know. And do you know how I know? Because I sought the bastard out. I searched the galaxies, wandered the cosmos, imploring Him to show Himself ... but, guess what? *He's not there!*"

London was just about to respond when the restaurant's manager came over to the table. Several of his waiters and busboys were hovering in the background, not really offering actual menace. The detective could see at a glance that it was a standard tactic, one used on the loud or the inebriated to help calm them down quickly. Disturbances were bad for business, were bad for a social atmosphere's reputation. Thus they had to be dealt with quickly, yet delicately.

"Sir, could I ask you please—"

"Shut up!"

All eyes turned toward London. The manager, his people, those observers at the tables all around, everyone had expected West to respond. To them, the detective had seemed the calmer, the more rational of the two men. Confused, the manager shook his head slightly, then began to talk once more. London ran over his words, shouting at him;

"Everyone understands that you're just doing your job—that you have to do it. We get it." Pointing at the blonde man, the detective added, "But, trust me when I tell you that dealing with this person is not part of your job."

"But, sir—I ..."

"No!" London snapped the word meanly, giving it the sound of breaking glass. "For your own safety, and everyone else's, just stop talking and back off. I'll handle this."

In between the two, West cackled deliciously. Rubbing his hands together, he threw his head back and tittered, pounding his feet rapidly against the floor, closing his eyes in the face of such high amusement.

"You'll handle me," he said with an amazed giggle. "Well now, that is what the scavengers in the cheap seats have been waiting for."

The manager looked about the restaurant, not liking what he was seeing. Far too many customers were hurrying, gulping food, agitatedly looking around. The line at the cash register was long and growing. As he saw one particularly nervous looking older woman simply drop a great handful of bills in one of his waitress' hands and head for the door, he decided enough time had been wasted. Catching the eye of the check out girl working the register, he nodded to her, their prearranged signal for her to go ahead and dial 911. Turning back to the table before him then, he interrupted the proceedings forcefully, turning his voice up to its most masculine volume as he announced;

"Sir, I'm going to have to ask you and your party to leave. I caution you that I have already telephoned for the police. You've caused more than enough trouble for the rest of our patrons. It's time for you to go."

West stared at the manager, eyes wide, pressing his lips together tightly, desperate not to laugh. His unblinking eyes were filled with a righteous assurance that life was bringing him all he wanted from it. His head bounced on his shoulders as his entire frame began to vibrate from his excitement.

"You heard the man," he finally said, his voice low and even and aimed at London. "It's time for me to go."

As all eyes focused on the Life-A-Day Man, he suddenly simply winked out of existence. A small rush of steam displaced his exit, curling around his chair. Many who had come forward stepped closer to the table, the manager actually reaching out to touch the now empty chair gingerly, as if it might be scalding hot—or as if it were the chair itself which caused West to disappear.

Then, suddenly, West reappeared in his seat.

"But, wait ..."

The doctor managed to only say the two words before the restaurant filled with screams. Customers raced for the door, all thoughts of paying their bills or seeing what happened next flying from their heads. Some simply joined in the rush to avoid their checks, others were swept up in the panic, fearing that perhaps the building were on fire. Those who saw what had happened in the center of the restaurant, however, ran out of blind panic. They did not know what they had seen; they did not care. They simply knew they did not want to be—were afraid to be—anywhere near the slender blonde man with the sinister smile.

"It dawned on me that I didn't get to finish my meal," West said. "Not that I'm actually all that hungry. But," the doctor turned his eyes toward the manager—still standing there next to him, paralyzed by his inability to comprehend what he had just seen, "you never know when a snack will come in handy."

And, so saying, the Life-A-Day Man reached his hand out toward the manager and sucked the man's life essence from his body. It was an instantaneous act—one performed at the speed of thought. There was no preparation needed, no long moment of anticipation. One microsecond the manager was there—eyes wide, trembling mouth moving silently—the next he was gone, replaced by a wisp of steam and Herbert West's giggling laugh.

More screaming, and far more stampeding ensued. The waiters and busboys who had originally congregated to help intimidate the doctor ran off in terror with the rest—worse than the rest. Chairs were thrown through the restaurant's large plate windows when the main doorway proved inadequate to handle all the desperate traffic mindlessly rushing for the street. In a medium-sized handful of seconds, London and McNeil were alone in the center of the restaurant with the Life-A-Day Man.

"I always heard that New Yorkers were rude," West commented. "Give me Boston any day."

"You monster!"

McNeil's face was streaked with tears. Her hands balled into tiny fists, she shook with rage as she shouted again;

"Monster!"

The doctor turned and stared at the woman as if inspecting a sample slide. He analyzed her as if seeing her for the first time, his indifference keeping her at an impersonal distance.

"You know," he announced finally, "I do believe this pretense at pleasantry has grown boring. I think I'll just take our ill-tempered bag of estrogen here and be on my way."

West reached out in McNeil's direction, but London threw his will across the table at the doctor, growling;

"Leave her be."

"My, my—my, my, mymymy ... my ... at long last our noble hero shows his regal temper. Tell me, oh, won't you, please—is this the big moment we've all been waiting for, Mr. London? Are you finally ready to 'handle' me? Yes?"

"I said," the detective answered, slapping West's taunting aside, "leave her be. I don't pretend to have a solid grasp on all this, but I do know one thing—I have had enough of you. Gather yourself up and take a hike. Leave this world, and be about your business."

Another small phrase rested on the edge of London's tongue—violent debate within his skull held it in place. Half his brain demanded its addition to the threat, the other half shrieked just as violently that it be withheld. As the detective went through all the arguments within his head, common sense withdrew from the debate, refusing to comment, seeing disadvantages and advantages both. Trusting his first instincts, the Destroyer spat out the rest of what he had been wanting to say all along.

"Or else."

"You don't frighten me, Mr. London," said West, reaching his hand out toward McNeil. "But you do fascinate me. So—let us put our little rivalry to the test—shall we?"

The Life-A-Day Man closed his fingers, attempting to jerk the woman's life from her body with the gesture. The detective intervened, throwing an energy shield between McNeil and the doctor. West nodded, acknowledging the interference, then casually doubled his efforts to steal the priestess's life energies. Again London threw masses of power in his way, blocking his efforts.

"Impressive, detective. Like a child who manages to amaze his elders, but only because they haven't really entered the contest yet."

"You will not harm her."

London stared unblinking, his body tense, muscles hardening over, veins pumping furiously. Energy crackled about his head and shoulders, and everywhere throughout the restaurant things began to simply unravel as his need for fuel broke them apart. Both men knew that while matter could neither be created nor destroyed, it could be reformed. Where West was getting his power, London could not tell. But, it was easy to see how the detective was feeding his defenses. All about the trio, chairs fell to dust, tables softened, toppled into goo, plates and food and napkins and menus all simply boiled away into wisps of colored air.

"What will you do, Mr. London, break the entire planet down into its basic elements, all just to defend one insignificant female? Are you so short-sighted?"

West's voice was challenging, but the edges of his face showed hints that he had not expected his opponent to show either such resolve or such stamina. He upped the drain aimed at McNeil dramatically to see what the detective would do and was both surprised and delighted when London matched him evenly. True, the doctor was working his end of their competition calmly— dispassionately, really—while the detective was hunched over, straining, breathing hard. But regardless, despite the wave of sweat breaking out across London's forehead, McNeil's form had not begun to compromise. Despite West's best efforts, her physical structure was still intact.

"It's sad you've got such a messianic attitude about you, Mr. London," hissed the doctor, his displeasure growing evident, "we might have made great companions."

"Never going to happen, scumbag!"

"Tiresome gnat!" West exploded with fury suddenly, his rage shaking the weakened foundation of the restaurant. "You are *nothing* to me!"

The doctor physically moved on McNeil. The air around the threesome vibrated with color—a wall of black densing around the woman and London, hot scarlet and oranged billows sparking violently where the Life-A-Day Man came in contact with the shield. West struggled against the thickening dark of the wall, driving his fingers forward, lightning shattering outward from his flesh, cracking apart the atoms of the detective's defense.

"A noble try, Mr. London," sneered the doctor, his delicate hands inches from McNeil, "but the better man, as always, prevails."

Saying nothing, London reached out and grabbed McNeil's wrist, pulling her to himself. Dragging forth every ounce of stability around him, the detective heard the distant sound of the sidewalks outside collapsing into the ground. As the ceiling came crashing down around the trio, London managed to push the Life-A-Day Man back a handful of steps, as he shouted;

"She's not yours! Let the whole fucking universe fall—you don't get *her!*"

West repositioned his glasses on his face. Taking a deep

breath, he stepped forward once more, saying softly;

"Indeed. And how exactly do you propose stopping me?"

London's face went dark, his soul cooling to its lowest temperature. His lips pursed grimly, he stared at West, then lowered his head a fraction to look into McNeil's eyes. The priestess nodded her head, telling him;

"Dies On The Right Day was the only one of us aptly named, but we were all well chosen."

The detective continued to stare into the woman's eyes, forcing his way into her soul, needing to know that he understood exactly what she meant. As if to emphasize her words, McNeil nodded sharply, then closed her eyes. Without another word, London opened himself and sucked away every atom of the priestess before the startled West could react. He took her, heart and hair and pocketbook, leaving not so much as a shred of lint for the Life-A-Day Man to claim.

As sirens blared outside the restaurant, signifying the arrival of the police summoned some one-hundred-and-eighty-seven seconds earlier by the no longer existing manager, Dr. Herbert West took a step backwards from his opponent and said;

"My, my, well ... you certainly showed me, didn't you, sir."

London stood hunched over, his body aching from the recent contest. As he drew in a deep breath, the Life-A-Day Man smiled, bowed, and then began to slowly fade away.

"You are clumsy and untutored," West whispered, "but you are filled with wonderful surprises. I believe I shall take a moment's rest and then return to finalize our dealings."

The detective wanted to shout, wanted to force their confrontation then and there, but the doctor declined. Finally winking out of existence, his voice came out of the air to ring in London's ears;

"Go home, sir. Lunch does not seem to be our meal. I'll see you after dinner, instead."

Outside the restaurant, a score of police were working their way from the still-solid sections of the roadway across the treacherously crumbling sidewalk to the porous walls beyond. Not wanting to have to explain what had happened, not knowing how, the detective summoned the remaining atoms of the restaurant to himself. The building simply dematerialized, the strength of its elements refreshing London instantly. Then, before he could be spotted through the rising billows of soot and dust, the detective stepped through time and space and returned to his office.

Knowing he had accomplished nothing.

Dreading whatever was to come next.

# CHAPTER
# TWENTY-SIX

"OH, TEDDY, WHAT ARE you going to do?"

London could not help but note Lisa had said "you," not "we." He did not find anything cowardly or off-putting about the distinction. There was no doubt whatsoever over who was going to have to face the Life-A-Day Man upon his return. The detective had told the others, all of whom had waited at the Agency offices, everything that happened at lunch. For a great while, none of the others said anything, all waiting to see how Lisa's question would be answered.

"Well," he said at length, "first thing we'd better do is go over whatever you've been able to find out about this guy."

"Now that's the boss I signed on with."

Morcey's quip reflected the attitude of the entire room. There was not a person present who was not frightened—not Pa'sha, the weaponeer, nor Penjii, who had prepared for the next few hours his entire life. Neither man was afraid to die; their fear came from the fact that despite their best efforts to the contrary, their deaths might be useless.

Hoping to avoid such a fate, the team bent to the task of filling in London on what they had uncovered during his absence. They did not know if what they found would be useful, but they had to try. At least, as Morcey said, once they had their target's name, they had something within their grasp with which to work.

As the detective had confirmed earlier, the Life-A-Day Man had existed on the Earth as a quite normal human some hundred years previous. He had been born in a small town in

Massachusetts, where he had stayed for most of his life. He grew to manhood there, raised by two aunts after a lightning strike had devoured his parents and his home in unstoppable waves of fire. Determined to become a healer, he attended the local medical college and received his degree.

"But that's where the trouble started," Morcey told his partner. "His big kick was raising the dead. Seems he started experimentin' with bringin' things back to life as an undergraduate. The college didn't like what he was up to. Neither did anyone else, apparently. Mainly because he wasn't very good at reanimating the deceased."

"What do you mean?"

"West could only reanimate the flesh," Pa'sha explained. "He could not find the soul to stuff back inside with the rest. His experiments left monsters where gentle hearts had once resided. All his trials, on animals or people, all the same horrible results."

London took in what he was told without comment. Every scrap of information that could be found on Dr. Herbert West revealed the story of an obsessive personality on the trail of an unreachable objective. But, the detective wondered, when had the moment come when the physician had become a god? Further details told the story. Reports on the doctor after he left New England became muddled. There were unconfirmed stories that he had been torn apart by his own creations—more than once—then he himself was reanimated by an unnamed assistant.

There were also horrible, sinister rumors of him working with the Nazis in the concentration camps. Their need, it had been supposed, was for reanimated soldiers to send to the Russian front. His need was simple to guess—more bodies to work with—fresher bodies, bodies as close to the moment of death as possible, close enough to capture the soul and entrap it within its reanimated carcass.

There were no indications that any of his work in Germany had shown much in the way of practical results. But, Pa'sha's shadow connections had allowed him to uncover American government reports from some sixty years earlier that filled in the missing pieces for everyone. West, captured in Germany by American forces at the end of the war, was sent to the states to continue his work.

"They sent him to Roswell, New Mexico. They had a body there they wanted reanimated in particular."

Truth began to pour into London. Lai Wan told him of how she had laid hands on the report, of how the sincerity of it had flooded over her.

"Apparently, West used his reanimating fluids on the remains of an alien they were holding there in storage. No spaceship had fallen from the skies. The alien itself was observed crashing to the Earth. Examination of the body left the investigating scientists convinced that the creature had the ability to fly the currents of space unprotected." Lai Wan took a short breath, shuddered slightly, then continued, telling London;

"When the alien was reanimated by the doctor, something went terribly wrong. the two somehow fused together. West was left with all of the creature's secrets, all of its abilities."

As the room went quiet, she added;

"Herbert West was shown by accident what you were purposely shown by Fate—that for those with the strength of their convictions, anything is possible. He is a man without doubts, Theodore, and thus he wields the power cosmic as do you—but with none of your restraints."

"So, from the moment of contact with the alien, he knew how to manipulate the fabric of space and time."

"No," corrected the psychometrist, "at first he was believed destroyed. His resurrection at that point seems to have been a thing accomplished almost atom by atom. Once he had finished his reassembly, however, that is when all trace of him disappears from the records of this world."

London pondered all he had learned for a long moment. He had kept the powers he had been given at arm's length, using them only when absolutely necessary. He did not wish godhood, feared its corrupting force. Moments like the one he had been forced to face in the restaurant disturbed him greatly. Indeed, he was still more than a little shaken over the destruction of Maura McNeil.

Yes, he understood that the woman had come to his office to give her life for the cause. She had arrived on his doorstep that morning, believing that she would be torn apart, her soul extracted, digested, and that she would exist as only energy to be wielded in a greater cause long before sundown. He had done not only what he had had to do, but what had to be done. There had been no other choices open to him, but still, the fact that he had been able to make such a decision made his blood run cold.

West had to be opposed, had to be shown there were those ready to make whatever sacrifices were necessary to deny him the victory he sought. London understood that. But, such knowledge was poor comfort for the man who had been forced to disassemble the priestess, and to store her soul within his own. He could hear her within his head, as he could faintly make out Dies On The Right Day and their other companions.

The problem rested, he felt, in the fact he could only "faintly" hear them.

"You know, I remember when the idea of breaking down objects, especially living ones, sucking down their tasty juices ... I just ..." the detective made a hopeless face, then fumbled forward to finish, saying, "It didn't used to be so easy."

"Hey, it's good to have skills."

London wheeled on his partner with a murderous look in his eye. He knew Morcey was only kidding him, knew the sci fi film comedy from where he had taken his reference. But the words wounded him, gave his paranoia free rein to accuse him of all manner of crimes. As he turned, everyone in the room felt the horrible heat radiating from him, the anger turned into energy. Realizing his mistake, Morcey told him;

"Hey, sorry boss; I was just, you know, lightenin' the mood.

Not very well, ah, obviously. But ... hey," the ex-maintenance man gave his partner a serious glance, holding his hands out open as he added, "you know I take this stuff serious as you."

"I know," answered London. The detective's muscles could be seen flexing and unflexing under his shirt sleeve. His body was in spasm, wanting to expel his minor rage, not daring to do so. Forcing a monstrous smile onto his face, he warned his partner;

"I got no problem with jokes. It's just the fact that I always have to worry, if I tell somebody to 'go to hell' in a moment of anger, will I be able to get them back?"

"Glad you were able to hold off," Morcey responded, half-serious, half-joking. "But then, who knows, I mean, it's where all the party animals end up. Might not be so bad."

Lisa rolled her eyes. Pa'sha laughed.

"I'm tellin' ya," added Morcey, wagging his finger, "you Christians, you're all so serious about the afterlife. It makes you awful tedious at times."

Lai Wan gave the balding man a twinge of a smile. Goward reached for his drink, his head shaking back and forth. Penjii's confusion showed on his face. London took note of the Hindu's consternation and then began to chuckle himself. Morcey handed the detective a hip flask he sometimes carried. Whenever he did, it was always for a special occasion, and thus filled with Frangelico, an Italian walnut liqueur he enjoyed.

"Little fru-fru juice, boss?"

Neither the detective nor Morcey were big drinkers. London usually preferred wine, if anything—the ex-maintenance man was more at home with a domestic beer. An older immigrant on his staff when he ran the custodial department had introduced Morcey to the liqueur, however, and his coffee had never seemed quite right without it ever since. Knowing what the flask held, London held out his hand and said;

"Yeah, what the hell."

Feigning terror, Morcey ducked under the detective's

outstretched hand. As London blinked, his partner came back up, handing him the Frangelico, saying;

"Sorry, but you panicked me there, throwin' around words like 'Hell' and all. Now I'm all worried and shit ..."

"I'm not going to live this one down, am I?" he asked, accepting the flask.

"Hey," answered Morcey, his tone as serious as cancer, "you get us out of this one, I'll find a way to put a cork in it outta appreciation."

As the ex-maintenance man grabbed up his coffee cup, London unscrewed the top to the flask. Extending it to where he could rap it against Morcey's mug, he did so, saying;

"Deal."

Then, the detective shut his eyes and took a long swallow of the sweet liqueur. While he did, he allowed his mind to slip back to the morning. Feeling the pine-scented air on his face, hearing the children and dogs, tasting the sea on the wind once more, he tucked his fears back inside the box from which they had momentarily escaped. Handing his partner back his flask, believing in himself once more, he said;

"All right, let's get it together and get ready to kick some ass—shall we?"

"Damn!" responded Morcey, loudly and with enthusiasm. "And people wonder why I love workin' here."

# CHAPTER
# TWENTY-SEVEN

"SO, TEDDY, DO YOU have any ideas?"

"I'm thinking on it, sweetheart, that's for sure."

"Ohhhh," she said with a degree of forced mock panic, working hard to disguise the true panic she was feeling. "Now we're in trouble."

"Jee'zus, everyone I know is a comedian today."

Lisa apologized, laughing as best she could as she did so. London smiled at her over the table, his eyes filled only with mischief. The meeting at the detective's office had broken up rather quickly after the discussion of West's past had been completed. London had forced himself to decide upon a course of action, given the others a few instructions, and then decided the one thing he needed was a good meal. That thought in mind, he had taken Lisa to The Loaf, their favorite eatery on the east side of Greenwich Village.

"How's your salad?"

The pair liked the place because it was more than just a restaurant. The multi-functional building actually contained a number of services, the chief ones being the restaurant, a health food store, and a holistic clinic.

"I think they could have changed the lettuce a little quicker today, but everything else is all right."

As a choice of eateries, when London had first taken Lisa there the place had been quite a surprise to his future partner. She had not expected such from a private detective. Now, however, it was the place they generally headed to first whenever they wanted to get away from the noise and pulse of the city.

"Ummmm," answered Lisa. Turning bits and pieces over within her own bowl, she asked absently, "You know, I realize it's a health food place and all, but would it kill them to put some hard-boiled eggs out at the salad bar?"

"Well, no—it wouldn't kill them ... but I think they're more worried about killing the baby chicks."

Lisa stared into London's smile. She watched him as he shoveled a forkful of raw mushrooms and alfalfa sprouts into it, watched him chew with it, listened while he pointed at her head and asked;

"Something going on in there I should know about?"

"Not really—no ... I don't think so."

"Wow, if that didn't set off my Guy Alarm, I don't know what could. What's up, little missy? What're you thinking now, and how much trouble is it going to cost me?"

Lisa put her fork down and took a short breath. She looked at London once more, his quiet eyes, gentle face. She ran her gaze over his soft, short hair, noting how its unruly rows could manage to seem unkempt no matter how diligently he combed or brushed it. She stared at his mouth again, ran her eyes over his lips, thought about the taste of them for the thousandth time, then answered his question.

"You know, normally you don't really tell someone that asks that question anything serious. Not unless you're in the middle of a war or something."

"Your point being ..."

"I'm saying that we *are* in kind of a war right now, and that if you really want an answer, I just might be scared and tired enough to give you one."

"I'll admit we're in a battlezone," the detective said. "But, I think West will give us a few more minutes."

"Some kind of psychic intuition?"

"No, just an old fashioned hunch," admitted London. "Probably more of a prayer than a fact. But, who cares? Whatever you've got on your mind, com'on, sweetheart, spill—

until something happens, you've got as much right to talk as anyone."

The young woman nodded, dropping her eyes toward the table as she swallowed hard. Then, looking back up, she said;

"You saved my life a few months back; I'm sure you remember." London nodded. Lisa coming to his office had been the trigger that had introduced him to the thousand worlds beyond most people's comprehension he now seemed to walk on an almost daily basis. "I thought you might."

"It was ... memorable."

"That's one way to put it," she admitted, adding quietly, "Another is to say that you barely survived. When you were finally able to get out of bed, you were old—feeble. The power had used you up—wrung you out. Or, so we thought for a while. Then, that very first day you could walk again, the vampires showed up. By the time you took care of them, you were young again—yourself. You—the you I'm looking at right now."

"That's all right," London asked, allowing his voice a hint of trepidation. "Isn't it?"

"It's fine," she told him. "It's wonderful. Where I'm going is that it was only a short time after that ... that Geneva happened. And then, after that woman showed up, and everything that happened at the Grand Canyon ... it's just that you've started using more and more power—incredible amounts some times." London started to answer, but Lisa cut him off, saying;

"No, don't worry. You don't have anything to explain—not to me. Not about her, or anything. I understand what happened with her, how you got cocky, thought you knew everything— you are a man, after all."

"Hey," answered London good-naturedly, "is this how I get to spend my last minutes, with everybody taking shots at me?"

"No, I'm sorry. I am. I didn't bring her up to embarrass you. Honest. It's ... I just wanted to say ..."

Lisa looked down at the table once more for a moment, then looked up again. Her eyes had gone clear, newly colored with defiance. Her nostrils flaring slightly, she finished;

"Teddy you need to take the gloves off this time. You need to cut loose. I know what's in your head. You're seeing the past, New Jersey, and lower Manhattan and Geneva and all, but you've got to forget all that."

"Tall order, sweetheart."

"Be tall enough to take it, then," she snapped. "You keep trying to be the good guy. A white knight, an honorable man. You can't do that this time."

"But ..."

"No!" Lisa said the word quietly, but with force enough to cut London off. Not giving him a chance to begin, she reached out, her fingers wrapping around his wrist as she pleaded;

"You can't play with this bastard. He's cold inside. Dead. He has no soul. Maybe he lost it when he was reanimated, or maybe he never had one. I wouldn't have thought such a thing possible six months ago, would never have been able to say such a thing—now, if you told me the streets were filled with chimpanzees riding ostriches, all of them waving pitchforks and wearing jackets that said 'Satan's Simians,' I'd just ask you who we could bill to get rid of them.

"Paul, Pa'sha, the professor ... there isn't a one of us who isn't ready to die right along side you to do what we know has to be done ..."

"Nobody *has* to die. Taking care of stuff like this, it isn't our job, you know. We—"

"Yes," Lisa said softly, raising her other hand up between them, two fingers reaching out and touching the detective's lips—electricity flowing from him to her and back again. "Yes it is our job. It's *your* job for certain. You know it and so does everyone else. You're God's right-hand man. You're the only hope this planet has."

"Hey, yeah," he answered with only a hint of nerves showing in his voice. "That makes this all easier."

"Oh, hush," Lisa told him. "It's true and you know it. And

if a city gets leveled—even if it's one the rest of us are in—then that's what has to happen. And you've got to know that."

London stared across the table at Lisa, his gaze brushing through the falling layers of her chestnut curls, deep into the warm sky blue of her eyes. He did not like to look at her while being forced to think of the possible end of the world. He wanted to think of her in other ways, softer ways. He had since the first moment he had seen her, heard her voice, breathed in her essence. She was, so very often, his first thought in the morning, as well as his last thought at night.

On the one hand, however, Fate had so complicated their lives that despite the overwhelming intensity of their feelings for one another, they had never yet even found the time to be with each other, to do more than merely kiss. But still, the idea of allowing her to be incinerated, simply to save a few billion people he did not know—

"Listen to me," he told her, catching hold of her retreating wrist with his free hand before she could bring it back to her side of the table. "I know how much real estate I've totaled trying to live up to whatever Destiny or whatever has saddled me with. And I know the way I wish my life had gone since I met you, and how it's turned out instead."

London closed his mouth, his lips forming a hard line for a moment. Then, exhaling through his nose, his eyes locked with Lisa's, his hand holding hers, her hand holding his, he looked into her eyes and admitted;

"I know there's no one else to do this job. Believe me, if there was, I'd walk out that door with you right now and never look back. But, I tell you this, I will face that demented son of a bitch down, and I will find a way to stop him. I didn't know what I was going to do the first time any of this started up, or any time after that, but I've always found a way—and, I'll find one this time, too ... somehow.

"For you."

Lisa smiled. She more than believed the detective, she

knew he would prevail, could feel it throughout her body with a complete and utter assurance. Moving one of her fingers slightly, she gently scratched London's palm. As he looked at her, she widened her eyes to their fullest, then asked;

"You know, for a hardboiled tough guy, you make me wonder. I mean, I can't help but notice how ... ah, chaste, shall we say, our relationship has been."

London's own eyes went a bit wider. Tilting his head to show both interest and appreciation, he listened intently as Lisa continued.

"I was thinking, what with the end of the world being possibly right around the corner ... again, if you were in need of ... say ... a little pre-battle distraction ..."

"Sweetheart," interrupted London, "I can see spending nearly a year now in the big city has had quite a shocking effect on your morals. I also want you to know that when that time comes, and I'm not saying it's all that far off, it'll be to celebrate us stopping something like West, not because we're afraid we can't."

"I'm sorry ..."

London stopped her from saying any more.

"Shhhhhh," he whispered. "You've got nothing to be sorry about. If you think I don't want you, that I haven't wanted you since that first moment ..., well, then you wouldn't be the genius I know you are. Right now, however, what I need to do is finish eating and get ready to wring this guy out. When I think that—"

The detective stopped short as their waiter returned to the table with the dessert they had ordered. It was a specialty of the house, a small personal fruit pie baked to order while the customer waited. The pair had ordered strawberry. As the waiter left, the two stared at the misshapen oval before them.

"That is the sickest looking pie I have ever seen."

"Some last meal," joked London. Both had ordered the special in the past. Both knew it would taste far better than it looked.

"That's the problem with vegans, man," the detective continued. "All they know is health, health, health." Raising his voice, he said to the restaurant in general;

"Would a little aesthetics kill somebody?"

Lisa giggled. Taking her knife, she aimed it for one particularly odd lump and began to saw away at it, saying;

"Look, just a little trimming and it'll be as nice and round as anything Betty Crocker could have made." Then, after her attempt fell something short of her expressed expectations, she said;

"Teddy, what were you thinking, cutting up our pie? Now you've ruined it."

Laughing, London played along, grabbing his own knife. Starting to saw away from a different angle, he told her;

"Me? I've got to take the rap for this thing? No way; I'll fix it. You'll see."

In minutes the two had made a huge mess out of the dessert. Their knifes, fingers and a growing section of the table were covered with bits of crust and strawberries. They howled with laughter, however, cutting their unrecognizable dessert into smaller and smaller pieces until finally, London was left with but one untouched strawberry to attack. Holding his blunt table knife as if it were a scalpel, he said;

"Don't worry, I think this last little repair will ..."

And then, as the knife began to slice into the solitary lump of fruit, the back of his mind whispered—

*Split it, yes. Right down the middle.*

"Teddy," Lisa said, suddenly startled by the look on the detective's face. "What is it? Are you okay?"

"Yeah," he answered. "I think I am. I think we're all going to be all right."

And then, before he could say more, his cell phone rang. Trying to answer it without getting more than a minimum of strawberry goo on his jacket or the phone, he found himself in communication with Pa'sha.

"Time, little brother," said the weaponeer, his voice tired—concerned. "Lai Wan has found him. Our Mr. West is back, has reappeared over the mountains near Denver."

"Thanks," answered London. "I'm on my way."

Breaking the connection, the detective unconsciously broke down the remaining smears of pie stuck to him at the atomic level and absorbed the energy of it into himself. As his eyes met Lisa's, she could see it was time for him to go. He handed her his wallet, telling her to take care of the bill.

"I'll see you when I get back." Looking at his wallet, he told her, "Hey, if there's anything left in there after you clear our tab, why don't you go out and get something frilly?"

"Frilly?" she said the word as if she could barely understand it.

"Hey, you wanted a hardboiled tough guy, didn't you?"

When she smiled, his only response was to take her in his arms and finally throw his lips against hers. He kissed her softly for a moment, then pulled her to him with a force matched only by that which she used upon him. Waiters stopped and stared. One old couple sighed, their hands unconsciously reaching for one another. Several youngsters snickered. Most in the large complex failed to notice.

Finally, after the long moment had spent itself, London pulled back his head, then whispered;

"I love you."

"Yeah, then go prove it. Go slay me a dragon."

*Split it, yes. Right down the middle.*

The detective smiled, then headed for the door. Dem's da kinda woids wez use.

# CHAPTER
# TWENTY-EIGHT

DARK CLOUDS ROLLED FORWARD over the towering landscape casting thick shadows in all directions. Far behind them, brilliant flashes of lightning scorched the terrain below, setting multiple fires, the accompanying thunder almost enough to blot out the Life-A-Day Man's words as he said;

"My, my, look who's here."

Dr. Herbert West hung calmly in the air over the Rocky Mountains, the blackening sky growing wide behind him, seeming to actually be bending around him. The blonde man did not appear to be standing on air, but rather seemed draped across it, as if reclining on some sort of invisible lounge.

"And you were expecting who else, exactly?"

"My, my ... on this dreary, unevolved, backward little rock, filled with its wretched, yammering mixed-breeds and low-lifes? Why, no one else but you, good sir."

As a gentle rain began to fall, London floated forward out of the still-blue half of the sky, doing his best to keep his nerves steady. He knew West would be studying him. Hoping to feed his adversary's over-confidence, the detective allowed the Life-A-Day Man to take note of that from which he was drawing his power. London permitted a faint gray tinge to filter through the energy he was creating for himself by disassembling various sections of the mountain peaks below them. The detective had never really considered where those things he battled—those staggering horrors that so well understood the use of the power cosmic—had found their resources. He always seemed a child to them, tearing apart matter to fuel his powers.

*Like some manner of brainless fool burning antique chairs to power a steam engine,* the back of his mind whispered, *while heaps of coal sat all about, begging to be used.*

"Yeah," he told himself, "well, I guess, no more of that."

"No more of what?"

The detective flinched, startled to realize that West could actually hear his thoughts.

"Just the crazed murmurings of a wretched, yammering low-life," answered London in an outrageously broad British accent. "Nothing someone so grand and vastly important like yourself needs concern 'isself with, guv'ner."

West shrugged, his face darkening as if the detective had managed to hit some sort of nerve. Stretching his arms, the doctor stood up and away from his imaginary recliner, then addressed London. Allowing himself to drift on the breeze as the sky darkened all around, the blonde man pulled at his sleeves, at his coat tails, straightening his apparel as he said;

"I want to make one final appeal to you, sir. I have been a great long time a wanderer. I have travelled far, and I confess to a certain weariness. I mean to say, if you've obliterated one planet ..." West made a twirling motion with his hand to suffice for the remainder of his sentence.

"Anyway," he continued, "I would like to point out a fair obvious fact to you. We are, in this universe, you and I, utterly unique individuals. I can, at present, destroy you utterly with barely a thought. I do not wish to do this, though."

"Well, that's good to hear. But, if I might ask ... why not?"

"Because, sir, I would much rather have you at my side. To think of the marvels we could witness, could achieve—a combining of our powers, side by side—"

"You are just one crazy bastard, aren't you?" London's interruption stung the doctor worse than any blow might have. "You are so far pulled into your tiny little world that deep down inside, you really believe I could turn my back on ... well, hell, on everything—on the entire world, and just let you do what you please with it."

"I will do what I please with this world," West sneered, his voice growing thin and cold, "whether you stand with me or not."

"Whatever you say, tiger." London moved his head back and forth on his neck, stretching it to its limits to loosen its muscles. "Since it looks as if we're going to be throwing down here, you have any rules you want to propose? Time limit? No punches below the belt? You're not a Marquis of Queensbury man, are you?"

"Are you in such a hurry to die?" The doctor shook his hands before him in frustration, so great his agitation that he nearly jostled his spectacles from his face. Straightening them unconsciously, he shouted;

"Have you not ached for company, for others like yourself? When you were first ... enhanced, didn't it make you stare at the sky, dreaming of when you finally wouldn't be ... alone?"

"Man, I couldn't explain myself to you if I tried, Doc," London sighed. "You picked a path a long time ago. So did I. You lost your parents. I lost mine. We're alike in a thousand ways; I won't deny it. But there's a wall between us as thick as discomfort and as hard as misfortune."

The detective had more to say, but the Life-A-Day Man put his hand up, stopping him. Swinging his fingers back and forth in a dismissive fashion, he cried out over the increasing fury of the oncoming storm;

"Enough. Limited as is your vision, you are true to it, and proper respect to such maturity must be paid. But," the doctor snapped his fingers together, pointing them at London, "if you insist on posturing, then ..."

The fingers came together, fisted—

"You must ..."

Then exploded outward, flinging forward what energy they had collected—

*"Die!"*

The power to shatter any score of the mountains below and swallow them whole flashed across the sky and slammed against the detective. Or, more exactly, against the steeled air in which he had sheathed himself. The blast shredded his defenses, stripping off one millimeter at a time, burning them, curling them, peeling layers away faster than they could be replaced.

"Nice try, fancy boy—but expected."

London vanished from sight, flashing through the ebony sky at supersonic speed to bring himself around behind West. Fast as his attack was, however, the detective's target had long fled the spot where he had been, shifting himself through space and time to appear behind the position he had been occupying. London arrived at the now empty position just in time to be caught in a wave of pounding sound and color bright enough to set his shoulders, neck, head and hair ablaze.

"Jesus Christ!"

The detective snuffed the flames out with a thought, instantly pumping antibiotics and steroids to the burns.

"Calling your friends in for support already?"

West laughed at his callous reference to London's exclamation. His arms folded across his chest, the blonde man slowed his movements to where they could be followed by the naked eye. Setting himself into a circular path around the detective, moving at a greatly reduced seventy to eighty miles an hour, he dared London to take another shot at him. Trying to control the pain throbbing through his back and head, the detective spat;

"I don't keep such exalted company."

"I do," said West quietly. "But you wouldn't understand."

"Try me," shouted London, throwing jagged bolts of energy at his opponent. The doctor shrugged them off casually. Wiping his brow as it grew heavy with rain, he said;

"I knew the concept of God, of our Heavenly Father, the Creator Almighty was nonsense—knew it was a sham from the first moment I heard it. As any person of intellect realizes sooner or later, man is the creator—god his invention. But that's not to say *all* gods are false. Oh, no!"

West sucked all the air out the region, leaving London gasping for a moment. Then, while the detective created his own, the Life-A-Day Man ignited the oxygen he had stolen and threw it in combination with the remaining hydrogen at his foe. The resulting explosion filled the storm-darkened sky with burning colors—violent oranges and reds that illuminated the encroaching darkness. Stepping out of reality at that moment, however, London not only avoided the pyrotechnics, but he was able to return at an angle which brought him in behind West where he dealt the blonde man a crushing blow to the back of his neck.

Grabbing the doctor, the detective threw the pair of them into a suicide dive with his weight driving them toward the mountains below. Throughout their plunge, London continued to pummel West with enhanced blows. Then, a split-second before impact, the detective dove off to one side, allowing the doctor to slam into the wet granite landscape beneath them. Landing next to the impact crater, London searched for signs of West. He found his first when the Life-A-Day Man burst through the ground and hurled the detective back up into the outer atmosphere.

"You can not best me with such antics," he told London, his voice higher, more strained in the thinner air. The detective was slightly distracted by the darkness so close above his head, the blanket of stars serenely set just outside the last layers of the atmosphere. "Indeed, you can not best me at all. I have destroyed gods, Mr. London. And you are naught next to their might."

"I don't get you, Herbie," the detective shouted. "First you say there is no God, then you talk about wrestling with Him. Which is it—is there a God or isn't there, cupcake?"

"Are you so dense, you actually can not understand me? There is no grand Christian God, no white-bearded counter of souls, taking attendance on Sundays, wresting with his own creation over a harvest of souls about which he cares nothing.

The contemptible little figures men babble over, Yahweh, Allah, Shiva—they are fairy tales only. But I have met *real* gods, Mr. London, and I have bested them."

On the last word of his sentence, West filled the air with daggers of molten consciousness and hurled them at London. The detective re-established his shields just in time, turning his body at such an angle so that he would only have to repel one of the horrid weapons. The Life-A-Day Man's burning thought tore at London's safeguard, singeing his most recent memories before it finally fizzled out. As the pair drifted back down into the thicker regions of the atmosphere, standing just above the raging storm, West said;

"You've met at least one of them. I believe you hear its name as Q'talu."

London hung motionless in the moist air. The name was one he had certainly heard, belonged to a thing he remembered meeting all too clearly. It was the merciless blackness he had encountered when first Lisa had come to him, the same heartless god-thing he had forced from the Earth at the cost of some two million lives.

"I stopped it aeons ago—locked it away with all of its kind, safeguarding this world of ours for all time."

"What are you talking about?" asked London, truly puzzled. As best he knew, the elder gods had been locked away from the world by various sorcerers in ancient times. "I know something of what knocked those monsters out of the park—but I've never heard your name mentioned."

The doctor lifted his hands to the attack once more, but London held his up, signalling a pause. As West halted his next strike out of curiosity, the detective kept his hands in their defensive pose, asking;

"Com'on—give out with it. You talk about trampling worlds for eons, but we both know you only got started in the late forties. Granted, that's a lot of days full of world killing, but its not a  billion years. You want me to take you seriously, get serious. Explain yourself."

The tall, slender man with the pale blue eyes and the unconsciously sinister grin, walked calmly through the storm churning there in the upper atmosphere toward London's side. Instinctively, the pair began to descend back toward the Earth. His features announcing that he was about to lay the winning hand on the table, West spoke softly as he told the detective;

"I have acted exactly as you think I did, living day by day, finding a new world to make my plaything each morning. Sometimes I played with their religion, sometimes their politics, most often just their blindness and their greed. But after a while, it became all too easy."

The storm now firmly enveloped the two figures hanging in the sky. As the wisping matter of the dark clouds passed around and between them, static from the occasional lightning discharges filled their bodies, making their hair stand on end. Barely noticing the change outside of the disturbance of the semi-regular thunder claps, the doctor continued his story.

"Bored, I began to wander through time as well as space. The alien's mind I had merged with, it was filled with theories, but I made them real. I found ways to shift the boundaries between dimensions; I crossed over into multiple parallel universes—and I destroyed all I found."

West drifted closer to London, brushing his way through the thickening cloud cover.

"And then, I finally found it ... the center of all existence. And the being that dwells there, slumbering in madness—the thing they call Azathoth."

London's eyes went wide. He had heard of the blind god, the one that lay in constant sleep. The legends he had come across claimed that Azathoth dreamed all of reality, and whatever it dreamed was made so. Instantly. Without question. They also said that if the mad god ever awoke, all of reality would wink out of existence. Instantly. Without question.

"I had encountered many of the other things that ravage

the lands between space and time. Glaaki, Shub-Niggurath, Bokrug, Shudde M'ell, even Golgoroth, the forgotten old one ... contesting with them was diverting, exhilarating, sometimes even closely decided. But then, then I found Azathoth."

Lightening from the clouds splattered against both the detective and the doctor, but neither man took notice. Their attention fully devoted to one another, they ignored the elements, London listening as the blonde man confided;

"As I said, I was bored. Destruction was futile. Playing the nurturing god was an infantile pursuit. But here, with Azathoth, here was *opportunity*."

The storm, completely encircling the pair, began to grow in its fury. As the wet darkness swelled, filled with the violent scream of thunder, the doctor finished his story.

"All my life, I had strained against the notion that anything had created me. I did not accept it. And therefore, I proposed to awaken Azathoth, to prove that man and man alone was the shaper of his destiny. The other gods opposed me, of course, but I knew they would, and thus I took my stance on Earth, throwing up barriers that would keep them from our world for all time."

London stared in sheer amazement. He knew everything West was saying was true—could feel the honesty of the blonde man's telling vibrating there in the sky between them. As he merely listened, the doctor told him;

"Then, free from their interference, I made my best attempt at capturing Azathoth's attention, by injecting the sleeping god with my reanimating potions."

"You what?"

"A billion, billion gallons," West's demeanor became loud, his voice wild and frenzied. "An ocean of it, I soaked it in my fluids, filled it, blasted its very being with it ..." And then, the doctor's tone went cold and low as he continued.

"But Azathoth did not awaken. It writhed out of control; bubbling there at the center of all infinity, it crushed solar systems in its madness, obliterated galaxies, burping monstrous belches of confused pain—and then, when I thought I had failed utterly, I noted movement in its center. Watching, praying, spellbound I was as one great amorphous section of it heaved aside, and one great eye was revealed. I hung in space, staring, unable to react and then it happened.

"There was a shudder throughout reality, and the great eye opened, then closed."

"But ..." the single word was all London could fashion. His mind closed down on him, refusing to consider the idea before him no matter which way he tried to view it.

"It was a blink, a momentary interruption of the hideousness's dream, but it saw me—it *saw* me—and *I did not vanish!*"

Hope fell away from the detective as if thrown out the window of a speeding car. Even if he desired its return, slamming on the brakes only slowed his moment away from it. Panic joined forces with hatred and self-preservation within London's soul, throwing him forward into action, not caring what path he chose as long as he dragged them away from thinking about West's words, or the chilling laughter which now emanated from him. As he did, though, the blonde man taunted the detective, sneering;

"Out of ideas, are we? No more tricks? Perhaps it's time for you to call on your friends after all."

London was just about to respond when suddenly a voice caught both men off guard.

"I can't claim to be a friend, but how about an acquaintance? Will that do?"

And, as the detective and West both turned, the form of Anton Zarnak floated into view.

# CHAPTER
# TWENTY-NINE

"GRACIOUS," EXCLAIMED WEST, HIS eyes growing wide, his smile wider. As the one-time defender of Earth drew closer, the blonde man removed his glasses, absently wiping their wet lenses on his equally soaked jacket as he said;

"Isn't this simply marvelous. Another trained monkey who thinks his ability to hurl excrement makes him some manner of threat."

London simply stared, trying to make sense of the facts before him. When he had left the debilitated Professor Guicet at 13 China Alley, the detective had thought that was the last he would see of anything connected to Zarnak. The man had passed through the doorway on Mt. Meru—the final threshold. It was supposed to be the one and only crossroads *to* all places *from* all places.

"Apparently," the doctor said to London, his tone strained—tense, "the difficulty of return from that particular beyond has been exaggerated."

The detective noted the fact that Zarnak was speaking to him, but that his eyes never left West. There had been a grimness to the doctor when they had met earlier, but nothing approaching the level London now sensed within the man. He had passed beyond the massive doorway in the mountain, going on to face an enemy the detective was in no way certain he could best, and had refused London's help. Now, Anton Zarnak seemed, not so much worried as he was cautious. The man who had marched into battle against a god-thing the detective could not begin to comprehend was now suddenly hesitant—moving carefully. Warily.

"So," said West, considering the latest arrival, sliding his glasses back into place, "the great Dr. Anton Zarnak. I believe I had actually heard of you, back when the limitations of the flesh still meant something to me. Back in the long ago of my youth. Tell me, physician to physician, are you preparing to break your Hippocratic oath?"

Zarnak hung in the air casually, his manner suggesting boredom if nothing else. Shaking his head slightly—sadly—he finally focused his attention upon West. Looking him up and down, he allowed their eyes to lock, then said;

"You, sir, are an abomination, and an embarrassment. This world is a far better place when you are not a part of it."

"A matter of perspective only," countered the blonde man. Smiling coyly, his head bowed slightly, West added, "but such a debate could drag on for untold hours, all of them tedious. And I do have a schedule to keep. This modern age, I understand, is all about speed, and I have always strove so to fit in."

West turned his head from side to side, stretching his neck muscles. Reaching up to his head, he ran his hands over his hair, squeezing the water from it as he demanded;

"So, if you do have something you would like to accomplish, or say, a little dance you wish to perform, by all means, please good sir, do get on with it. I would ever so like to get on with a few things, killing Mr. London here, destroying this wretched planet ... dinner ..."

As West chuckled to himself, Zarnak floated forward, placing himself between London and the blonde man. Reaching inside his jacket, he once more pulled forth the mask of the high priest of Yama and began chanting;

"*Sub pat'kiaa, yef yef gerdic trum'el kuna.*" As the words spilled out of him, the doctor sent a thought into London's brain, telling him;

"Be ready."

And then, as his chanting continued—

*"Yama hidie'ay, Yama gibgib'conna gibgib'conna."*

Once more the detective witnessed a curling mass of ambrosial flesh and fire swirling into existence. As a violet mist began to crackle with lightning, the doctor called out;

*"Trum'el kuna, Yama hidie'ay, Yama gibgib'conna gibgib'conna bing shem!"*

As it had the first time the detective had witnessed the summoning, the cloud continued to metamorphosize. As West watched with obvious fascination, the hazy mist began to dissipate, replaced by a growing ball of living fire. Impossibly, a mouth filled with jagged fangs sprouted within the center of the blazing sphere, the hideous maw topped by a trio of terrible, unblinking eyes. As the god-beast neared completion, the blonde man clapped his hands several times, saying;

"So, a touch of that old time religion, eh? What an intriguing idea ... how do they put it these days, back to basics?"

"This is your only warning, West," responded Zarnak. Holding his hands before himself just so, the position of his fingers obviously keeping the raging fire god at bay, he said, "leave now. Go somewhere else. Anywhere. I would rather spare this poor world any further damage from your hands if possible. If you refuse, though, then you will be destroyed."

As West considered Zarnak's words, behind the blonde man a second rift began to appear. As London watched, a coiling mass of boiling flesh, long and thick and covered in hairy scales that glowed with a dull orangish hue began to slide through into the atmosphere there above the mountains, forcing the very storm apart with its arrival. The detective's eyes grew wide. Although its appearance was somewhat changed, he knew what approached.

Part of his mind marveled. When London had taken charge of Guicet, had let Zarnak go through the doorway, he had believed the elder magician was going to perform the same holding action as his predecessor. Now, he found the man had not only beaten the horror, but like the Yama thing before it, had tamed the second horror as well. Suddenly believing they might actually stand a chance, hope began to build within the detective, even as West grinned, saying quietly;

"So be it, my good doctor, what must be ... must be."

And then, with a motion far too quick for the human eye to follow, the blonde man threw himself forward into the very heart of Yama. Somehow, impossibly grabbing handfuls of the insubstantial creature, West tore the monstrosity asunder, flinging the loosen fragments downward to smash against the countryside below. As Yama bellowed in unbelievably agony, the second horror moved in on the blonde man from behind, even as Zarnak turned and streaked across the sky to London's side.

"We must fall back—*now!*"

As the detective followed the doctor's warning, both of Zarnak's apparent lackeys fell on West, tearing at him, smothering him. As London felt a surge of hope, Zarnak shook his head grimly, tugging at the detective's sleeve, pulling him along through the rain-filled air to a greater distance.

And then, suddenly, both men heard a small popping sound coming from behind them. Before they could turn, the sky turned purple, filling with thunder and flame and a ruinous din which knocked the pair from the sky.

# CHAPTER
# THIRTY

"**W**HAT THE HELL WAS *that*," shouted London, his words garbled, his mouth filled with soggy frost.

The detective thrashed in the rain-encrusted snow bank in which he had landed, trying to right himself. He had been flung at a tremendous rate by the power of the unexpected explosion and thus driven deep.

"Something very wrong, I'm afraid."

Zarnak floated just above the frozen wave of perpetual snow there on the mountain top. The blast had caught the elder magician off-guard as well, but he had years more experience in such matters, and recovered quicker than London, catching himself just before impact. Above Zarnak and the detective, the crushed color of the sky vibrated, the deep indigo with which it had been shot through slightening, lessening, falling backward through the spectrum toward a more recognizable blue.

"What," wondered London aloud, "did your boys wipe out West? What's bad about that?"

"There would be nothing amiss with that outcome in my book," answered Zarnak, his eyes looking westward, back along the way they had been thrown, "but that is not what happened."

As London turned his head, looking off toward the horizon as well, he mentally willed the range of his vision to increase, to focus on their far point of origin. The detective hated crossing the line to the other side, playing with the physical laws of nature. He distrusted those who did so, and he did not like being forced into situations where he had to do it himself.

"Enough nonsense," whispered one of his ancestors, the ancient voice hissing in his brain, "drop this endless wondering. Attend to that which must be attended."

"There is no other choice."

One by one those that had gone before him—young and old, male and female—threw their advice at him. They were not unanimous—no family ever is—but their collective suggestions were as overwhelmingly close to it as possible.

Throwing off hesitation, only the slightest part of his mind taking a moment to hope he was not stepping off into damnation, London opened himself completely to the power available to him. Only seconds had passed since he had dragged himself upward out of the snow. Already, though, the detective and Zarnak were in trouble. The sky had completely reverted, all traces of the explosion long spent. Only the storm remaining.

So too disappeared were all traces of Yama and whatever the thing from the other side of the door had been. *Had* been. Both of the monstrous creatures eons old. Both of them slaughterers of billions. Destroyers of worlds. Both of them gods. Both of them obliterated by the Life-A-Day Man.

Both of them snuffed out of existence by Dr. Herbert West, who only an instant after eradicating a pair of unbelievably powerful beings was on the hunt for more.

"Mr. London, Dr. Zarnak ... come now. Time for another round, don't you think?"

As he spoke, the blonde man snapped a bubble around his opponents with a thought, only to be instantly countered by Zarnak who bent the bubble inside-out, tossing it around its creator. For a split-second, the elder magician and London had been without air, floating in vacuum—everything familiar to them instantly eliminated. When the reality of oxygen and atmosphere and the noise of life slammed back into being, ricochetting off the detective's skin, he narrowed his eyes, focusing on West.

"That's it. That's enough."

London threw a jab at the Life-A-Day Man from five

hundred yards, flinging the force at the blonde man with every intention to smash him—his brain flooded with images, his will screaming to bring them into being. West's head shattered, brain tore asunder. West's jaw torn away, spine erupting through the back of his head. West's neck—

The blonde man moved his wrist, just enough to place his hand in the proper place at the proper angle to deflect the blow. A split-second later he shifted it just far enough to the left to stop a similar blow thrown by Zarnak. Then another from London. Another from Zarnak—

Over and over the doctor and the detective took shots at West, forcing him backward, keeping him off guard. Keeping their entire mental focus centered on their enemy, never relenting, burning energy at a tremendous rate, gathering it from anything solid at hand without discrimination, for there was no time.

"He's tiring," thought London, knowing he was not humoring himself. Knowing he was not confusing mere hope with truth. "Wiping out Yama and his pal, it took him down further than he's letting on—"

While the detective pressed their fight onward, holding West at bay, Zarnak redirected his will, gathering several mountaintops and flinging them upward through the raging storm, not so much hoping to kill their enemy, or even hit him. But to possibly distract.

"He might even be lying to himself ... maybe we're the first real challenge he's had in a while—"

*Maybe ever—*

The quartet of peaks, hundreds of thousands of tons of rock came slamming upward into the upper atmosphere, one to each side of the blonde man, one directly beneath him, one slashing toward the most likely spot to which he would transfer himself. West sensed the massive disruption in the air flow currents, took in the closest objects, the back of his mind planning a retreat. Rebuffing London's last blow, the doctor threw himself out of space and back into it—

Directly in the path of Zarnak's last mountaintop.

West's cry filled the sky, a horrid, unbelieving echo of shock and surprise that traveled beyond all horizons. Across the face of the world in every direction, people stopped what they were doing—even if they were sleeping—and by the billions, they looked up. Their energy focused for an instant on the monstrous, terrifying sound they had just heard. And, by throwing worldwide attention at West, by directing their attention toward him, they undid everything Zarnak and London had accomplished.

Shattered beyond recognition, the influx of psychic energy gave to West everything he needed to once more reconstruct himself. Barely able to stay aloft, Zarnak coughed, fatigue stooping his shoulders. He had thrown everything he had into the last maneuver. He had squandered strength, thrown years of life into one massive attack—and the manuver's very success had doomed it.

Close by, London flashed a glance at the elder magician, the detective knowing without asking that he was suddenly on his own. Zarnak needed time to recover.

"Like it or not," he thought, "it's our round now."

As West stretched his arms, he began to giggle. In the millisecond during which he felt himself dying—an inch from destroyed—he had known failure, experienced losing, had been forced to acknowledge he actually still could be beaten, and that it was too late to do anything about it. And then, Fate had changed the rules and given him a second chance.

"You know," the blonde man whispered, his words sailing directly to those two sets of ears he wanted to hear him, "my hat's off to you gentlemen. You actually killed me. Well done. I must admit, you've convinced me."

Threading his fingers, West pushed his hands away from himself, cracking the bones in his fingers, palms and wrists, as he said;

"I don't believe it would be wise for me to trifle with you any longer."

London knew he had only seconds to act. Not knowing what else he might be able to try on his own, the detective opened himself to suggestions, flashing through all his memories, looking for connections he might have missed, not yet made, listening to his ancestors, weighing every idea ...

And then, the back of his brain reminded him—

*Split it, right down the middle.*

The best of all the random ideas he had flashed through his brain returning to him, London concentrated on the air directly in front of West. Focusing his attention, he channeled it inward—downward—until he could actually see a microscopic dot of matter there in the air before his target. Gently, as the blonde man's tittering began to come to a close, the detective guided the insignificant cluster of atomic matter inside West's mouth, and then, as he threw a shield around himself and Zarnak, rather than absorbing the atoms for energy, he split them open instead!

# CHAPTER
# THIRTY-ONE

T HE SKY ABOVE COLORADO tore itself asunder—exploding with a violence previously unheard by any living soul. The storm which had existed around the trio of combatants was torn apart, the air baked, burned, used up, thrown out of the sky—shriveled. Useless. It that split-second, the near torrential rain disappeared, the clouds banished. Indeed, in all of a sphere some several miles in diameter, everything whatsoever had disappeared utterly except for Anton Zarnak and Theodore London.

And the Life-A-Day Man.

"Well, that was rather unsporting."

West hung calmly in the air, his clothing gone, his limbs and upper torso charred, his head mostly missing. From where his words were emanating the detective could not tell. As he noted writhing tendrils of flesh beginning to sprout from the blonde man's neck, spines of bone cracking their way upward along with them, London felt himself slip over into panic. Without thinking he repeated his attack, splitting atoms all across West's body. The explosions were massive, energetic, blinding, but of little use. The doctor had already shielded himself against any such further attacks. The force did not reach him. In moments, Dr. Herbert West was reformed. Clapping his hands, he rendered London applauds.

"Oh, bravo, bravo, my good man—I must admit, nicely done. You were waiting all along to do it, too, weren't you? Making me think you could only consume energy. Oh, a worthy stroke, sir."

"You miserable bastard," snarled London, anger coming

dangerously close to overwhelming him. "You're the one who focused the attention of the elder gods on Earth. You're the reason they just keep coming back here ... and coming back and coming back!"

West shrugged his shoulders, wagging his head in a cavalier manner. Enraged by the sight, London threw himself at the doctor. Flying through the air, he slammed into the smaller man, doing his level best to grasp the doctor around the throat. West worked to repulse his attacker, but could no more remove him from his person than London could effect his own attack.

The two rent the fabric of time, shifting in and out of realities, slamming one another against and even through the various dimensional walls they passed by, but to no avail. The two were evenly matched, had access to the same degrees of limitless power, and simply could not harm one another.

Finally, falling back into the realm of Earth, the specific reality which had given both men birth, the two landed in the Middle East, somewhere in the vast desolation of the Sahara. The ground beneath their feet was composed of sand alone, their view in all directions the same. The sky above them was brightly lit and cloudless.

"My, my," tittered West, "whatever will we do now?"

"We keep at it," growled London, part of him wishing he could have found his way back to Zarnak, part glad to be on his own, "until one of us is dead."

"Now, is that any way to treat a guest?"

The detective spat a wad of gummy, blood-thick mucus into the sand. Fixing the doctor with his gaze, he said;

"It's the only way to treat a mad dog like you. You can't be allowed to go off on your own—to even exist. You're too dangerous and you have to be stopped. And ... I finally think I know how."

Really," drawled West in a derisive, supercilious tone. "And where did such an idea come from? Divine inspiration?"

"Funny you should say that."

The doctor inspected his newly reformed sleeves, making certain they were to his liking. While he played, London told him;

"You know why you started looking for a way to reanimate the dead? Why your brilliant young mind went down that particular path? I'll tell you. You were looking for mommy."

West's fingers dropped his sleeve, his eyes shifting upward, focusing on the detective far quicker than he would have preferred.

"My father died when I was just a baby, but my mother lived until I was in my teens, so I understand somewhat. But you, you lost both your parents, early on. No father to teach you how to be a man, no mother to love you."

West's eyes narrowed to slits.

"Poor little lost boy, cursing God for his loss, unable to accept the realities of life."

"I shall warn you now, sir," growled the blonde man, "you are treading on dangerous ground."

"Oh no," responded London with mock horror. Putting a hand to his mouth, he asked, "whatever will you do—threaten to kill me, to murder the world? Heavens, no—"

"Heaven, indeed," snapped West. "Leave the pleasant fictions for the mooing herds. Do not insult me with such words. There is no Heaven, for there is no *God!*"

The detective smiled. Slowing his breathing, calming himself, emptying his mind of conscious thought, he answered;

"Of course there is. The God that took your mommy away from you is out there—and you know it. And the fact that he was able to steal her away left you afraid of him. Oh, you've looked for God, sure you have, but in every place you were certain *not* to find him."

"If there actually is such a creature, anywhere out there, then it is a poor and cowardly thing," spat West, "one that refuses to face me."

"Yeah, you keep telling yourself that, cupcake." London

laughed slightly, shaking his head with a sad, dismissive air. Smiling at the blonde man, he allowed his eyes to fill with pity, saying;

"Face you. We're talking God here. The *real* God—not that sad sack of ectoplasmic nightmare you got to notice you. Azathoth is just another creation of whatever it was that constructed everything around us."

As London kept his voice steady, tone even, West began to shake. The tremors were slight things, barely noticeable, except for his hands. The doctor bit at his lower lip as his fingers continued to vibrate, half from rage, half from fear. Pretending not to notice, the detective offered;

"Think about it, Herbie ... put the old Bible stories aside, and what is the most common agreement? It's that God is everywhere. Whatever he is, he *is* the universe. But, if you actually want to have a chat with him, then where are you supposed to go to find him?"

London thumped his chest lightly—

"That would be right here—in the human heart. And you know what I think, I think you know this's true. I think a part of you's known it all along. That no matter how hard you've tried to reject everything you were taught—everything you know, deep down inside—that buried in that internal, secret place in the soul you don't believe you have, that part of you that you haven't visited in the last billion years, that you still know that there *is* a God."

West drew a deep breath through his nose. Then, his pupils shrinking drastically, staring at the detective with an emotion which as of yet had not played across his face, he growled;

"And thus your plan is to bore me to death by preaching to me?"

"No—I plan on giving you the proof you claim to have been looking for all this time."

And then, the hatred that had been building on West's face suddenly dissipated. Intrigued, his eyes filled with a moment of wonder as he asked;

"Are you serious?"

The doctor meant his question. He had no doubts that London was a being of equal capabilities as himself. As the blonde man rolled the possibilities over within his mind, he realized at once that a person such as himself who actually did believe in a Supreme Being might possibly be able to find one whereas he had not. The tiniest rays of hope cracking through the darkness within which he had wrapped himself so many eons previous, West asked;

"Do you really believe you can do this?"

Reaching down into his soul, London quietly extracted the essence of Dies On The Right Day.

"Yes, I do."

As the doctor considered what he had been told, the detective added Ling and Na'ruma's spirits to the mix as well. He blended the energies, stirred them, riled them, got them ready for what he was planning.

"And tell me, how do you plan on proving to me that there actually is a God?"

Acting with the speed of thought, London released the soul of Maura McNeil into the blinding bomb of saintly energy, telling West;

"By sending you to one of his creations."

The doctor blinked. London released the four spirits, hurling them directly at West as he screamed;

"*Go to Hell!*"

A blindingly bright doorway opened behind West as the quartet of souls splashed against him. The doctor screamed, burning as the wash of energy sizzled against his flesh. One by one, the stored souls seared their way through the blonde man, tearing at his atomic structure, forcing him backward, inching him toward the gaping crack in the ether.

Violent shards of color blasted forth from West's eyes, his fingertips, flashing off into the sky, splattering across the horizon. The four souls which had prepared throughout their lives to face the Life-A-Day Man tore at the monster they had trained to battle, but their combined force was not enough. As London watched their struggle, he could see they did not have enough power to drag West down to that dark and terrible pit from which there is no escape. Knowing what had to be done, the detective thought;

"You're going to be needed. Are you ready?" And, on the other side of the world, the man calming sitting within London's office thought back to him;

"I have been ready for this moment my entire life. Do as you must, sir."

And, with bitter regret, the detective bent the space between his office and the Sahara, pulling Mr. Penjii to his side, and then hurling him forward. Ready and willing for the moment, the older soul cast off all notions of self, reducing himself to nothing more than energy, throwing himself into the struggle. West, seeing what had happened, understanding that a sacrifice had been made—blinked. It was but a split-second of confusion, but it was enough. As his mind wavered, denial of what he had witnessed blinding him for the slightest of moments, the doorway snapped forward and engulfed the doctor, then snapped shut, disappearing back into the nothingness from whence it had sprung.

London sat on the sand and stared blankly at the spot where the Life-A-Day Man had disappeared. Any moment, he feared, the madman would simply reassemble himself, stroll forward out of nowhere, and make some other patronizing remark.

But, one moment turned into a second. And then a third.

And then, something blew past London's face.

His mind immediately leaped to a suspicious conclusion, but his heart felt no evil presence, and he calmed himself, searching instead for the mote which had caught his eye. He did not find the first one he had seen, but it did not matter. He found another.

And then another.

Looking up into the desert sky, the detective blinked, not believing his eyes. He stood then, stretching out his hands, catching the small, insubstantial nothings in both hands.

"Snow flakes," he whispered, marvelling at the sight.

"Snow."

He laughed at the word, at the concept, continued laughing as the tiny bits of ice spread across the sands, melting at first, then quickly catching, lowering the temperature until they began to stick. The detective's laughter finally slowed, and he looked about himself once more. Then, finally he repeated the word with acceptance;

"Snow."

After which London started walking, not caring in what direction he was headed, only glad that there was air to breath, and a God to thank for each precious lungful.

"Duties are not performed for duty's sake, but because their neglect would make the man uncomfortable. A man performs but one duty—the duty of contenting his spirit, the duty of making himself agreeable to himself."

Mark Twain

# A PERFECT MOMENT

VRENTEN OF SPERICA HAD not reached the rank of enjele because he was a member of the royal family. If anything, his birthright had worked against him mightily after his decision to join his world's military. Not that such mattered to him. He had succeeded despite his title. As he told his fellows, he had never been overly interested in politics. Who would rule, would rule, he knew. And in all honesty, he could care less whose behind filled the jade throne.

"I'm certain you're curious as to why you were called in."

Enjele Vrenten broke his proper, forward gaze just long enough to indicate that his superior was correct. The twelve planets of their solar system were maintaining a reasonable peace with their neighbors in the galaxy, no upheavals mentioned on the news, no national disasters, his personal record clean—he could not even begin to cobble together the beginnings of a guess at what could have caused him to be roused at such a time in the morning—let alone to be summoned on the run to the ge'het's private office. He sensed a raw level of tension in everyone around him, however, including the ge'het, which intrigued him greatly.

"Just what in seven suns is going on around here," he wondered. Hoping he was betraying none of his interest on his face, he added, "and could it possibly, just once, be something even a touch exciting?"

Ge'het Krec stared at the officer before him, then looked down at his desk. The commander allowed himself one deep breath, then sufficiently steeled, looked up once more, saying;

"You're being offered a mission, Vrenten. One so important, and most likely dangerous, that the word 'offer' was not a mistake. Normally such an undertaking would have entailed an extensive training period. The officer first chosen was prepared for seven months."

The enjele's heartbeat sped up, despite the iron grip he was exerting over his emotions.

"But, five hours ago, he was murdered."

When Vrenten remained rigidly at attention, the ge'het sighed, then said to him;

"Release, Enjele. Your control is proper and admirable, but now is not the time. What you're being asked to consider, you deserve the right to ask questions—"

"As you deserve the right to hear what questions I might ask, eh, sir?"

Krec smiled. Such honest impertinence was just one further assurance they had chosen wisely. Pulling a pair of smokers from the box on his desk, he tossed one to Vrenten, then allowed the officer to light up as he did so himself. Across the desk, the enjele inhaled deeply, his mind racing. Whatever was going on, it was at least twice as big as he had suspected. Clearing his mind, he asked;

"Murdered by who, sir? Do we know?"

"We *suspect* ... but we can't prove. It doesn't matter. It's the Atthans."

Vrenten grinned internally over the fact he managed to keep his eyes from going wide. Nodding gravely, he settled into the chair his superior indicated, letting the ge'het fill him in on what he needed to know.

"We're going to be at war soon. Matter of weeks, whole system be on fire. No stopping it. Attha's been spoiling for a turmoil. Making alliances, pushing borders ..."

Krec stopped himself as if realizing there was no need to explain the obvious. Bowing his head for a moment, he raised it again, took a long drag on his smoker, then said;

"Thirty-eight thousand years, that's how long we've been recording our history. We've been around a long time. Seen a lot, learned a lot. And yes, even we, the great and wonderful Sperican ... even we've made some mistakes. Your mission, Vrenten, if you accept, is going to be to correct the most serious one of those mistakes our people ever made."

The enjele exhaled, releasing a large cloud of smoke into the room. This time, he allowed himself to smile. Allowed his self-pleasure to be observed.

"After all," the back of his mind whispered in triumph, "what could it possibly matter *now?*"

TWO HOURS LATER, VRENTEN stood on a launch platform in a heavy assault tactical suit, his head fairly reeling from all he had learned. Every ten thousand cycles, time and space shattered, the walls of the universe collapsing for a time—inter-dimensional chaos known throughout the galaxies that shared information as the ShatterTime. A secret history of expeditions and wars, unknown to anyone but the ruling class. And the last time around, they put their foot into it.

Big time.

Last time, they had lost the Light. The divine power that had created their world, their culture, their entire way of being. An unlimited source of energy which the government's chief wizards had nurtured and experimented with for millennia. Gone, allowed to slip through this idiotic breech which befell the universe—all the universes possible—every ten thousand cycles. In frustration, the college of sorcerers had been able to follow its movements, but had been unable to do anything to recapture it.

The Light, Vrenten had been informed, had fallen into a pattern, revealing itself upon a planet named Earth every twenty-five hundred years. It was there—now. And it had to be recovered—it had to be brought back.

Now.

Which would not be accomplished easily, the enjele was assured, for the natives had knowledge of the Light, and would not release it easily.

"It must be returned to the council," Krec had pressed upon him, the commander's voice laced with desperation. "Attha spent a planetary ransom in an attempt to make certain this mission fails. You must thwart their desires, Vrenten. The Light must be returned, for if it is not, our world dies!"

Of course, the enjele had accepted. How he could he not? After all, this was a mission worthy of a warrior. This was a deed worth doing. As he waited for the breech to open, his excitement was something he could feel in his fingertips, hear in the air around him, taste it there as well. He had a device he was assured would lead him to the Light. He had been given any weapon he had asked for. He had but a handful of days to find the lost power, liberate it from wherever it was being held, and return it to the council.

Madness, he thought, unable to stop grinning. The greatest madness a man could ask for.

And then, suddenly the air turned a thin yellow, hazing over before him, filling with the scent of fresh halinbred buds. It was the sign—the breech was opening. Stepping forward without hesitation, the enjele moved into the shimmering disruption and in an instant ... was elsewhere.

His new reality slammed against him with the force of a falling mountain. His armor caught the blow and dispersed it with typical efficiency, shattering the landscape around him as it did so. With a thought he commanded his visor to locate whatever force had hit him. His suit responded, turning him in a rapid arc until he saw—

"What in the seven suns is *that?*"

Staggering tall, improbably wide, the wildly constructed lifeform waddling across the cityscape before the enjele left him too startled to immediately respond. The thing was too oddly put together. There was no central trunk, no core hub of construction, no nucleus from which its appendages might sensibly fall. It was insanity given flesh, and the sight of it transfixed him—crippling his ability to react.

"Look out!"

Vrenten had only paused for the briefest of moments, stunned as he was by the maddeningly impossible thing before him. But, in the scant seconds his brain had needed to scan the horror, it had taken note of him. The first blow he had received from the creature had been but the merest edge of one meant for another. Now, as the enjele stared forward, blinking hard, struggling to focus his mind, he realized the thing was about to direct its next attack at him. Was doing so even as he fumbled to respond.

"*Down!*"

The earthling that had shouted at him a second earlier had now thrown himself against the enjele, knocking him to the ground an instant before another of the monstrosity's beams had left its body. The force tore the atmosphere open, filling the air with fractured atoms, frying their edges, clogging the defenders' lungs with the stink of ozone. Behind the pair, several buildings shook violently, then collapsed inward upon themselves, filling the area with a monstrous cloud of rapidly-swelling dust and debris.

"Quick," shouted the earthling, his speech translated by Vrenten's suit, "we've got to move—now!"

The enjele shook his head within his helmet, trying to clear it. The indicator link within his helmet showed him that the Light was indeed within his immediate vicinity. Everything had worked as Krec's experts had hoped. He had been delivered directly to his objective.

"Gather intelligence," he told himself. "You're already in the right spot, and you have days to complete your mission. Best guess, that whatever-it-is possesses the Light. Make certain. Only way to find out—interact. Get what information you can from the local."

Standing, Vrenten assumed the same hunched over stance as

the earthling and then followed it as it ran into the billowing dust. The pair ran a very short distance, then the earthling grabbed at the enjele's arm, pulling him around the corner of what Vrenten assumed was a building of some sort.

"Thank you," the enjele heard his suit translate. "I believe you may have saved my life."

"Night's not over," answered the native. "Might need you to do the same for me, you know."

Vrenten used the moment to study the life form. The earthling was not so terribly dissimilar from himself. Squatter, far more hairy, an extra finger on each hand—but still, bipedal, two eyes, set forward, still actually possessed teeth, but close enough to normal to find some sort of common ground. The fellow did not seem to be carrying any weapons. He was fully clothed, but not armored.

Not naked or wearing face paint, thought the enjele, they build cities. At least there's some level of civilization.

As Vrenten was taking his tally, the native asked;

"You military?"

"Yes," he answered honestly, not seeing any harm, needing to establish some sort of basis for communication.

"What're your orders?"

"Making it up as I go along," the enjele replied.

"Yeah," agreed the earthling, "tonight, aren't we all?"

"What is that which you combat?"

"No idea," answered the local. "Crap has been popping out of thin air all day. One damned thing after another. My tech people tell me we're in for a bad bout for up to a week."

They understand the breech, thought Vrenten. Nodding, he began to run a fast inventory of his weapons, making certain that not only had everything transferred through the breech along with him, but that none of it had suffered damage either during the transition or the attack. As he did, the native said;

"This thing here, though, we're thinking it's the worst that's going to come through. Doesn't have a name we can put to it.

Just a whole lot of nasty that's gotta be stopped."

Vrenten frowned slightly. His information was that the Light existed on this world. The creature before them, however, appeared to have arrived as he had—through the breech. Then he thought, Krec had told him the lost power interacted with the planet on a cycle, much like the one causing the breech.

Thing slides through the breech, he thought, possesses the Light ... possible—

"Time to move."

The enjele heard the local's words, but as the earthling ran quickly toward the shadows created by the growing debris cloud, Vrenten answered—

"Yes, time to move, indeed," and hit his vertical thrusters, throwing himself a rapid fifty feet into the air. A flaming gelatin shot through with vibrant strands of a green lightning splattered against the ground where the two had been, thrown at the spot by the towering horror. Ready for battle, the enjele snapped one of his firearms into his left wrist cradle and spat;

"I can deal heat, too, ugly."

With a thought, his zelcator reached out in every direction, pulling all the thermotic energy within a hundred yard radius to itself, and then converted it to a tight beam and sent it pulsing back toward his foe. The purple/pink stream of incalescence scintillation tore across the area between them at the speed of thought, splattering against the monstrosity, burning through the first two layers of its semi-metallic scales.

As the creature roared, spitting its anger into the sky, Vrenten smiled, thinking;

"Oh, if you liked that ..."

Snapping a much bulkier unit onto his other wrist, the enjele thought the proper release sequence and then braced himself as his converter ranged through the available atmosphere, scooping all available metallic atoms and converting them into inch thick, yard long segments of a type of razor wire which it flung with terrible force into the monstrosity's flesh.

As the creature howled, its raging bringing the sound of breaking glass through the ever-billowing debris cloud now covering a several mile radius, Vrenten chuckled. He had followed a science-driven, esoteric attack with one of standard metal. It never failed to catch such enemies off guard. He knew the thing had been bracing its defenses for a like attack and thus had suffered far more damage when his fester spears had struck home.

Maintaining what he assumed was a safe distance, allowing his suit to fall into a standard bob and weave pattern, the enjele switched the fester attachment back to its place on his utilization rack, and was pulling down another weapon—one he had always wanted to see used against something capable of withstanding its power—when suddenly, his mind froze as it heard a black and choking thought—

*worthy*

A great, mocking bellow splattered across the landscape, and then the towering horror threw forth a second volley of flame and lightning—one several hundred times the diameter of the first. Although Vrenten's zelcator had been left armed, it could not begin to pull the heat energy from the air being created at that moment. The temperature of the enjele's armor rose dramatically, even as the maelstrom of electricity sluiced through every circuit it could find.

His suit stunned, Vrenten fell helplessly toward the ground, even as his monstrous foe slid forward a massive cephlopodic length to ensnare him. But, before the enjele could fall into the outstretched appendage, his native ally leapt into the air, making an incredible, unassisted jump which not only brought him in contact with Vrenten, but allowed him to shove the soldier out of the horror's grasp. As the two of them hit the ground some distance away and began to roll, the enjele shouted;

"Behind me!"

As he had thought, the monstrosity followed up its attack by hurling another overwhelming blast of flame and current their way. Vrenten knew not all of his offensive equipment would be back on line yet, but he was certain he could count on his armor's defensive net to protect them. As the enjele's suit actually rebuilt its power from the energy being thrown against it, he shouted;

"I'll be topped off in a moment, but if you have anything you could throw at that thing, this might be a good time."

"Well," answered the earthling, giving Vrenten a short smile, "I guess I can't let you have all the fun."

The enjele could not help but admire the native. He wore nothing but standard civilian issue, carried no weapons of any size—oh, his indicator had marked the fellow as carrying several small metallic items on his person, but they were trifles—and yet he was ready to move forward against the monstrous shape before them. Watching the gauge on his forearm, knowing it would still take several seconds for his regen-unit to finishing charging his circuits, Vrenten thought;

"You will be avenged, good sir."

And then was struck speechless.

Sucking down a deep breath, the native braced himself, then extended his arms, pointing his hands at their foe. The fellow took a moment to shout;

"I gave you a chance to move on, but you wanted to dance. Well then, let's shake it, baby."

As the creature threw itself forward, it was suddenly stunned as if hit by a battery of pulse cannons. No discharge left the native's hands, at least, none the enjele's eyes could track. His armor, however, was better equipped. Running through his visor's various range modes, he found one which revealed the truth. Through some unexplainable power, the fellow had converted matter from all around them into energy and hurled it at their enemy. His systems instantly calculated the mass, letting him know that some ninety-six tons of rubble, buildings and street had been reduced to their basic atomic matter and then directed through the native and against the creature. In amazement, he whispered;

"Gralg, stuff a dilly."

Vrenten's armor revitalized as the monstrosity fell over backwards. As it slammed against the ground, the enjele shouted;

"Did you kill it?"

"Possible," answered his companion, not turning to look at him. Indeed, Vrenten noted immediately that the fellow did not even break his defensive stance. As the native turned his head from side to side, his eyes straining against the still swirling billow all about them, the enjele began to do the same, asking;

"What are we looking for?"

"The other two."

Vrenten froze, not from fear, but self-reproach. Sending a mental command to his armor, he had the location of at least one of the creatures instantly. Even as he began to inform his companion, his radar located the second.

"That way," he said, pointing toward the west. "One half as close as the other."

"Headed this way?"

The enjele looked to his scanner for a movement reading, when suddenly the atmosphere was shattered by a terrible, drilling scream, a pounding clang of uncomprehending fear and sadness which signaled the final breath of the thing he and the native had just dispatched. Double checking his scanner, he said;

"They are now. You ready for two of them?"

"I could use a breather. How about yourself?" When Vrenten agreed, the native extended his hand, touched the enjele on the shoulder, then said;

"Brace yourself."

Vrenten was about to ask what his companion meant when suddenly he found himself shifted through space to a point in the city quite a good distance from the site of their combat. Outside of the dust cloud for the first time since arriving on the target planet, he looked about at the primitive poured stone buildings, wondering if his newfound friend and his race had been walking upright for even fifty thousand cycles. Then, remember what had just happened, he looked at the native with even more respect than he had after his last show of power and said;

"You teleported us—with but a thought!" Trying to get his mind around his own words, Vrenten asked;

"Forgive the question, but what are you? Some local god come down off the mountain, or something equally entertaining?"

The fellow bowed his head a bit, a gesture the enjele accepted as a universal one for indicating embarrassment. Understanding, knowing on so many levels what his words had done, Vrenten immediately extended his hand, saying;

"Forgive the armor. Enjele Cormac Vrenten. Pleased to meet you."

"Likewise," said the native. Taking the fingers of the enjele's glove in a grasp rather than his wrist as Vrenten had expected, the fellow gave them a slight shake, then released his grip, adding;

"Theodore London. I'm assuming 'enjele' is some rank I just don't recognize. I'm a private detective myself. Although, obviously, I can throw around a bit more power than most guys."

"I noticed."

"Yeah," answered London, his face not changing. "I noticed you noticed. And that you didn't freak out while doing so. Can I assume you've seen a bit of the strange in your time?"

"A bit ... here and there."

And, in that moment, Vrenten made a decision. His armor had confirmed moments after his arrival that the local atmosphere could support his life functions adequately. Reaching upward, he thumbed the tab which would recess his helmet. As the metal and frosted glass collapsed into its partitioned chamber, the enjele smiled as he noted the change in London's expression as the fellow took note of his alien features.

"Yes," he said, the sides of his own mouth relaxing as well, "I'm not from around here."

"I didn't think so," answered the native. "You had that 'elsewheres' feel to you. But then, so much stuff the last few hours has, it's hard to tell friend from foe. Well, that being the case, welcome to New York City."

"Much appreciation."

"No problem. But, if it's not too being too nosey, might I ask what're you here for? Not that I'm looking to turn down help, but why'd you join in?"

Checking his scanner, seeing that the second two creatures had but just reached the site of their fallen third, Vrenten answered;

"My world lost something valuable the last time this disruption came through the universe. I have been dispatched to retrieve it."

"And you're thinking this trio has what you're after?" When the enjele answered in the affirmative, London told him;

"Well, you're welcome to whatever they've got once we're done with them." Vrenten started to answer, but as the warning alarm he had set on his scanner beeped, he said instead;

"Our targets are on the move again." Once more he was about to say one thing, only to receive a further notice from his armor which caused him to replace a pleasantry with something far more urgent.

"London," he snapped, "bad news. My instruments reveal that our foes are far more powerful than their fallen comrade."

"I was afraid of that," answered the detective, not seeming terribly surprised. "I never met these boys personally, but I know the type. Symbionts, sort of."

"They are sharing power. With the death of the one ..."

"The other two are now each fifty percent stronger. Maybe only thirty-five or forty, but ... still feel like joining in?"

Vrenten stared at his companion, marveling over the fellow. Amazed not only at his power level, but at his easy acceptance of facing such monsters, he found himself asking;

"If I might pose a question—"

"Shoot."

"You know why I am doing this, what I have to gain. What is your motivation in this—if such is not ... nosey?"

"Hey," answered London, smiling again, "as I told a buddy of mine a long time ago, any guy who jumps into a monster fight and asks questions later is all right by me."

The sound of buildings being knocked over stole the pair's attention for a moment. The enjele let his companion know that their foes were moving directly toward them once more. Nodding, London said;

"Anyway, this job of stopping crap like this kind of fell into my lap a while back when I unexpectedly came into a little extra power. Do I want it? No ... not really. But, there's no one else who can handle it, so ..."

The native shrugged his shoulders, the sight of the gesture making Vrenten chuckle. He had met hundreds of beings from other worlds within his own universe. Yet never, he realized, had he ever understood one from another race so completely, trusted one so utterly, as this one.

"Has there ever been an Atthan that shrugged its shoulders," he thought, "or did so for so utterly the right reason?"

"Let us go," responded the enjele, hitting the tab to close his helmet once more, "we have more monsters to kill."

And then, before London could respond, the brutish things were upon them. The first of them slid through the dusty haze, its body reformed into a defensive mass of far-reaching appendages. All the grasping lengths were armored, all were covered with harshly staring eyes and screaming mouths. At the sight, the native indicated that Vrenten should become airborne. The enjele did so, just avoiding a massive attack as the horror flooded the area with an over-whelming barrage of fire and lightning, the power of it consuming the ground where they had stood downward to a level of some sixty feet.

Not worried about his companion, certain the clever London could not only avoid so obvious an attack, but that he had most likely meant to draw the thing's fire, Vrenten did what he knew was expected—he slammed the creature with everything he could. Hoping that the monstrosities shared experience as well as power, he unleashed his razor wire lengths first.

"Yes!"

Expecting the shape-shifting beast to simply create passages through its body to allow the bladed edges to pass through itself harmlessly, he immediately followed the blast from his one arm with a second from his other. Unleashing a new weapon, he sent out his full complement of directional explosives. The bombs followed the razor wires along their trajectories, but then at a signal from the enjele they switched course, all streaking to the closest heat source—in this case the monstrosity's body.

Vrenten cued his armor instantly, moving himself some thousand feet backward seconds before the explosions began. Sixty detonations rang out, shattering much of the horror from the inside. Again the air was fried by the unexpected burst of pain which radiated from the second beast. Scarlet agony blasted from the monster in all directions—but not enough to indicate its demise. Although damaged extensively, the beast had no true form. It could remake itself into any form it desired.

If, of course, it was given sufficient time.

"Nice set up, Vrenten," London's voice rang in the enjele's ear piece somehow, "let me see if I can do it justice."

Vrenten's armor placed the native for him instantly, hanging in the sky well above their foe. Watching him at the proper frequency, the enjele saw the entire action as it was happening. Again using whatever power it was he possessed, London disassembled the buildings the creatures had destroyed, and even the body of their fallen companion, and turned it into a pure beam of colorless power which he drove through the beast. Spearing it to the ground, he pushed with all the force he could muster, tearing the remainder of it into shreds too small to allow reassembly.

And then, the native fell from the sky, done in—overwhelmed.

Throwing all the power he had into his rear jets, Vrenten rocketed forward, swooping in at just the right angle to hopefully intercept the falling man without injuring him. Upon reaching London, the enjele then hit his upward thrusters, changing his trajectory radically just as the third creature blanketed the area with a holocaust of blazing energy.

"Thanks ..." the native managed weakly.

"You called it earlier, didn't you," answered Vrenten, angling to move both of them out of range before the last of the monsters figured out what he had done. "I had to do something to even the score between us."

"Well, here's hoping someone pins a medal on you ... if that's what they do ... when you get back, back—"

The enjele ordered London to save his strength. He could feel his companion's weakness. Knew that he had not done a perfect job of catching the native as he fell. Something had snapped in London's side. Landing them down far enough away from the last of the monsters to give them a moment, Vrenten said;

"You are injured."

"Yeah ... not the first time."

The fellow started to say more, then suddenly coughed, vomiting out a thick, sticky fluid, the purpose of which the enjele was certain he knew. The native had been more than just slightly damaged. From the way the color of his skin was changing, it was obvious he had been hurt severely. Setting London as carefully as he could on the ground, his back supported by some manner of large plant, Vrenten took stock of his situation.

The last creature was approaching. It would be upon their position soon—with not only its own power, but that of its fallen brothers as well. And, this one he would have to face alone. His companion, brave as he was, looked as if he would certainly die if he went into battle once more.

Still, his mind whispered to him, this isn't our concern. We are here for the Light. Nothing more. This fellow's just trying to save his world. If we get the power out of that thing, his world is saved. What does it matter if he dies, if he gets what he wants out of it?

The enjele did still possess the device that was supposed to make his task simpler. Krec had called it a 'drainer.' Said all that had to be done was to slap it against whatever it was that had captured the energy of the Light, and that would be that. His world's divine power would be reclaimed. He would be a hero, to all—everyone. Forever.

If London can just attract the thing's attention long enough for me to fly in from behind—

And then, suddenly, a different notion struck him. His locator was supposed to bring him directly to wherever the Light was. To whatever or whomever had claimed it. The locator had brought him into the vicinity of the first of the creatures. That was true.

But it had brought him to within feet of London.

His eyes flashing wide, Vrenten was as horrified as he was certain he was correct. The creatures were not what had taken possession of the Light—

*Anyway, this job of stopping crap like this kind of fell into my lap a while back when I unexpectedly came into a little extra power.*

The enjele remembered the native's words—

*Do I want it? No ... not really. But, there's no one else who can handle it, so ...*

"It's not them ..."

"Hey," asked London weakly, staring up at the enjele, "something wrong, pal?"

Vrenten's mind swam for an answer. All he had to do to complete his mission was to merely touch the broken man at his feet with the drainer. The Light would be his. His world would be spared.

"And his will *die!*"

The final condemnation from the back of his mind stung the soldier, forcing him to look away. As he did, the warning alarm in his armor alerted him to the position of the last creature.

Whatever he was going to do, he was going to have to do it soon.

Reaching his hand down to London, the enjele asked;

"Like the last time, do you think you can attract the thing's attention?"

"I can give it the old college try."

"Then do so," answered Vrenten, helping his companion to his feet as carefully as he could.

"I believe I have an idea."

And then the enjele rocketed off, hoping his decision would only doom one world and not two.

"SO, if I understand you, enjele," snarled Ge'het Krec, "you used the drainer on this monster, not this London, and drained its energy instead? You came home without the Light? You disobeyed orders? Is *that* what you're telling me?"

When Vrenten responded that the ge'het was correct, the officer stormed across his office and threw himself into the chair behind his desk, demanding;

"And can you tell me *why* you did this? And while you're at it, why you bothered to come back afterward?"

"Sir, it wasn't right. The fellow saved me—more than once. His world needs him. Needs him to have the Light. More than we do."

"And what makes you say that?"

"Sir, we've survived without this Light for ten thousand cycles. If we can't beat the Attha without it, the *Attha*, for the sake of pity, then we don't deserve to survive."

When Krec said nothing in response, merely continued to sit and stare at him, Vrenten realized he had not responded to all he was asked. Clearing his throat, he added;

"I returned, sir, in the hopes the energy drained from the creature might be enough to serve. And ..."

"Yes—"

"It wasn't right to leave you with your neck the only one in sight when they came looking for a place to bury their knives. Ah ... sir."

No longer able to contain his joy, Krec stood, reaching out to grasp Vrenten's wrist, shouting;

"You magnificent bastard, I told them you were the man for the job."

It took a while for the ge'het to explain the entirety of what had actually been going on to Vrenten, but eventually the enjele came to realize what had truly happened.

"So I'm not in trouble?"

"None."

"There never was anything called the Light?"

"Not at all."

"This was just a test ..."

"Let's not make too little of it," said Krec, indicating that the enjele should take a seat. "Ever since our people have become aware of this event, we've put it to good use. Only the Supreme knows, and then only when he's told by those who carry the secret. One in the military—that's me right now—one of the faith, one in the populous. Between us, when the time comes, we look over the available candidates, and one is chosen to be tested."

"Tested for what ... ah, sir?"

"To be the Supreme, to rule. To strengthen the blood. To sweep out the old. Look, my boy, you know your history. Ten thousand back, the Gorben dynasty, ousted overnight. Suddenly a new line of succession."

"But ..."

"New ideas, new ideals, comfort and waste thrown out. Respect for all revived. Something we've been losing the past few thousand years. Something—"

Krec continued to talk, and Vrenten did hear most of it, but he could not concentrate on the individual words. He had, in a perfect moment, turned his back on all that had been expected from him, and instead had done what he had felt was truly right.

"And by doing so," the back of his mind whispered, "I have gained ..."

His words trailed off as he realized he could not actually tabulate all that he had acquired.

"Everything," the same voice whispered from the back of his mind, comforting—chuckling. "Everything that shall be for the Sperican people from now on, will be of your design."

"At least," he reminded himself, enjoying the sounds of Krec telling him what a splendid fellow he was, "for the next ten thousand cycles, anyway."

L ONDON slid into the booth seat being offered to him by a tall, thin man with thick black hair, save for the white streak which zig-zagged through it back from his temple across his head. The detective held his side as he moved to make certain he did not bump it against anything. As he parked himself carefully with a sigh, the man on the other side of the booth commented;

"You really should have that looked at."

"I'll be fine, Doc," answered London. Signalling for a waitress, he added, "but, thanks for the heads up on that guy."

"You have your job," said Anton Zarnak with a tired smile, "I have mine."

When the waitress arrived, London ordered a black coffee with amaretto. His friend merely pointed at his glass and nodded, indicating that he simply wanted another of the same. As the woman headed back to the bar, the detective said;

"You think things will quiet down out there soon, Anton?"

"Got a long way to go, old friend," answered the other. Fishing in his pocket, he pulled out a pair of twenties, placing them on the table just as the waitress returned. As she moved the drinks on her tray to spots before her customers, London's friend turned to her, tapping the bills as he said;

"I got this. Give my friend another on me. The rest is yours."

The woman gave the fellow the brightest smile she owned. He nodded, then turned back to London.

"You going to make it home all right?"

"I'm not totally helpless." The detective took a sip of his coffee, then added, "although I doubt I'll be much more help on this one. You going to be able to handle things?"

Zarnak set down his empty glass—which London could have sworn he never picked up, let alone drained—and slid himself out of their booth. Slipping his hat on, he said;

"If I can't ..."

London nodded, toasted his friend with his cup, then watched as he made his way to the door. As the detective made to pick his cup up again, he winced, realizing he had moved too fast. Of course, he thought, he could simply use the same energies he had utilized earlier in the evening to heal himself. But that, he knew, was a cheat. Fate had handed him the power it had to use in the service of others, not himself.

As a part of his mind criticized his thinking, reminding him that ribs took a painfully long time to mend on their own, he reached for his mug but waited to raise it as he noticed the waitress returning. As she stopped at the table, he asked;

"Yes?"

"I hate to be like this, but my shift is ending, and I was just wondering ... were you going to have anything else?"

"No," London answered softly, sympathetically. "I'm not much of a drinker. Go ahead, take it. I'm sure you earned it."

Grateful, feeling somewhat playful, the waitress pocketed the twenties, asking the detective;

"What makes you so sure?"

"We all earn what we get ... sooner or later."

London drained his mug then and began the slow process of removing himself from the booth. When the waitress asked if he needed help, he told her to wait, just in case he did. Making it to his feet without too much trouble, he thanked her, then headed for the door. As he did, she called out;

"Hey, your buddy, he was nice. What's he do for a living?"

"Well, he used to be a doctor. Now," the detective thought for a moment, then with a smile, he finished, "Now, he's more of a salesman." The woman considered the detective's answer for a moment, then asked;

"Yeah ... what's he sell?"

London stopped, then turned and said in a voice only the waitress could hear;

"Hope for the future."

"Crap," she said, unconsciously patting the twenties in her apron, "he's got a worse job than mine."

London nodded, resuming his march to the door, wondering if his friend Anton might not have a worse job that everyone. Everyone else, indeed.

# SUPERNATURAL INVESTIGATORS
## of C.J. Henderson

**Thirteen tales of spine-tingling terror and bravery.**
www.mariettapublishing.com

CPSIA information can be obtained at www.ICGtesting.com
Printed in the USA
LVOW040938110113

315274LV00001B/232/P